T0130164

ALLIE FINDS ANOTHER BODY

I was going through my project documents, trying to figure out where the snafu might have come from, when Ursi hissed and let out a growl that would make a mountain lion proud. By the time I looked up, her back was a feline version of the St. Louis Arch and her tail was a bushy, black-and-orange feather duster.

"What's wrong?" I went to her and bent down to figure out what had her freaked out. Seconds later, I sprang back upright as my blood ran cold.

Ursi had uncovered a human finger.

Forcing myself to maintain some semblance of calm, I grabbed a decent-sized piece of mulch and scraped smaller wooden pieces from the finger. It only took a few scrapes to reveal an entire hand.

"Oh, God." I fell to my hands and knees and vomited. The hand wasn't fake. Or warm.

Something told me it was attached to an entire body.

With trembling fingers, I dialed 9-1-1. I broke out in goose bumps when I told the dispatcher I needed to report a dead body...

Books by J.C. Kenney

A LITERAL MESS
A GENUINE FIX

Published by Kensington Publishing Corporation

A Genuine Fix

J.C. Kenney

LYRICAL UNDERGROUND
Kensington Publishing Corp.
www.kensingtonbooks.com

LYRICAL UNDERGROUND BOOKS are published by
Kensington Publishing Corp.
119 West 40th Street
New York, NY 10018

All Kensington titles, imprints, and distributed lines are available at special quantity discounts for bulk purchases for sales promotion, premiums, fund-raising, educational, or institutional use.

Special book excerpts or customized printings can also be created to fit specific needs. For details, write or phone the office of the Kensington Sales Manager: Kensington Publishing Corp., 119 West 40th Street, New York, NY 10018. Attn. Sales Department. Phone: 1-800-221-2647.

Lyrical Underground and Lyrical Underground logo Reg. US Pat. & TM Off.

First Electronic Edition: July 2019
ISBN-13: 978-1-5161-0857-2 (ebook)
ISBN-10: 1-5161-0857-4

First Print Edition: July 2019
ISBN-13: 978-1-5161-0860-2
ISBN-10: 1-5161-0860-4

Printed in the United States of America

Chapter One

It was the best of times, it was the worst of times. Actually, it was the best of times. Full stop. I turned on the coffee maker and wandered into the living room of my apartment. While the machine gurgled away, I looked out the window. The view from my perch on the second floor was incomparable. On this sunny September morning, I could see from the shops of Washington Boulevard below me all the way to the verdant green woodlands of nearby Green Hills State Park.

My tortoiseshell cat, Ursula, better known to one and all as Ursi, bumped her head against my shin and meowed as the aroma of fresh dark roast wafted in from the kitchen. Between an apartment I loved, a job I adored, and a group of family and friends who made me feel welcome and safe, life was good.

After spending almost a decade on my own in New York City, it had taken some time to get used to small-town living. But now, ten months after returning to my hometown to run my late father's literary agency, I'd settled into a routine that was as fulfilling as it was comfortable.

"Ready for breakfast, girl?" I carried Ursi to the kitchen, scratching her ear on the way. I barely had time to pour her food into her Hello Kitty bowl before she attacked her breakfast with the ferocity of a lion feasting on the day's catch. Between the energy she spent on our regular walks around town and her prowling around our spacious living quarters, Ursi had become an eating machine.

Even though I never seemed to fill her bowl enough to satisfy her, she was content in her new, window-filled surroundings as much as I was. On top of that, her status as the only cat in town who took her owner for walks had made Ursi something of a local celebrity.

Despite my best efforts to downplay it, I couldn't deny my status as a local celebrity of sorts, too. It came with the territory of solving the first murder in Rushing Creek, Indiana, population 3,216, in thirty years. I was proud of the work I'd done to solve the case, but all things considered, I would have preferred that Thornwell Winchester, the father of my best friend Sloane, hadn't been murdered.

The memories of those dark times, as I searched for a murderer in the days after my own father's death, still woke me up at night in a cold sweat and probably would for the rest of my life.

Several doors were opened to me during that rough time, though. They were openings I walked through without an ounce of regret, and they led me to where I now found myself—happy, healthy, and living the dream every day.

"What's on today's agenda?" I pushed down the lever on my toaster to warm a blueberry bagel.

Ursi responded by winding herself through my legs and then sauntering off to the living room and settling herself on her perch in front of a window. Evidently, napping, eating, and monitoring her surroundings were the items on Ursi's calendar.

"Another day of guard-kitty duty. What would I do without you?" When the bagel popped up, I spread a thick layer of Nutella on both pieces, filled my Cobb Literary Agency coffee cup, and took a seat at the kitchen table.

I had a jam-packed schedule on this fine Thursday. First up, I needed to finish editing a client's thriller manuscript. I'd been up until three the night before reading it and had sky-high hopes for landing a contract offer from a publisher in record time. After that, Ursi and I needed to go for a walk. Then I was scheduled to spend the rest of the day contacting editors to whom I'd sent proposals. I had five books currently under consideration by various editors and was confident I'd land contracts for all of them.

Ultra-productivity was critical today, because the next four days were filled with activities totally unrelated to my literary agency. Tomorrow, I was scheduled to check in at the under-construction Winchester-Cobb Memorial Park. As chair of the committee overseeing the park's construction, I visited the site every Friday to make sure work was progressing on schedule.

Saturday was set aside to help Sloane finish packing and then move her into my brother Luke's house. She and Luke deciding to cohabitate before exchanging wedding vows wasn't sitting well with my dear mother, but everyone else in town was happy they were getting married.

After Saturday, the only thing on my mind was spending Labor Day with my honey, Brent Richardson, and Sammy, his golden retriever. It was a ninety-minute drive from Rushing Creek to his current workplace in Terre Haute, Indiana. That meant weekends and holidays were pretty much the only time we got to see each other in real life.

"Okay, girl. Let's do this." I bit into the bagel and savored the combination of gooey and crunchy goodness. I wiped bagel crumbs from my mouth to keep them from ending up between the computer keys and opened the thriller manuscript.

Ninety heart-pounding minutes later, I let out a yelp and almost knocked my coffee off the table when there were three rapid, sharp knocks at my door. With a groan, I closed my computer. It wasn't fair that I had to walk away from an amazing story with only fifteen pages to go.

Ursi gave me a *meh* as she leapt from my lap. She landed on the hardwood floor without a sound and gave me a look over her shoulder as she padded to the door to let me know she expected me to open it.

"Hey, girlfriend," Sloane said when I opened the door. She scooped up Ursi and kissed her fuzzy head. "Oh. Hi, Allie."

"Whatever." I rolled my eyes as my best friend and I shared a laugh.

When we were together, the laughs came easy and often. It was good. I closed the door, and we got comfortable in the living room. Ursi started purring as loud as a lawn mower the nanosecond she got settled on Sloane's lap.

"You sure you don't want a cat of your own?" Ursi loved me in her own mysterious feline way, but she had formed an undeniable bond with Sloane during the days after Thornwell's murder. I'd suggested more than once that Sloane adopt a kitty, all to no avail.

"You know I couldn't betray Ursi like that. Besides, Luke says he's allergic to cats." She scratched my pet under her orange-and-black chin. "So little Miss Ursula gets all my love. Don't you, girl?"

Signaling her agreement, Ursi purred even louder.

My heart warmed at the sight. Sloane was my best two-legged friend, and Ursi was my best four-legged friend. The fact that they were besties made my life, which was pretty great, even better.

"So, what brings you by?" My gaze drifted to my computer. I needed to get back to work. Sloane's reason for stopping by unannounced must have been important, though. She never visited without texting first.

"Brace yourself." With a devious grin, she waited until I was leaning so far forward in my chair that I was literally on the edge of my seat. "The diner begins serving their seasonal apple pie at eleven."

My stomach growled, and my mouth started watering as visions of the most glorious pastry on Earth danced in my head. The Brown County

Diner served their fruit pies on a seasonal rotation. September was the pinnacle of apple picking season in Indiana, so the diner would be serving my favorite pie until mid-October, when it would switch to pumpkin.

I glanced at the antique clock hanging on the wall above the television. A wedding present from Thornwell, for decades it had hung in Dad's office. Mom gave it to me when I moved into the apartment. The hands, which kept perfect time, were currently pointing at the ten and the eight. *Twenty till eleven. That manuscript isn't going anywhere.* "Let me get Ursi's leash."

A few minutes later, my four-legged friend led us out the door and down the stairs. On the first floor, the door on the left opened to Renee's Gently Used Books, and the door on the right opened to the Sock Shoppe. I'd spent more than I cared to admit at both places,

Sloane leapt ahead of us and opened the front door. "Keep moving, girl. We can't let your mom get distracted by the new books."

"You mean like that one?" As we passed in front of the bookstore, I pointed at a hardback copy of *The Endless River* on display. It was Thornwell's final book. Published nine months after his death, it had maintained its lofty perch at the top of the best-seller lists for almost two months now.

My bestie stopped and placed her fingertips against the glass of the bookstore's window. As she stared at her father's work, she wiped what might have been a tear from her eye.

"Are people really calling it his best book ever?"

We resumed our trek to the diner.

I nodded as pride swelled within me at the small role I'd played in the book's publication. "A few people in the industry have mentioned the Pulitzer Prize and the Man Booker Prize."

"Wow." She shook her head. "Dad had his act together at the end, didn't he?"

"That he did."

An elderly couple staring at us with open mouths kept me from saying more. People often gave Ursi and me strange looks when we went for walks. Ursi ignored the stares. I had to make an effort to keep from laughing at the often-comical looks.

We got moving. There was glorious pie to be eaten. A few minutes later, we turned a corner, and the diner came into view. My stomach growled again. "I think they heard that in Bloomington." Sloane bumped her arm with my elbow. "I'll put our order in."

While she was inside, Ursi and I got settled at one of the handcrafted, wrought-iron tables in front of the diner. Despite my status as a local celebrity of sorts for solving Thornwell's murder, when I was with my feline companion, I still had to dine alfresco. On a glorious, sunny morning like today, with Ursi at my feet, grooming herself in preparation for a nap, I had no complaints.

A few minutes later, Angela Miller, the diner's owner, emerged with a platter laden with two massive pieces of pie and a saucer of milk. Sloane was right behind her with a carafe of coffee in one hand and two mugs in the other.

"How's the best literary agent in town today?" Angela placed the pieces of pie on the table and the saucer on the sidewalk next to Ursi.

"Given that I'm the only literary agent in town, I'm good. How's the campaign?"

"Overwhelming." Angela brushed a strand of black hair out of her face. "I didn't expect running for mayor would be so time-consuming. On the other hand, I'm loving every minute of it."

"I think you'll be a fantabulous mayor." Sloane wiped whipped cream from her lips. She was already a third of the way through her piece. "And it's not just because this is the most delicious pie you've made ever."

Angela put a hand on her hip. "If memory serves, you said the exact same thing about my blueberry pie a few weeks ago."

"Because it's true," Sloane said through a mouthful of the heavenly smelling pastry I hadn't even had a chance to taste yet. "You are an artist, and your pies belong in that art museum Allie always talked about when she lived in New York."

"The Met or the Museum of Modern Art?" Angela propped one arm on the other so her chin fit on her fist. Thanks to the compliments, her undivided attention was on Sloane.

"Both, actually." My bestie scooped up a massive forkful of the pastry and took a picture of it with her phone. "Totally going on Instagram."

"That's high praise." Angela gave her a knuckle bump. "I need to get back inside, but that may have scored you another piece."

"Let's go then."

I chuckled as they went inside. Sloane's youthful exuberance was the perfect yin to my reserved, introvert yang. She had an irrepressible spirit that hadn't been extinguished by having to cope with her father's murder. It made me proud, and thankful, to call her my friend.

When I finally took my first bite of the pie, my taste buds exploded in ecstasy. Sloane hadn't lied. This might have been Angela's best pie ever.

As the two of us dined with deliberate slowness, a police cruiser pulled into a parking space not far from us. While Sloane was my oldest friend, the officer who emerged, Jeanette Wilkerson, was one of my newest friends. We exchanged greetings, and Sloane asked her to join us. Despite the invitation, I couldn't help wondering if it was my bestie's attempt to go for a third piece of pie.

"I'm afraid I can't. On my way to see Jax Michaels, so I'm stopping for a coffee to go."

"You going to arrest him?" Sloane's eyes narrowed.

"Sorry, guys. Not this time." Angela gave Sloane's shoulder a gentle squeeze. Jax had been Thornwell's property manager for years until Thornwell fired him for failing to do work he'd been paid for. Sloane still held a grudge against the man. "He's complaining someone keeps stealing his CANNON FOR MAYOR yard sign. Says it's happened three times now."

"Serves him right," Sloane said with enough venom to paralyze a bison.

"Any idea who's doing it?" I put my fork down.

Rushing Creek's current mayor, Larry Cannon, had been in office for almost eight years. Our relationship over the last year had been a roller-coaster ride, but, in general, he'd done a good job. Despite that, I'd jumped on the Angela Miller for Mayor bandwagon early.

"Probably just kids causing trouble, but the chief wants to send a message that we won't put up with stuff like this." Jeanette tipped her cap to us. "See you around."

After Sloane and I finished, we took a circuitous route back to my apartment. I wanted to tease her that she needed the longer route to work off the calories she'd ingested, but I couldn't. It was too perfect a day to be snarky.

Besides, as a professional trail runner, Sloane was in top physical condition and burned through calories like an airplane burned through jet fuel. Some extra sugar and carbs from time to time never seemed to hurt her race performances.

Instead, we went over the game plan for Sloane's move. As we talked, she held out her left hand so the half-carat solitaire engagement ring could catch the sunlight.

"At times, I still can't believe we're getting married." Her goofy grin warmed my heart. She'd had a crush on my brother since we were kids, but it wasn't until the last year that their relationship had gotten serious.

"And I can't believe Luke had it in him to come up with such an amazing ring."

"I know, right? Your bro is full of surprises."

"And we'll stop right there before we get into TMI territory." We exchanged a high five. Thanks to years of practice, we made perfect contact without even looking at each other.

As we parted ways a little while later, I took some time to soak in my idyllic surroundings and incredible luck. I'd made a spur-of-the-moment decision to leave the literary agency I had been working for in New York to come home. The decision was working out better than I could have ever dreamed.

I had family and friends close by. I was my own boss, with a book on the best-seller lists. I even had a boyfriend, even if we only saw each other on weekends. As I unlocked the door to my apartment and got back to work, I had a feeling some exciting things were in my future. I couldn't wait to find out what they were.

Chapter Two

By the time my head hit the pillow that night, I'd finished edits on the thriller manuscript and sent it to my client with my comments. The manuscript would sell quickly, in days rather than weeks or months, so I couldn't wait to get it back with her final edits. I'd also spent the afternoon on the phone with editors at various publishing houses who were reading manuscripts I'd submitted.

I actually woke up before my alarm went off Friday morning, so, after a breakfast of mixed fruit and an English muffin, I put on my walking shoes and grabbed Ursi's collar. "How about a trip to the park, missy?"

Ursi looked up from her food bowl, licked a paw, and trotted to the front door.

All righty, then.

Winchester-Cobb Memorial Park wasn't a park. Yet. It was a fifteen-acre parcel of land that had been part of Thornwell's one-hundred-twenty-acre estate. Sloane inherited the property and donated the fifteen acres to the City of Rushing Creek so it could be developed into a park. She made a single request when she donated the land and the funds to build and maintain it.

She asked for the park to be named after her father and my father.

The city graciously accepted the donation and assembled a steering committee to oversee design and construction of the park. Mayor Cannon asked me to serve as the committee chair. It was a kind offer I couldn't refuse and was the first step in rebuilding the fractured relationship between us.

As steering committee chair, it was my job to serve as the liaison between the city parks department, which was overseeing day-to-day construction, and the community at large. Given that the park was being named in part after my father, who'd been my hero and mentor, I took the role seriously and visited the park at least once and often twice a week.

My visits typically consisted of saying hi to whoever was working on the site that day and making sure we were on schedule. I jotted down notes so I could report back to the committee on progress and any issues that might have arisen since the last meeting. I also took pictures and posted them on social media. I wanted to build excitement for the park's opening, which was scheduled for the second weekend in October. Just in time for the annual Rushing Creek Fall Festival.

I glanced at my watch when we arrived. It was a little after seven. The only sounds were the chirps of cardinals among the rapid hammerings of a woodpecker. "Doesn't look like we'll be talking to anybody today, girl. Come on. Let's take some pictures."

From the park's main entrance, we headed toward the area where a gazebo was to be constructed. I envisioned the structure as a draw for special events, like concerts and weddings, as well as a destination spot for family portraits and graduation pictures. I hoped to host book-related events there, too.

When the gazebo's construction site came into view, I halted so abruptly that Ursi yelped when her harness brought her to a surprise stop.

"No. No. This is all wrong."

The scene was equal parts confounding and panic-inducing. A dump truck was parked on a gravel path that led to the cleared area where the gazebo was to be built. The truck's bed was raised, and a full load of mulch, twenty cubic yards, had been dumped right where the structure was supposed to go.

I pulled up the construction schedule on my tablet. Three truckloads of mulch, sixty cubic yards in all, were scheduled for delivery today. They were supposed to go to the playground, though, not the gazebo.

"Come on, girl." Ursi and I double-timed it to the playground construction site to see if there was anyone who might have seen something. Nobody was to be found. After a park-wide search confirmed we were alone, we went back to the mulch pile.

A peek inside the truck's cab yielded no answers, so I called Luke. I figured that, since he was the superintendent of the parks department, he'd know if there was a change of plans that hadn't been communicated to me. While I was waiting for him to pick up, Ursi began straining against the leash. Evidently, she was finding the mulch pile irresistible.

"Go ahead. But don't go potty. It's a mulch pile, not a litter box, and I don't want to clean up after you." Once I unhooked the leash, she trotted to the edge of the pile and started sniffing and digging, as if she was a dog.

A growl escaped my throat when I got Luke's voice mail. "Hey, bro. We've got a problem at the construction site. Call me ASAP." After leaving the message, I texted Sloane in the hope she could tell me where her fiancé was.

I wanted the mess cleaned up before it threw the construction schedule out of whack. We were on a tight deadline, and the last thing I could afford was to lose a day because of a silly mix-up.

I was going through my project documents, trying to figure out where the snafu might have come from, when Ursi hissed and let out a growl that would make a mountain lion proud. By the time I looked up, her back was a feline version of the St. Louis Arch, and her tail was a bushy, black-and-orange feather duster.

"What's wrong?" I went to her and bent down to figure out what had her freaked out. Seconds later, I sprang back upright as my blood ran cold.

Ursi had uncovered a human finger.

Forcing myself to maintain some semblance of calm, I grabbed a decent-sized piece of mulch and scraped smaller wooden pieces from the finger. It only took a few scrapes to reveal an entire hand.

"Oh, God." I fell to my hands and knees and vomited. The hand wasn't fake. Or warm.

Something told me it was attached to an entire body.

With trembling fingers, I dialed 9-1-1. I broke out in goose bumps when I told the dispatcher I needed to report a dead body.

Discoveries like this weren't supposed to happen in Rushing Creek, Indiana. Sure, we had crime like petty thefts, drunk and disorderly conduct, and the occasional domestic violence report. But a capital crime like murder? No way. Especially only eleven months removed from the town's first murder in thirty years.

I was sitting on the ground in a daze when an officer dressed in the familiar indigo uniform of the Rushing Creek Police Department approached me. It was Matt Roberson, the police chief, who also happened to be my former brother-in-law.

He squatted down to look me in the eyes. "I'm here in response to your call. Can you show me where the hand is?" His voice was quiet, almost gentle, and had a calming effect.

"Ursi was digging and found the finger." My hand was shaking like an autumn leaf in the wind as I pointed toward the mulch pile. At the mention of her name, my kitty trotted to me and curled up in my lap.

Matt used a pen to push away more wood chips. He pulled on a rubber glove and placed his fingers on the wrist for a few seconds. Evidently unable to find a pulse, he said a few words into his radio. Chief among them was the word *coroner*.

I held Ursi when Luke jogged up to us. "I came as soon as I got your message." He ran his hands through his hair. "The work order was clear. I can't believe they screwed this up. I'm calling Parke Landscaping right now." He took out his phone.

"Don't do that." Matt got up. "This is an active crime scene."

Luke rolled his eyes. "It's just a delivery snafu, Matt. Anybody seen Georgie? He was supposed to tell the driver where to dump the load." He started scrolling through his phone.

"Don't." Matt took the phone from Luke. "My office received a call this morning from Parke reporting one of their trucks was missing. And Allie found that." He pointed at the exposed hand.

Luke's eyes went wide as the color drained from his face. "What the...?"

"You got a shovel in your truck?" Matt asked. When Luke nodded, Matt told him to get it. "I want to ID the victim as soon as possible."

As Luke sprinted to his truck, a Rushing Creek police cruiser pulled up next to the dump truck. Jeanette popped the trunk and took out a role of police tape and a handful of stakes. "What have we got, Chief?"

"Unidentified vic under this mulch. We need to clear enough to remove the body." Matt took a few of the stakes. "After we cordon off the area, take Allie's statement."

The scene was more surreal than a piece of M. C. Escher artwork. I was sitting in a police car, telling my friend about discovering what looked like a murder victim, while my brother and brother-in-law worked to uncover the body. The only normal thing in the scene was having Ursi curled up in my lap, asleep.

While we talked, a rescue vehicle rolled to a stop next to us. Two firefighters jumped out and, after some discussion, joined the shoveling effort.

"Is this really happening?" A hot tear rolled down my cheek. "It can't be real. Tell me it's an elaborate prank pulled by some high school kids."

"I'm sorry, Allie." Jeanette handed me a bottle of water.

When I finished my report, we sat in silence as the work continued. A few minutes later, the firefighters fetched a gurney from an ambulance that had just arrived. They lifted the uncovered body onto the gurney and placed a white sheet over it. Pieces of mulch dropped to the ground as they adjusted the sheet.

I squeezed Jeanette's hand and closed my eyes in a futile attempt to keep the tears at bay. "I've never seen a dead body like this. After last year, I thought I was tough. God, I was so wrong."

"You weren't wrong. Everybody reacts to a crime scene differently." Jeanette handed me a tissue. "Especially ones like these, which we don't see very often."

With a sniff, I dabbed at my cheeks. "Am I allowed to know who it is?"

"Of course." Jeanette got out of the car.

While she went to find the answer, I tried not to think, but my overactive imagination took the reins and spurred my brain into a full gallop. Who was the victim? How did he or she die? Was the death painful? Did I know the person? What would drive someone to take another person's life?

With no answers to be had, I hugged Ursi and scratched her ears. In response, she licked my cheek. It never ceased to amaze me how so much of the time she played the role of a standoffish cat perfectly, but in the year and a half since I'd adopted her, she *always* knew when I was hurting. And was always there to give me love and support.

I drew strength from that. As Jeanette opened the door to the cruiser, I was going to need it.

"The deceased's name is Georgie Alonso. Did you know him?"

My mind reeled as the news hit me like a kickboxing blow to my midsection. I knew Georgie Alonso. We had a history.

It wasn't a good one.

"Yeah. We were in the same class in high school. I don't want to speak ill of the dead, so I'll leave it at that." I looked out the window. Another police officer had arrived. This one was putting on plastic gloves as he strode toward the dump truck.

"I want to go home. Will you take me? I don't think I'm up to walking." I'd reached my limit. The only thing I could feel was a tidal wave of exhaustion crashing down on me. I wanted some chamomile tea, my bed, and a lighthearted rom-com to read.

"I'm afraid I can't do that. Matt has some questions for you and needs me to talk to the people at Parke Landscaping about the truck being taken. I can drop off Ursi on my way."

The hair on the back of my neck stood on end as I handed Ursi's leash and my door key to Jeanette. I broke out in goose bumps when she wouldn't make eye contact with me during the handoff. *Keep it together. I didn't do anything wrong.* I drained the water bottle, took a deep breath, and got out of the car.

With an unsteady gait, I made my way to Matt, who was talking to Luke. My brother enveloped me in his arms. "It'll be okay. Just be straight with Matt." He hugged me. "I told him I'd break the news to Lori. I don't want her finding out through the grapevine."

Good Lord. I hadn't had time to process how this would affect Georgie's girlfriend, Lori Cannon. Three years behind me in school, Lorelei Cannon, known to one and all as Lori, had been quiet but always had a smile whenever I said hi.

She was a math whiz, too. We were in the same calculus class my senior year in high school. I always figured she'd end up working for some Wall Street investment bank on the East Coast. Guess I missed on that prediction.

Lori was the mother to Georgie's five-year-old daughter, Brittany. And the only child of Larry Cannon.

The situation had just gone from bad to worse.

I crossed my arms and looked Matt in the eyes. He met my gaze, and we stood there, silent, for what seemed like forty years but was probably only four seconds.

"Jeanette said you have a few questions for me."

"I do." He flipped a page in his little cop notebook. "What time did you arrive at the park?"

"Sevenish."

"Did you see anybody else or talk with anyone else before you called Luke?"

"No."

Matt's pen scratched on the surface of the paper as I recounted the efforts I'd taken to find someone. His silence as I spoke was unnerving.

"Any reason why you came to the park so early this morning?"

"I'm an early bird. You know that." The hair on the back of my neck, which had relaxed, was back standing at attention. As the implication of Matt's line of questioning dawned on me, my throat went dry. "You can't possibly think I had anything to do with this, do you?"

"I don't think anything, right now." He flipped his notebook closed. "But I have more questions. Let's go to the station so I can ask them there." He put his hand on my arm to guide me toward his car.

"Wait a minute. Are you arresting me?"

"You have a history with Georgie, and you discovered the body. That makes you a person of interest. That's all it does, though."

Person of interest. I'd read enough books to know what that meant. As Matt opened the passenger door of the car, there was no doubt.

I was the main suspect in Georgie's murder.

Chapter Three

I'd ridden in Matt's cruiser once before. The circumstances between then and now were as different as ice cream and liver and onions. At least he was kind enough to keep the handcuffs on his belt and let me ride in the front seat.

My shoes scuffed against the black surface of the asphalt parking lot as he led me toward the municipal building. Once indoors, I leaned against Matt's arm for support as he guided me past his office and the officers' desks and into an eight-by-eight room containing a table and two chairs.

A blanket of icy fear enveloped me as Matt closed the room's steel door and gestured toward the chair on the far side of the table. The chill from the aluminum seat seeped through my leggings, and a shiver ran through me. The painted cinderblock walls radiated the cold. I rubbed my forearms to generate some body heat.

"Is this the time when I ask for a phone call or to refuse to say anything without my lawyer present?"

"You're not under arrest." Matt sighed and massaged his temples as he took his notebook out of his pocket. The embossed Rushing Creek Police Department logo on the cover blinded me for a second when he flipped it open. With the pace of a turtle that seemed deliberate, he removed a pencil from the same pocket.

"Then why am I here?" I placed my palms on the wooden tabletop. The rough texture of the aged surface scraped against my palms and sparked a flame of indignation that elbowed the shock into the corner. "This is your interrogation room, right?" I pointed at a window covering on the wall to my right. "Let me guess. There's a two-way mirror behind that curtain. Am I right? Do you have a camera hidden somewhere that's recording us?"

"Calm down." Matt popped a square piece of gum into his mouth. Over the previous winter, he'd managed to kick his cigarette habit with chewing gum, but it was rumored he replaced his Juicy Fruit with Nicorette when he was agitated. Evidently this was one of those times.

"How many times in the history of everything has someone actually calmed down when you said that?" The flame inside was spreading throughout my limbs. The warmth of righteous indignation urged me to press for an advantage. "The answer is none. With that out of the way, will you please tell me why we're here instead of in your office if I'm not a suspect and all you want to do is ask me some questions?"

"Police procedure. Nothing more, nothing less. And the more argumentative you get, the longer this will take." He tried to stare me down.

Sloane and I had been waging staring contests since we were eight, so I was more than prepared to meet his gaze. I'd reached fifty-nine using the trusty one-Mississippi, two-Mississippi silent counting method when Matt got to his feet.

I leaned back and smiled. *I owe you one, bestie.*

"Fine. Have it your way. For the record, we aren't being recorded. The thing is, in the aftermath of the Winchester investigation, some questions were asked regarding the unusual access to case information you may have had."

"My best friend's father had been murdered." Resentment propelled me to my feet. "It was also the first murder in this town in thirty years. If you ask me, the only thing that should matter is that the case was solved."

"So, the end justifies the means?"

"In some cases, yes. Like that one." I stared at the acoustical ceiling tiles. "Come on, Matt. I'm more than willing to tell you everything I know, but I didn't kill Georgie. What's this really about?"

"I can't give the appearance of playing favorites. You were the first person on the murder scene. You had a bad history with the guy." He flipped to a blank page in his notebook. "Let's play this by the book. Tell me again what time you got up this morning?"

Two hours, a doughnut, and two cups of coffee later, Matt closed his notebook. "You know the drill. If you remember anything else, call me. Don't leave town. And..."

"And what?" A headache had set in, I had to go to the bathroom, and I wanted to hug my kitty. I was *so* ready to be out of there.

"Stay out of this. Let me and my officers do our jobs." He opened the door. "Please."

"I'll take it under advisement." With as much dignity as I could muster, I swept past him and marched down the hall, avoiding eye contact with a police officer at his desk.

Jeanette met me at the door. After a glance at Matt, she walked me outside. "From the way your boss raked me over the coals, you sure you want to be seen with me in public?" I massaged the back of my neck to relieve some of the tension that had built up during the interrogation. This was turning out to be one of the worst mornings of my life.

"Yes, I do. I believe you, Allie. I'm sure Matt does too, but he has to—"

"Play it by the book. I know. He told me."

Jeanette put on her department-issued aviator shades. I was envious of how cool they made her look. "With the election a couple of months away, Matt's under the microscope. All of us in city government are. Anything that varies even the tiniest bit from protocol could become an election issue. Matt doesn't want the department to become a political football. I don't want that either." She shook her head and stared at the ground.

"What are you not telling me?"

"That if we're going to catch Georgie's murderer, we better do it fast, before the heat gets turned up so high it burns us all."

* * * *

I'd just inserted my key in the lock when my front door swung open.

My mom wrapped me in her arms and hustled me to my couch. "Oh, little one. I can't believe what's happened to you. Are you okay?" Her sky-blue eyes were red-rimmed with tears, but her jaw was clenched. I knew that look. She was mad, undoubtedly at Matt.

"I'm fine."

As Ursi jumped onto my lap, I looked around the living room. Luke was there, along with my sister, Rachel, who was staring out the window, tapping her foot in rapid-fire fashion. "That son of a—"

"Watch your tongue, young lady," Mom said in a sharp tone.

"He arrested Allie." Rachel spun on her heel, her long, blond hair covering her face as she turned. "How can you defend him?"

"I'm not defending him. There's no need for vulgarities. Besides—"

"He didn't arrest me." Cradling Ursi in my arms, I went to the kitchen and poured myself a tall glass of water and took a long drink. While the cool liquid was refreshing, what I really wanted was a big glass of wine.

Drowning my sorrows would accomplish nothing, though, so a drink would have to wait.

"He did, however, tell me I'm the main suspect." I returned to the living room and plopped down next to Mom, keeping my kitty close to my heart. "Good times, huh?"

"That's stupid. Everyone knows you wouldn't do something like that." Luke's phone went off. After taking a minute to read the message, he brushed his brown hair from his eyes and texted a response. "I need to get back to work. Larry wants to meet with Matt and me." He gave me a kiss on the head. "Hang in there, sis. I'll talk some sense into Matt."

"So, he didn't arrest you, but you're his main suspect." Mom frowned. "Where does that leave you?"

"As a casualty of municipal election silly season." Rachel took the open spot on the couch, leaving me in the middle. She gave my knee a squeeze and looked me in the eyes. "Everyone in Larry's administration is under the microscope. They're not going to cut you any slack and probably won't be as willing to work with you as they were with Sloane's dad."

"A minute ago, you were calling the man names and now you're defending him?" The heat of Mom's frustration nearly scorched me as she glared at my sister.

"No. I'm just…" My sister closed her eyes and ran her fingers through her hair. "I overreacted when I called him that, and I acknowledge it wasn't helpful to the situation at hand."

In recent months, Rachel and Matt had been attending post-divorce family counseling. There was no chance of them reconciling, which they both admitted without remorse or recrimination, but they were committed to improving their relationship for the sake of Tristan and Theresa, their twin children. Her comment was proof the counseling was working.

I gave Rachel's hand a reassuring squeeze. She was a Type A personality through and through. Making such an admission, which she probably perceived as a sign of weakness, couldn't be easy.

"Jeanette hinted at the same thing when I left the station." I turned to face Mom. "To answer your question, I don't know where this leaves me. What I do know is I'm not going to hide here in the apartment like a frightened bunny. I've got too much to do."

"I don't like any of this, but if you say so." Mom gave me a hug. "I need to get back to the office. Patients are waiting. I'll call you later. Promise me you won't do anything rash."

"Allie's too smart for that, Mom." Rachel opened the front door and gave Mom a hug. "If there's one thing I've learned in the last year, it's that your youngest child knows how to take care of herself."

"Laying it on a little thick, weren't you?" I asked when she closed the door behind Mom. "I appreciate the kind words, but..."

"Mom needed reassuring. You know as well as I do she's not been the same woman since Dad died. The less she needs to worry about us and Luke, the better."

Rachel was right. Mom was the strongest woman I knew, but the eleven months since Dad died had taken their toll. It wasn't like she was falling apart. Far from it. She still went to work as a primary-care physician every day, attended Mass every Sunday, and never missed the twins' activities.

She'd lost weight, though. And was using more concealer to hide the dark circles under her eyes. And she had called Luke twice asking for help because she'd locked herself out of her car.

Little things, perhaps. But they hadn't gone unnoticed by my siblings and me. Mom knew my sibs and I met for dinner every Wednesday at Rachel's restaurant, the Rushing Creek Public House. What Mom didn't know was we used that time to compare notes.

We were worried about her. We also knew she was too proud to talk to her children about her struggles. So, the three of us kept an eye on her and reported anything that concerned us.

It made me feel good to be helping Luke and Rachel with Mom. My sibs had covered for me when Dad got sick and I was living in New York. In doing so, they bore my share of the duties, both physical and emotional, during the final two years of his life. It was a debt I could never repay, so at least I could help with Mom and the twins now that I was back in Rushing Creek.

"Good point." I smiled. "I guess that means you have to compliment me whenever Mom's around."

My sister laughed. "Don't get your hopes up." With a sigh, she plopped down on the couch. "So, what are you going to do?"

"Whatever it takes to prove I didn't do it."

"You know I love you, right?" When I nodded, Rachel took a deep breath. "Do you think getting involved in this is a good idea?"

In the past, I would have taken her question as a swipe at my competence as an adult. I knew better now. My sister and I would never be best buddies; we were simply too different for that. But over the last year, we'd come to see the best in each other, to trust each other, and to accept each other for who we were.

"Believe me, I'd love to stand aside and leave things to the Rushing Creek PD, but based on my not-so-lovely interrogation with Matt, I'm already plenty involved."

Rachel shrugged. "I figured you'd say that, but I had to try." She gave me a hug. "At least promise me you'll be careful. No life-endangering escapades, okay?"

"Okay. Pinkie promise."

We wrapped the pinkies of our right hands around each other. It was a gesture to confirm the great importance I placed on the pledge.

After Rachel left, I gave Ursi a few kitty treats and chuckled as she gobbled them up in seconds. If the morning's events had traumatized her, they hadn't affected her appetite. It was easy to conclude they hadn't bothered her at all when, after a drink from her water fountain, she strolled to a sunny spot on the floor, curled up, and went to sleep.

While Ursi used napping to recover from the morning's events, I chose note taking. I went to my office and grabbed a battered spiral notebook from a bookshelf. I wanted to write down everything I had told Matt while it was still fresh in my mind. Doing so in the office, with its minimal distractions, would help me stay focused.

The office was the apartment's second bedroom. At twelve by twelve, the room wasn't overly spacious, but it met all my work needs. One wall was made up of floor-to-ceiling bookshelves. They'd come from my dad's office. There, the shelves had been filled with copies of his authors' published books. Here, there was only one book, on the top right shelf. Within the next few days, I'd be adding another, though. I had faith that, in time, my bookshelves would be as full as Dad's were.

Good things were happening in my life. I kept that in mind as I eased into my work chair. It was an executive model, made of polished wood and leather, that was handcrafted by a furniture maker in town. Sloane and Brent had given it to me as a housewarming gift. It was comfortable and roomy enough that I could share the seat with Ursi when I worked.

In other words, it was perfect.

I rolled up to my desk, an antique made of Indiana hardwoods, which was against the wall opposite the bookshelves. The desk, and the vintage Underwood manual typewriter occupying a corner of the work surface, also came from Dad. They were constant reminders of his legacy as a literary agent and made me thankful I'd chosen to keep his business, the Cobb Literary Agency, alive.

As I opened the notebook and took a pen from the WORLD'S GREATEST AUNT mug the twins had given me for my birthday, a tiny flame of anger flickered to life inside me. I had agent work to do, but I had to set that aside for a different kind of work.

Someone had killed Georgie Alonso. Circumstances made me the prime suspect. I needed to clear my name. And to do that, I had to find the killer.

Chapter Four

After spending an hour making notes, it was high time for some stress relief. I still wanted a drink but instead spent an hour in a high-intensity session with my kickboxing bag. After that, I rewarded myself with a delivery dinner from Marinara's, the pizza restaurant in town, and a glass of wine. I ended the day by reading a client's manuscript in bed with Ursi curled up at my feet.

When I woke up Saturday morning, my mind was clear, and I was ready to get to work. Today wasn't a day for agent work, though. It was a day for physical labor.

Moving day.

Mom, due to her devout Catholic beliefs, wasn't happy with the development. She was about the only one, though. My best friend and my brother were getting married the weekend before Halloween. The invitations had been sent, the reception hall had been reserved, and Sloane and I were going to Indianapolis for her final dress fitting coming up in a week. In my book, the fact that they were moving in together was a formality.

They were getting married. That was what mattered to me.

So, with a light heart, I gave Ursi a kiss on the nose and hopped on my bike for the ride to Sloane's apartment. Between walking my cat and riding my bike everywhere, including to get groceries, a lot of people around town said I was eccentric. While the label was an attempt to find an inoffensive way to say I was weird, it didn't bother me. I'd spent years in New York City without a car, after all, and didn't want the hassle and expense that came with owning one.

Besides, the walking and cycling helped keep me in shape, and Rushing Creek was small enough that I never had to go very far for anything. Even in snowy or rainy weather, I could get around without much difficulty if I was careful and dressed for the elements. If there was an item I needed that wouldn't fit into the basket in front of my handlebars or the saddlebags on either side of the rear wheel, I borrowed a car from someone in the family. I pushed the trigger on the bike's bell as I pedaled past Creekside Chocolates and waved at the store's owner, Diane Stapleton. The joyous *ting, ting, ting* made me smile. Normally, the happy sound made me laugh. Given the circumstances, I'd take the smile.

Much of southern Indiana is hilly, and Rushing Creek fit into that description. The rolling hills, and the twisting-and-turning roads that came with them, made for great recreational experiences for motorists, motorcyclists, and elite road bicyclists. I was none of those, so the trek uphill to Sloane's apartment complex included a climb that always left me a touch winded.

Today, I breezed right up the hill and coasted to a stop next to Luke's truck without a hint of labored breathing. Either my physical condition was improving or I was benefiting from an extra dose of murder-influenced adrenaline. My money was on the latter. It was a nice thought for it to be the former, though.

The door to the apartment opened as I was about to knock. "Yay! It's A.C. the K.C., here to fight the evil forces of putting kitchenware into moving boxes."

"Hey, you." My cheeks warmed as my bestie hugged me and spun me in a circle. Outside of my family, she was the most important person in my life. We'd grown up together, learned to ride bikes together, gossiped about boys together, and had more than a few drinks together. The most important achievement in my life was solving her father's murder. I'd do anything for her.

I hated her new nickname for me, though.

A.C. the K.C. was short for Allie Cobb the Kickboxing Crusader. Kim Frye, the reporter for the *Brown County Beacon*, our local weekly newspaper, had given me the nickname while reporting on how I used my kickboxing skills to help catch Thornwell's killer. Most people forgot about the nickname as the news cycle turned to other topics, like the start of high school basketball season. Not Sloane.

"You two going to make me do all the work?" Luke's voice came from the bedroom. A few seconds later, he appeared, carrying a brown moving box labeled WINTER CLOTHES in red ink.

"Not make you. Let you, honey." Sloane kissed him on the cheek as he made his way toward the door.

"That's gross. How many times do I have to ask you not to kiss my brother when I'm around?" I held the door open for Luke.

"Just wait until you see the kiss I'm going to give her at the wedding." With his hazel eyes glittering with mirth, he bumped me on the shoulder as he made his way through the doorway.

I closed my eyes, stuck my finger in my mouth, and acted like I was going to barf. "I've come to help, and you two are torturing me. With friends like you, who needs enemies?"

Sloane put her arm around me. "We just thought we'd try to keep the mood light after what happened." She led me to her couch. "Sorry I couldn't make it to your place yesterday. I was in Indy all day helping my mom look for a dress. How are you?"

"Better than yesterday." I was pleased with my initial round of note taking but didn't want to think about my predicament. For one thing, I wanted to give myself time to mull over what facts I knew, along with what assumptions I'd made.

For another, I wanted this day to be about Sloane. She'd been through so much in the past year. After losing her father in such a horrible way, she deserved to be happy. My mission was to make her happy, even if that meant getting hot and grimy from schlepping boxes from one place to the other. All my energies were directed toward helping her.

"Allie, you should know better than trying to lie to your best friend." She leaned toward me. "Did you get any sleep last night?"

Sloane was one of the few people who knew about my sporadic bouts with insomnia, which were brought on by high levels of stress. They'd gotten almost unbearable during the time of my dad's death, but the move from New York to Rushing Creek, combined with the use of aromatherapy products, had mostly cured the problem.

"A full nine hours." I normally slept between six and seven hours, so nine was a huge number.

Her wide eyes proved I'd convinced her there was nothing to worry about, so I shifted the conversation. "How did the dress shopping go?"

"Not as bad as I was afraid of. She's down to two dresses and plans on making a final decision by the end of next week." Sloane's relationship with her mom wasn't good, but they were working on it. Her report made me warm inside. Family was important.

Satisfied we weren't hiding anything from each other, we got up and made our way to the kitchen. First, we emptied the cabinets of their contents, then we put the plates, cups, glasses, and similar items in boxes. While we worked, she told me about their day looking for a mother of the bride dress.

The wedding colors were sage, sandalwood, and cream. The maid of honor, which was me, and the bridesmaids were wearing sage-colored dresses. Sloane wanted her mom to wear something in sandalwood, since the flower girl, my niece, Theresa, was going to be in a cream-colored dress. Accompanying my friend step-by-step as she planned her wedding had been an interesting character study. At the start, I had no idea what to expect from my ultimate tomboy bestie when it came to wedding planning.

After helping her make decisions on everything from the wedding ceremony's location to the guest list to the buffet menu, I concluded Sloane knew what she wanted yet was the polar opposite of a bridezilla. When she made a decision, she talked it over with Luke before making it final. Then she was firm, yet gentle, that the decision was to be respected.

At the end of the day, she wanted one thing for her wedding. She wanted a day everyone would look back on with a smile. That included her mom. I had guarded optimism that the wedding would be a huge step forward in their relationship.

Once all the kitchen items were boxed up and labeled, we moved to the spare bedroom, where Sloane kept the supplies for her trail-running career, including a decade's worth of training notebooks, boxes of energy bars, and large plastic jugs of powdered nutritional supplements.

Luke yelled at us to get back on track when he caught us flipping through a photo album. She told him he could sleep on the couch tonight. When he tried to argue that the house was his, I reminded him that once they were cohabitating, she was in charge and had the final say in all matters. We shared a giggle when that seemed to shut him up.

As we loaded the final boxes into the truck and Sloane's Subaru, Sloane tossed a few questions about yesterday's events in my direction. I deflected each one, insisting that while it was horrible Georgie had lost his life, I had full confidence in everyone at Rushing Creek PD.

A few hours later, the three of us were sitting on the backyard deck of the happy couple's house, soaked in sweat but pleased with our efforts. While we sipped iced tea from pint glasses embossed with the Rushing Creek Public House logo, Luke tried to put his arm around Sloane.

"Yuk." She scooted as far away from him as the love seat would allow. "It's too hot for you to get all snuggly. You need a shower."

"Whatever." My brother rolled his eyes, but he was smiling. "We appreciate your efforts to make this day about us and not about you, Allie. We're worried about you, though. You want to talk about yesterday?"

Lacking the energy to argue, I told them everything, from the time Ursi discovered the finger to the time I concluded my note-taking session. "At this point, I'm not sure what to do next. I might sit tight and wait until I can get a copy of the police report."

Luke put down his drink and leaned toward me. "Check out Roger Parke. Georgie worked for him until he crashed one of Roger's trucks. Totaled it. Since he was on the clock, he had to take a mandatory drug test."

"And?" Dozens of possibilities were running through my mind. Given my negative attitude about the guy, none of them were good.

"He failed it. No surprise there. Tested positive for weed. Roger fired him that day."

"And you're privy to this information how?"

Rushing Creek was like any small town. Gossip and rumors spread faster than the pace of high-speed Internet. As I'd recently learned firsthand, though, accuracy often took a back seat to hyperbole.

"The mayor made Luke hire the bum." Sloane had a pinched look like she'd just bitten into a fresh lemon.

"What?" In the months since I'd moved back to Rushing Creek, there had been numerous situations in which I felt totally out of the loop, thanks to my dozen-year absence. This was the latest.

"Yeah." Luke scratched the back of his neck. "Lori was pregnant with Brittany at the time. Larry didn't want Georgie to be out of work."

Stunned into silence by the revelation, all I could do was shake my head. After what seemed like hours, I finally found my voice.

"You're suggesting Roger Parke killed Georgie because Georgie cost him money by crashing a truck? Years ago? Seems like a stretch to me."

"That's not all." Sloane traced a circle in the condensation on her glass. "Georgie claimed he got hurt in the crash. He filed a workplace injury lawsuit against Roger."

"Not so much of a stretch now, huh?" Luke finished his drink. "I'm starving. Let's continue this conversation at the pub. I'll buy."

An hour later, we were cleaned up and seated in our favorite corner booth at the Rushing Creek Public House. Luke had a pint of the pub's house brew, Rushing Creek Red. I had a glass of chardonnay. With a race two days away, Sloane had a sparkling water.

Our waiter, a young man with electric blue hair and Latino features, had just taken our appetizer order when Rachel slipped into the open spot next to me.

"I was wondering if you guys were ever going to get here." She added sweetener to her iced tea and lifted her glass. "To my brother and the sweetest woman I know, who's willing to put up with him. May you enjoy your weeks of living in sin until you get hitched."

We clinked glasses among warnings to Sloane to make sure Luke did his own laundry and reminders to my brother to leave the toilet seat down. The waiter brought the appetizer, an order of deluxe nachos served on a sixteen-inch pizza pan, and all conversation ceased.

"To what do we owe the honor of having you join us?" I scooped salsa and sour cream onto a nacho chip. The salty, spicy, and creamy combination sent my taste buds straight to heaven. "My compliments to your chef, by the way."

"Thanks." Rachel's blue eyes sparkled at the compliment. "We're going to feature them in the Taste of Rushing Creek during the Fall Festival."

While we munched on the nachos, the conversation turned to the unpleasant topic of Georgie's murder. Rachel wanted to know what progress I'd made, so I brought her up to speed, including the information from Luke and Sloane.

When I finished, she tapped her fingernail on the lacquered wooden tabletop. It was something she did when she was deep in thought. "Something else you should know about. Georgie hung out at Hoosiers a lot. And by a lot, I mean he was there almost every day after work. Talk to Willie Hammond. If anybody knows what Georgie was up to last Thursday, I'd put my money on Willie."

Willie Hammond was the brother of "Big Al" Hammond. Big Al, the owner and namesake of the restaurant that served the best burgers in Indiana, was one of my favorite people in the world. Willie, not so much. Where Big Al was like a giant-sized teddy bear and was always ready with a smile and a hug, Willie was like a real-life grizzly bear. You could feel his presence, even if you couldn't see him. If you weren't part of his inner circle, he kept you at arm's length, and if he felt you wronged him, he'd turn his back on you in the blink of an eye.

The Hammond brothers were a mere eighteen months apart in age, Willie being the elder, but miles apart in every other way. Their parents had owned Hoosiers for years, running it as a family restaurant that featured all kinds of pop culture memorabilia related to the state of Indiana. When they decided to retire and spend their golden years in the Florida sun, they turned the restaurant over to Al and Willie to jointly run it.

The brothers' visions for the restaurant differed as much as their personalities, and within a year, Willie had bought out Al's share of the business. Al took his proceeds and opened Big Al's Diner. With Al out of the picture, Willie turned Hoosiers into a sports bar. Both businesses had thrived over the ensuing two decades, but the split had caused a rift between the brothers that time had yet to heal.

"You think he'll talk to me?" It was no secret around town that Al and I were close. I ate at his restaurant at least once a week.

"Cheese and rice, we're not in middle school. Just because you babysat for Al's kids doesn't mean Willie's going to treat you like a loaf of moldy bread. I'm on a committee with Willie at the Chamber of Commerce. He's not so bad once you get to know him, and I'm one of his competitors."

"Rachel's got a point," Sloane said. "Couldn't hurt to talk to him. I mean, it's only your freedom on the line."

"Indeed." I looked at my dining companions one by one. They wanted to help, and their advice was solid. "I'll talk to both Roger and Willie."

"And let us know what you find out." Luke pointed his fork in my direction. "We'll do whatever we can. Got it?"

Later that evening, I scratched Ursi between her ears as I updated my Keep-Allie-Out-of-Jail notebook list with information I'd obtained during the day. There was much work to be done and not enough time to do it.

Exhausted, I let out a long sigh. "We'll take things one day at a time. Right, missy?"

Ursi lifted her head to look at me. Once she had my full attention, she closed her eyes at a languid pace and opened them again, a gesture of affection and trust. It was always a good sign to have my kitty in my corner.

My question to Ursi unleashed a torrent of other questions, though. All revolving around a factor that was my enemy—time.

When, exactly, did Georgie die? Was he dead before or after the mulch was piled on top of him? If he was at Hoosiers the night he was killed, when did he leave? When was the dump truck taken from Parke Landscaping? When was the last time someone who wasn't the murderer saw him alive?

As I got in bed and turned off the light, another question came to mind. If I could find answers to the timing questions, I could find the answer to this latest question.

Why did the murderer kill Georgie?

Once I figured that out, I'd find the killer.

Unless the killer found me first.

Chapter Five

I'll admit it. The reason I went to Mass every Sunday was more about spending time with Mom than saving my soul. Over the last few months, Sunday mornings had become our time. We met outside St. James Catholic Church, attended 9:30 Mass, and then had breakfast.

On this Sunday, the church became my sanctuary. For whatever reason, I didn't think about the murder until Father Edwards delivered his homily. During the priest's talk, he addressed Georgie's death and reminded us that, in the darkest of times, it was up to every one of us to be our own source of light. And that by sticking together in the spirit of service to others, our light would become so bright there would be no dark corners left where evil could hide.

The words resonated with me as I reflected on the past few days and how so many people had offered to help, without even being asked. Their confidence in me was empowering. Their unwavering belief in my innocence was, too.

Leaving the church, I made a promise that when I returned next week, Georgie's killer would be behind bars. It was a promise I had every intention of keeping.

"Let's go to the diner for brunch. I'll buy." With gray skies overhead, but no threat of rain, it was an ideal morning for the four-block walk to the Brown County Diner. Besides, my muscles were a little sore from all the packing, moving, and unpacking from the day before, and the walk would help loosen them.

Mom hesitated. "I was hoping we could have the morning for just the two of us."

"Uh-huh." I started walking. "You just want to get me alone so you can ask me all the questions you wanted to ask on Friday but didn't have the time and you're too scared to ask them in public."

"I am not." She caught up with me. "I simply want to have a nice, quiet visit with my daughter. Is that so wrong?"

"No." I smiled. "Except for the fact that your denial confirmed you want the scoop about"—I shrugged—"you know. You can interrogate me to your heart's desire at the diner."

"I can't do that."

That wasn't the response I expected. On top of that, her clipped tone was a decades-old signal she was hiding something. With my curiosity piqued, I turned toward her. "Why not?"

After looking around to make sure we were alone, Mom took a deep breath. "I have something that might help with your investigation. If I tell you, I'll be violating a patient's confidentiality."

"Then don't tell me. I'm in enough hot water. There's no need to add you to the pot." I started to move, but she took hold of my arm.

"I mean, when I tell you. This is too important. *You* are too important. So, let's go to your apartment where we can talk without being overheard."

Mom was a straight arrow and one of the pillars of the Rushing Creek community. If she was willing risk getting in trouble by sharing information, whatever she knew had to be huge.

"My apartment, then." I looped my arm through hers and forced a smile that I hoped didn't look forced as we headed for her car. "Shall we?"

* * * *

While I rummaged through the fridge to decide what to prepare for breakfast, Mom and Ursi entertained themselves. They were in the living room, batting a toy onion ring back and forth across the hardwood floor. Mom used her foot, while Ursi used her front paws. They were so caught up in their competition I had to tell Mom brunch was ready three times before she joined me.

"Breakfast burritos, eh? What's in them?" Mom spread a thick slice of margarine on a piece of toast. Sometimes she could be as finicky as the twins when it came to food. I enjoyed seeing her expression when she tried something new I'd prepared and liked it.

"Don't worry. Nothing too exotic. Corn tortillas, sliced bell peppers, poblano peppers, mushrooms, and grated cheese." I slid two small serving bowls across the table. "Be sure to add some salsa and guacamole. I made the guac myself."

She took a bite and raised her eyebrows. "This is great. Where'd you get everything?"

"Got the tortillas at the bakery. Everything else at the grocery. Even the avocado."

"Avocados in Rushing Creek. I see your browbeating the folks at the grocery is getting results." She winked as she dipped a piece of her burrito into the guac.

"The Barbours know what they're doing. It only took a little begging on my part." The current proprietors of Rushing Creek's grocery store were second-generation owners who'd been running the operation for twenty-five years. They'd remained in business because they were good people and smart businessmen.

One aspect of those smarts was reflected in their willingness to stock unusual items when a customer was willing to pay a premium for them. If I had to pay more to get an avocado in Rushing Creek than I would if I drove to Bloomington or Indianapolis, so be it. It was important to me to have thriving, local businesses. My agency was one, after all.

We got caught up on the local goings-on while we ate. It never ceased to amaze me how much could happen in a little town in a single week. And especially know much my mom knew.

"Do you know everybody's business?" I emptied my coffee mug and poured a refill from the ceramic carafe.

"Of course not, but it's my job to know what's going on in the lives of my patients. I need to pay attention. I never know when someone may say something about a new ache or a spouse who isn't sleeping. Maybe it's nothing, but I've lost count of how many times something a patient thought wasn't important turned into a diagnosis of something major."

"Okay. I get it." I took a drink. Hot coffee always helped me focus. "While listening to your patients, you get intel on everything, and everyone else."

"In a manner of speaking." Mom scooped up her last piece of tortilla and a stray mushroom. "Which is why I wanted to talk to you here. I know something about Georgie. It's something you need to know."

"I don't want you to violate doctor-patient confidentiality."

"And I don't want you to go to prison." She took our empty plates to the sink. It was as if she needed time to decide once and for all whether to share her secret. When she returned to the table, she spread her napkin on her lap. The debate had ended.

"When Matt was up for police chief, he wasn't the only candidate for the job. Tommy Abbott was being considered, too. A lot of people in town, myself included, thought Tommy was the better candidate."

"Why didn't he get it?" I'd gotten to know Tommy Abbott a little bit while I investigated Thornwell's murder. He seemed like a good cop.

"Right around the time the city council was interviewing candidates for the chief job, there was an incident. Tommy tried to arrest Georgie one night at Hoosiers. I'll spare you the details, but Georgie filed a complaint claiming police brutality. Tommy denied it, but..."

"With a charge like that hanging over Tommy's head, there was no way he was going to get the job."

Mom nodded. "Tommy's wife, Wendy, is one of my patients. Based on some of her comments, Tommy's never gotten over it."

"Can't say that I blame him." Mom knew all too well the heartache Georgie had caused me. Given the circumstances, I was glad she'd confided in me.

Revenge was a strong motivator. Still, was the loss of a promotion enough of a reason to murder someone?

"There's something else." Mom's tone sent a shiver down my spine. It was way too reminiscent of the tone she'd taken when she told me about Dad's cancer diagnosis. "A year or so after Matt was named chief, I saw Wendy for an emergency appointment. She had a broken arm and a black eye. She said she'd tripped in her backyard doing landscaping work."

"The classic battered spouse lie." I wrapped my arms around myself. When I was in New York, I did volunteer work with coworkers at a women's shelter. To this day, some of the stories I had heard made my blood run cold.

"Yep." Mom loaded the dishwasher. "I tried to get her to ask for help, but she said no. Wendy promised Tommy had never hurt her before. As far as I can tell, he hasn't since, either."

"Any other incidents of violence you're aware of?" I fetched my notebook and jotted down an abbreviated version of what Mom had told me.

"No. But Tommy has a bit of a reputation as a hothead."

I rubbed my eyes, then wrote Tommy's name on the page entitled "Suspects." To the right, I made three columns. I labeled the column on the left "Motive." I labeled the one in the center "Means," and the one on the right "Opportunity."

Revenge was a classic motive for murder. I put a check mark under "Motive." The man was a cop, so it was beyond doubt he had the means to do it. Another check mark went under "Means."

The only question that remained was opportunity. Tommy worked nights, but was he working the night of Georgie's murder? Did it matter whether he was working or not? I didn't know but was pretty sure of the answer. I put a check mark under "Opportunity."

After Mom left, I spent a few hours reading queries, the letters authors send to gauge my interest in potentially representing their books. I had a special e-mail address set up to receive queries, and since Thornwell's book had come out, it filled up if I didn't go through it at least twice a week.

As a one-person business owner responsible for all aspects of the agency, including revenue generation, having so much interest from authors was a good challenge to have. I was able to pay my bills, but just barely, so even with a potential murder charge hanging over my head, I couldn't afford to neglect my business.

Of the three dozen queries I read, four interested me. I responded to those authors with my standard request for the first three chapters of the book and a synopsis, a two-page summary of the entire story. After hitting the SEND key on the last of the responses, I sat back and let out a long, tension-releasing breath. I loved my job, and spending the afternoon on it left me energized and ready to tackle my final activity of the day—attending a meeting of the volunteers to elect Angela Miller mayor of Rushing Creek.

After the events of the previous year, I'd been hoping someone would run against Larry Cannon for mayor. I would have supported anyone—Luke, Diane from Creekside Chocolates, even the hedgehog that lived downstairs in the bookstore. Okay, maybe not the hedgehog, but I was convinced there were any number of folks in town who would be a strong alternative to Larry.

It wasn't that I didn't think Larry was a capable mayor. It was more that I didn't approve of some of his personal choices. I also didn't want him to run unopposed. After all, I was still influenced by my years in New York. In the last mayoral race in which I voted, six candidates received at least one percent of the vote. To me, someone being elected to public office without opposition was an insult to those who fought and died for our freedom.

Given that, I was overjoyed when Angela announced her candidacy. She had it all. A lifelong Rushing Creek resident, a business owner, and a parent, she could speak intelligently on any number of campaign issues. She was also outgoing without being fake. In short, she was the real deal, and I couldn't wait to get started working for her.

The excitement that was bubbling inside me as I walked into Angela's basement recreation room didn't last long. In fact, it lasted for all of about three seconds. That was the time it took for conversation to go from an excited buzz to nonexistent and for all heads to be turned in my direction. As I gave Angela a hug, someone made a comment just loud enough for me to hear. The words were an excruciating slap across the face.

"I can't believe a murderer would show her face in public like this." As I froze in mid-hug, Angela drew me to her. "I'll take care of it."

With her arm around me, she turned us to face the gathering. There must have been two dozen people in the room.

She cleared her throat and waited until all eyes were on her. "Thank you all for coming. I also want to say a special thank you to my dear friend Allie Cobb for being here. It means the world to me that the person who caught Thornwell Winchester's murderer supports me in this election. Allie put her life on the line to bring justice to our community. That kind of integrity is priceless, and I, for one, am not going to let silly rumors go unanswered when I know how much of a hero Allie is.

"Her selfless actions last year inspired me to take this leap of faith and run for mayor of our beloved Rushing Creek. I can't thank her, and all of you, for your faith in me. Let's get to work."

A flurry of activity followed as people went from chatting to specific tasks. Pieces of paper were taped to the white walls every ten feet or so. On the papers, in black marker, were written committee names. The committees ranged from Phone Bank to Voter Registration to Public Relations. Under the Phone Bank sign, a group of four people huddled around a document that had names and phone numbers on it. After some discussion, they headed upstairs, with their cell phones out, to make calls to Rushing Creek residents.

I tried to join the special events committee, then the fund-raising committee, but each time I was given the cold shoulder. Evidently, Angela's faith in me hadn't transferred to the rest of the volunteer force.

With the message received, I wandered to the signage station and began assembling yard signs. The colors of the signs, blue and white, were the colors of Rushing Creek High School. The fact that Angela had decided to forgo the more common red, white, and blue political colors and use a color scheme that voters would immediately connect with—those of the local school system—made me smile. It was a subtle way to connect with the school system, which was a source of local pride. She always had every detail covered.

A little while later, there was a tap on my shoulder.

"Impressive stack you've got there." Angela patted the pile of the assembled signs. "How many?"

"Eighty-four." My fingers were black from the grit on the wire sign frames. I wiped them on my jeans. "I'm not quite halfway through." "That's a great start. We'll hand them out at the Labor Day Festival tomorrow." She motioned toward the stairs. "I could use some help taking these to the car. Would you give me a hand?"

When we had the signs loaded into Angela's minivan, she took a seat on the back bumper and motioned for me to join her.

"I'm so sorry about the way you've been treated tonight. I'm going to have a word with a number of people, letting them know in no uncertain terms my opinion of you."

"Which is?" Angela's words were a balm to the aching wound in my heart. I wasn't one for self-pity, but in a way, the reaction I'd received from the others made me feel isolated, like I didn't exist, like I was a victim of the murder, too.

"I've known you since you were a toddler. You're a kind person. A good person. You're not the type to hurt someone, much less take another life."

"Unless it's self-defense." My mind drifted back to the time I used my kickboxing training to help me apprehend Thornwell's murderer.

"Very true. And I'm glad you weren't afraid to do what it took back then." She bumped her shoulder against mine. "Between you and me, I'd give almost anything to see video footage of the Kickboxing Crusader in action."

"I'm *so* glad there's no footage of that. I bet I looked like David trying to take on Goliath."

We laughed. At five-one and a hundred and ten pounds, I didn't make for an intimidating figure. All my life, I'd tried to make up for my lack in stature with smarts and quickness. That mind-set had served me well so far, but would it be enough to help me be up to the challenge before me?

"I don't know about that." Angela got to her feet. "What I do know is you're a fighter. And you're going to need to be one until Georgie's murder is solved."

"I know. Matt's basically told me I'm on my own."

"Unfortunate, but understandable. There's something else, though. Larry and I have our first debate in two weeks. He won't want to face questions about an unsolved murder."

"Are you saying he'll have me arrested if the killer hasn't been caught by then?" Larry and I were hardly friends, but even he wouldn't stoop to something so underhanded. Would he?

"No. At least, I sure hope not. What I am saying is don't let yourself be put in that situation." She placed her hands on my shoulders. "Find the killer before the debate, Allie. You solved a murder once. You can do it again."

"Thanks." I gave Angela a hug. Yes, I could do it again. I would do it again. I'd find Georgie's killer and do it before the debate.

It sure looked like my freedom depended on it.

Chapter Six

My life had been a roller coaster full of twists and turns the past three days. As I woke up Monday morning, it was with great hope that the day's portion of the ride would be a smooth stretch that went gently uphill. The night before, when I got home from Angela's house, I took a long hot bath using some bergamot oil to unwind. Then I curled up with a book, a bowl of popcorn, and Ursi by my side—in short, the most relaxing way to end the day.

Despite my troubles, Labor Day promised to be amazing because Brent was coming to town. His job took him around the state of Indiana overseeing the installation of genealogy equipment in local libraries. I teased him, saying he was a twenty-first-century vagabond living in a short-term rental for a couple of months before moving to a new community, where the process started all over again. He loved his work, though, and I loved hearing about his travels around the state.

A cold front had moved in overnight, bringing chilly temperatures and scattered showers. I wasn't going to let the dismal forecast ruin my mood. On the contrary, the weather had provided a perfect excuse to break out my brand-new Cobb Literary Agency fleece jacket. After all, it couldn't hurt to add some promotional efforts to a day of fun.

I was sipping a post-breakfast cup of coffee when a rapid sequence of five knocks on the door had me out of my seat. Ursi scrambled from her perch by the front window to race me to the front door. My kitty had learned that the pattern of knocks meant Brent was here. She was no dummy. He always had a treat for her, so her warm greeting was mostly based on the snack she knew was forthcoming. Hey, whatever worked to get my cat to warm up to my boyfriend was all right by me.

I opened the door and sucked in a little breath as my heart rate ticked up a notch. It had been two weeks since I'd seen Brent, and in that time, he'd started growing a beard. The stubble served as a rugged accent to his mid-length brown hair, which tended to fall in front of his round, steel-rimmed glasses. The brown, tweed sport coat and blue jeans completed the hipster librarian look.

"Aren't you dashing today." I stepped aside and gestured for him to come in. "To what do I owe the pleasure?"

"Simply happy to see you." He leaned down and gave me a kiss on the lips that made my heart flutter, then offered me a bouquet of flowers he'd been hiding behind his back. "Pretty flowers for a pretty lady."

I took the colorful mixture of red, orange, and purple daisies and placed them in a vase on my kitchen table. Ursi jumped onto the tabletop and gave the flowers a sniff. After gently pawing at a few of the lower-hanging petals, she curled up next to the vase, licked a paw, and stared at Brent, ready for her treat.

"I guess she likes them." I scratched her between the ears. "That makes two of us. Ready for the awesomeness that is the Rushing Creek Labor Day Festival?"

"Yeah, but…" He went to the living room and lowered his six-five frame onto the couch. "Before we go, I was hoping you'd tell me what happened at the park."

"There's not much more to tell." We'd spoken Friday night, and I'd assured him I was fine. He'd texted me the following two days, ostensibly to confirm our plans for today. I knew better. He'd been checking in on me.

"That's not what Sloane and Mrs. Miller said." He smiled and spread his long arms along the couch cushions. "Given the fix you're in, I thought I'd get into town early and do a little investigating of my own."

I didn't want to ruin the day by getting into a fight with my boyfriend. I didn't get to see him often enough, so being disagreeable would be a waste of time. Besides, I was curious to hear the details of his conversations.

"How about you tell me what they said." I slipped onto the couch next to him. "Then I'll decide if you have a future in private investigation."

"Fair enough. When I got to town, I dropped Sammy off at Luke and Sloane's house so he wouldn't be cooped up here in the apartment. She told me about the conversation you guys had at the pub. After that, I stopped by the diner for a cup of coffee. Mrs. Miller was there. She told me about the jerks you had to deal with last night." He took a deep breath. "And the deadline you're up against."

When he was finished, I tried to swallow, but my throat had run dry. The picture he painted was one hundred percent accurate and one hundred percent nerve-racking at the same time. I had a lot to do, and not a lot of time to do it, which was beyond frustrating. I'd been so looking forward to spending a fun-filled day with Brent, not thinking about Georgie's murder.

"What do you say we enjoy ourselves at the street fair while keeping our eyes and ears open? Later, we can discuss what we learned over something to eat, maybe at Big Al's."

I had a brain blast at his mention of the restaurant. I could try to pump Al for information about Willie. I wasn't happy with the thought of getting Al to spill the beans on his brother, but that was the cost of living life as the number-one suspect.

"I like the way you think." I kissed Brent and popped to my feet. "Let's go have fun and play investigator while we're at it."

Separated from the entrance to Green Hills State Park by the waterway that gave the town its name, Rushing Creek thrived on the tourist trade. Virtually every holiday that brought folks to the park was accompanied with some sort of street festival or celebration.

While all the celebrations paled in comparison to the massive Fall Festival extravaganza, each had characteristics that made them unique and entertaining. Memorial Day featured a salute to our fallen veterans and a vintage car show. The Fourth of July had a parade, and the day concluded with spectacular fireworks.

Labor Day was close to the end of summer, so Rushing Creek celebrated with a cookout. The community groups and local businesses offered something unique to eat or drink. A new catchphrase was developed for the event each year, but the locals preferred the unofficial slogan—"Eat your way through Rushing Creek."

Since it was still chilly and overcast when we stepped outside, we headed for Creekside Chocolates' hot chocolate, the most magical drink on Earth, in my estimation.

My friend Diane Stapleton was staffing a booth in front of the store. Samples of chocolate and other decadent morsels covered a blue-and-white-checked tablecloth. When she saw us, she stepped out from behind the booth.

"Hey, sista." She was wearing a T-shirt in a khaki shade that highlighted how richly brown her skin was. Her luminous black hair, which until a few months ago had been colored purple, was pulled back into a tight topknot. In short, even while working, she was gorgeous.

"About time you came to see me. I've been worrying about you all weekend." She gave me a hug. "Anything I can do to help?"

I waved her concern away. "I'm fine. It's nothing one of your hot chocolates won't take care of."

We chatted for a few minutes while Brent tried a few samples. I abstained since I was holding out to get my chocolate in liquid form.

When some people approached the booth, we moved toward the shop's front door.

Diane put her hand on my arm. "I've got my ears open. If I hear anything interesting, I'll let you know. You're not in this alone."

My eyes clouded over, and a lump formed in my throat. It took some effort, but I managed to swallow and blink the tears away. As Brent and I waited for our drink orders, it occurred to me that I'd spent so much of my time thinking about solving Georgie's murder, I hadn't thought of the effects of said murder.

A man was dead. He wasn't a good man. To be honest, I despised Georgie Alonso. That didn't mean it was okay to have his life taken from him. What about his family? How were Lori and their daughter coping?

Suddenly, it was sweltering in the shop. I slipped out of my fleece, but then had trouble breathing. I told Brent I needed some fresh air and bolted for the door.

I was at the metalsmith's shop, looking at some silver earrings with tiny books on the ends, when Brent joined me.

"You okay?" He handed me my drink. "If you want, we can go back to your place."

"No." I paid for the earrings and put them on. As I did so, I glanced at the sky. The clouds were parting. "I need to be out and about. I'm taking these earrings as a sign today's going to be a good day."

After a couple of hours wandering up and down the Boulevard, the nickname for Rushing Creek's main thoroughfare, sampling all kinds of food and drink, we arrived at the Chamber of Commerce booth. I'd always loved this stop since the Chamber served venison stew.

As a little kid, I'd always thought eating venison was partaking in something as exotic as dining on caviar while cruising the Mediterranean. Nowadays, the sampling of the stew meant one word that I'd come to learn was as important as anything in my life.

Home.

With an eyebrow raised, Brent sniffed at his bowl. I dove into mine like I hadn't seen food in a week. His over-the-top reluctance to try the stew was borderline hysterical.

"Chicken. What are you afraid of?" I devoured a spoonful that left my bowl empty and relished the tangy flavor of the local delicacy.

"You said this was deer meat." When I rolled my eyes, he handed his sample-sized bowl to me. "You eat it. I can't stand the thought of eating Bambi."

Our verbal joust was interrupted by a shift change among the booth volunteers. To much fanfare, Larry Cannon arrived on a bike wrapped in red, white, and blue crepe streamers. He was wearing a blue blazer that had a red, white, and blue button on the lapel emblazoned with the logo KEEP CANNON.

"Allie, it's good to see you again." The mayor shook my hand. "And you as well, Mr. Richardson. I was worried about the weather, but it's turned into a fine day, hasn't it?"

"That it has." I kept my tone friendly. Part of me didn't trust the man and probably never would.

On the other hand, he'd supported the proposal to build Winchester-Cobb Memorial Park without a moment's hesitation. He'd been the one who suggested I serve as the steering committee chair. If I needed to see him about anything related to the project, he made the time.

I couldn't escape the sense he was trying to make up for the abhorrent way he'd treated me in the past. Whatever the reason, the least I could do was act like an adult and respond to his olive branches in kind.

Larry cleared his throat. "Mr. Richardson, would you mind giving Allie and me a moment alone?"

Brent's eyes narrowed, but when I nodded, he shrugged. "Sure. I'll be looking at the stained glass in the next booth."

When we were alone, Larry shoved his hand in his pockets. "Chief Roberson briefed me on the unfortunate circumstances of Friday. I wanted to let you know I've instructed him to use any and all tools at his disposal to find the culprit. The *true* culprit."

"Thank you. I appreciate it."

He smiled. "Given the circumstances, would I be correct in saying that you won't be content leaving the investigation to others?"

"Yes." I chuckled as my cheeks got warm. "You know how I am."

He offered me another sample of stew. "You're a valuable asset to this community. I want you to know you have the full support of City Hall. If you need anything, don't hesitate to ask."

"I'll keep that in mind."

After looking at the stained glass and a few other artist's booths, I was ready to get off my feet. I suggested to Brent that we head to Big Al's. As tasty as they were, I'd had enough of trying the various festival offerings and was in the mood for a burger and fries.

The diner was buzzing with activity, as we'd arrived during the midday rush. After we got the usual round of hugs, Al seated us in a booth near the back. Jeanette walked in as we were perusing the menu. I waved at her to join us.

"Is it appropriate for you to be seen with a known felon?" Brent asked Jeanette as she eased into the opening next to me.

"Probably not, but at least my last meal as a police office will be a good one." She gave me an elbow to the ribs and winked.

After we ordered, I reached for my fleece. There was a small notebook in one of the pockets, and I wanted to jot down key observations as we discussed the case. I looked to my left, but it wasn't there. The same thing when I looked to my right. I even checked beneath the table. Still no luck.

"My fleece. It's gone." I looked at the coat rack by the diner's entrance, but nothing was hanging from it. I wracked my brain but couldn't recall where I'd left it. Panic built within me like the lava in a volcano about to erupt. I squeezed my eyes shut to slow the lava flow.

When I opened my eyes, Jeanette was talking into the radio attached to her collar. Brent was tapping away on his phone.

"I texted Luke to keep an eye out for it." He took my hand. "I know it's special to you. Don't worry."

"What's it look like?" Jeanette relayed the information I gave her into the radio. "It's sky blue with 'Cobb Literary Agency' embroidered with navy blue stitching on the left breast area. If you see it, let me know."

She gave my shoulder a reassuring squeeze. "Tommy just came on duty. He said he'll take a swing through the vendor area and ask around."

My friends' reassurances calmed me. "I know it's just a jacket, but it was new."

Al placed our orders on the table, and for a few minutes, all my troubles disappeared. The spicy curly fries left me in a state of pure bliss, and I didn't even care that I'd have to schedule an extra workout with the kickboxing bag to counteract the calories contained in the double burger with cheese and bacon.

Then I had a brain blast. "Speaking of Tommy, I've heard he's had some disciplinary problems in the past."

Jeanette wiped her mouth with a napkin. "I don't think I like the sound of this."

"I know you're all under the gun and can't be seen breaking any rules, but if he really does have a short fuse with a big boom, it could be relevant."

I told her what Mom said about Tommy missing out on the promotion, minus the domestic violence part. "If there's information in his file indicating he held a grudge against Georgie, it would be helpful to know, don't you think?"

"Of course it would." She sipped her diet cola. "I didn't want have to tell you this, but Matt took me off the case."

"Why? You haven't done anything wrong." In her eleven months since being promoted from reserve to full-time officer, Jeanette had been a model cop. She was smart, thorough, and caring. The Rushing Creek Police Department was lucky to have her.

"It's not that. Since you and I are friends, Matt thought it best to have someone else work the case." She stared at her plate, evidently as unhappy as I was about this development. "At least I still get to help with evidence collection if we need it."

"Sounds like more of this election-season silliness you were telling me about earlier, Allie." When Brent was unhappy, he frowned. When he was angry, he clenched his fists. At the moment, he was doing both.

"I'll see if I can figure something out and let you know." Jeanette slid out of the booth. "Since I'm sticking my neck out on this, you can pick up my lunch tab."

"When this is all over, I'll buy you a Surf 'n' Turf dinner at the pub. How's that?" The Surf 'n' Turf dinner was the most expensive item on the menu there.

"Deal." She gave us fist bumps. "We'll get you out of this. I promise."

When we were alone, Brent finally unclenched his fists. "I can't believe they're doing that to Jeanette, and to you. If I was in your shoes, I wouldn't want anyone else working on the case."

"No argument there." I let out a long sigh. "I get it. She has to be careful. Besides, she didn't say she wouldn't help, only that she had to be discreet."

While we finished our drinks, we made a list on a napkin of the places we'd visited over the course of the morning. Between the two of us, we came up with a thorough retracing of our steps.

As we exited Big Al's, feelings of confidence at finding the fleece battled with anxiety for supremacy. What if we didn't find it? Had I simply misplaced it, or did someone snatch it? If someone had snatched it, another question begged to be answered.

Why?

On the way home, we retraced our steps, and every vendor and storekeeper promised to keep an eye out for my fleece and contact me if it turned up. We even crossed paths with Tommy Abbott, who told us he'd asked around about it and would do so again later in the day.

By the time we got back to my apartment, we were tired from walking and disappointed with our inability to find my fleece. I told myself the jacket was only a thing and could be replaced in a matter of days. It still didn't take away the hurt. I was so proud of my first article of Cobb Literary Agency apparel.

And now it was gone.

I plopped down on the couch and let Brent get me a glass of water while I took off my shoes. Ursi jumped onto my lap and gave me a long look, her golden eyes letting me know she was sorry I was sad.

"You sure you're okay?" Brent handed me the water as he sat beside me. "Is there anything I can do for you?"

A few thoughts crossed my mind, which made my cheeks warm, but I nudged them aside.

Then there was the other thing. Since Mom was struggling enough with the bride and groom-to-be living in sin, I'd promised her I wouldn't let Brent stay the night when he visited. The bargain was silent regarding my trips to visit Brent, so I kept my mouth shut about that detail.

"No. I'm bummed it's gone, but I'll get over it. Thanks for being so patient while we looked."

"Anything for you." The conviction in his voice left no doubt he truly meant it.

We spent the evening chilling on the couch and watching Netflix. I made chicken Caesar salads for dinner since neither of us had much of an appetite after eating ourselves through Rushing Creek.

When it was time for Brent to go, he gave me a kiss, ruffed Ursi's tortoiseshell coat, and made his way out the door with a promise to do some research of his own to help the cause. He also promised to make his next visit a longer one. While I treasured every minute with him, spending only one day together wasn't enough.

Later, as I got ready for bed, my mind drifted back to the events of the day. Overall, it had been positive. The weather had cleared. The food was great. Brent had been the perfect companion.

And yet, I couldn't get the fleece out of my head. As much as I told myself I was being paranoid about a matter of petty theft, I couldn't escape a tiny voice in the back of my mind.

A voice that kept insisting the missing fleece was connected to Georgie's murder.

Chapter Seven

I slept the sleep of the dead Monday night, no doubt thanks to the seventeen thousand steps my fitness tracker had recorded. Refreshed and ready to tackle a new work week, I got right to work on my real job as soon as I finished my first cup of coffee. It was a big day. Check that, it was a momentous day.

Red Skies, the latest thriller from my client Malcolm Blackstone, was being released today. I would always have a special place in my heart for Malcolm. He had refused to leave the Cobb Literary Agency when Dad got sick. Then he encouraged me to take the agency's reins after Dad passed away. To top things off, he insisted I become his new agent.

If anyone in the literary world had my back, Malcolm did.

Reviews had been strong for *Red Skies*, and Malcolm's publisher had high hopes for it to follow the path of his previous book and land on the best-seller lists. I was a little more cautious in my expectations. It wasn't that I lacked faith in the story. I thought it was fantastic. At the end of the day, I simply thought it was too much to ask for the first two Cobb Literary Agency novels released under my watch to become best-sellers.

A girl could still hope, though. Right? I called Malcolm right after I poured my second cup of coffee.

"Congrats, buddy," I said as soon as he answered. "I'm looking at your Amazon sales ranking. You're off to a roaring start."

"Thanks. I couldn't have done it without you. I, uh…"

"Is something wrong?" The way his voice trailed off had me worried. Release day was a hugely important day in an author's life. It was a day to celebrate the months, sometimes years, of blood, sweat, and tears put into a book. Malcolm didn't sound as overjoyed as I expected.

"Well." He took a deep breath. "I heard about your recent troubles. At the risk of sounding selfish, is there any reason for this to worry us?" I stifled a laugh. God love the man. He was such a kind soul he couldn't come out and say what was really on his mind. To be honest, he had every right to be concerned. The thought of his agent landing in jail probably had him as frightened as a rabbit trying to hide from a red-tailed hawk lurking on a nearby branch.

"No reason at all." I put a cheery tone in my voice to try to relax the man. It was his day. He deserved to enjoy every minute of it.

"I spoke with the police department yesterday. They're pursuing several leads. We just need to give them time to conduct their investigation." It was stretching the truth far enough to almost snap, but I did chat with Jeanette. That should count, right?

"Glorious. I'm so pleased to hear that." His tone had changed like the sun coming out from behind a rain cloud. "I hope you don't mind me saying so, but now I can relax and enjoy the day."

"As well you should." We chatted for a few minutes about promotional efforts he had scheduled, including a tour of bookstores near his hometown of St. Louis.

By the time I signed off, I was as excited about the book's prospects as Malcolm. It was a great start to the day, so to keep the momentum going, I went back online and posted a handful of blurbs about *Red Skies* on social media.

Then I did something I should have done days ago. I made a post on the agency's private group site about my situation. The chat with Malcolm had served as a hard reminder that Georgie's murder, and my potential implication in it, affected a lot of people beyond me.

Including Thornwell's estate, I was now representing eleven authors. The nine clients I signed after Malcolm didn't have the history he and I did. I was remiss in failing to notify them about the situation earlier. While it was uncomfortable notifying them now, it was the right thing to do.

A few authors responded to the post with questions, which I answered with complete honesty. Okay, mostly complete honesty. They didn't know about the past Georgie and I shared. I was embarrassed enough having it resurrected among folks who'd known us both for years.

From the day I met Georgie, way back in first grade, I'd had a crush on him. He was the bad boy who could make my heart flutter with a simple raise of his eyebrow. It was a classic case of unrequited puppy love. All my classmates knew I had a thing for the boy with the long hair who spent as much time in detention as he spent in class.

Including Georgie.

I had enough brains and self-respect to stop him from ever taking advantage of me, though. It was simply beyond rational thought that he would spend time with a plain, bookish type when he could have a lot more fun with the girls who liked to party and didn't mind getting in trouble.

It was never meant to be and that was okay. Especially after he tried to sweet-talk me into the back seat of his car after a football game when we were juniors. When I said no for the third time, he put his arm around me and tried to guide me toward his car.

We hadn't gone two steps when Sloane appeared from out of nowhere, just like Batman, and slugged him. Georgie crumpled like a house of cards. As he lay on the ground, spewing cuss words and massaging his jaw, Sloane towered over him.

"Don't ever mess with my best friend. Got it?" He tried to get up, but she pushed him back to the ground with her foot and wouldn't let him up until he apologized to me. I had no idea the events of that night would come back to haunt me, but they did. In a big way.

Georgie worked hard to get back in my good graces, bided his time, and then asked me to the senior prom. I should have known his intentions were less than honorable, but I was so shocked I said yes. The whole situation was like a fairy tale, until he turned the dream into a nightmare by standing me up.

I was a modern-day Cinderella, with no ride to the ball, no Prince Charming, and no fairy godmother to make things right. That night was one of the worst nights of my life. There was no way I was going to share one of the worst nights of my life with anyone beyond a need-to-know basis.

On a lighter note, one of the authors asked if she could pick my brain when this was over so she could use some of the material for a book. I agreed but joked I'd only do it if she promised to include me in the acknowledgments as a subject-matter expert.

Spending time with my authors was like eating ice cream on a sunny day. For me, there wasn't much better in life. The time spent answering their questions also served as a reminder that I had a lot of good things going. I shouldn't lose sight of that.

After a trip to get groceries and a walk around the block with Ursi, I spent a few hours e-mailing editors to check on manuscripts I'd submitted for their consideration. I was thrilled to have a second Cobb Literary Agency book in the world, but I couldn't rest on my laurels. The next agency book wasn't scheduled for release until November, and it was critical to keep the wheels turning.

The e-mail exchanges with the editors were so promising, I felt as powerful as Wonder Woman. With a sense of invincibility coursing through my veins, I opened my case notebook and reviewed my notes.

It was time to start solving a murder.

* * * *

Parke Landscaping was situated on Lincoln Branch Road, northwest of town. The business was started by Roger Parke's grandfather as a timber-harvesting firm. As the decades passed and the tiny population of the area grew, the company shifted its focus to landscaping services and winter snow removal.

Nowadays, Parke Landscaping was one of the most important businesses in the county. If you were a homeowner who wanted someone to mow your lawn in the summer, Parke could do it. Needed leaves removed and gutters cleaned in the fall? Roger was who you called. It didn't matter if the work was for a residential, commercial, or even industrial customer. Parke Landscaping was your answer.

I'd had a passing acquaintance with Roger through my parents, which changed when the steering committee was formed. Parke Landscaping was doing a lot of work for us beyond mulch delivery, like planting trees and shrubs and starting the wildflower garden. Because of that, I'd gotten to know him on a professional level.

The man was old-school in every sense of the word. He went to work in blue jeans and a collared work shirt. If you couldn't find him in his office, odds were good he was either supervising a project somewhere or working on a piece of equipment in one of the company's barns.

His gray hair was short and his leather work boots clean. There was no smoking or cursing in Roger's presence, but he was known to enjoy a scotch on the rocks from time to time. He and his wife, Claire, were high school sweethearts and were happily married over forty years later. The oldest of their four children, Maggie, was Roger's heir apparent and handled the books so he could keep working in the field.

Roger was a straight shooter who had little time for idle chitchat and even less time for fools. I'd have to tread carefully around him.

It was after five as I pedaled my bike the three miles to Parke Landscaping. The early-September sun combined with the exertion from the pedaling to produce a bead of sweat on my brow. The effort, while mild, felt good. I loved walking, but cycling was fun, and its low-impact nature was a nice change of pace after all the steps the previous day.

I turned from the road onto a gravel driveway that was as smooth as an airport runway. It ran a quarter of a mile between rows of white pines and ended in a small parking area in front of a two-story log cabin. A steel farm gate, which was currently open, had been installed where the driveway ended and a paved parking area began.

An overhang ran along the front of the building and provided shade for the three wooden rocking chairs spaced evenly along the front porch. The structure reminded me of the Rushing Creek Community Center in style, all the way down to the green metal roof and polished brass PARKE LANDSCAPING sign that hung by the front door.

The thought of the community center took me back to the last time I'd visited that building—the day of my father's funeral. The fact that I was thinking of how both buildings intersected with death wasn't lost on me.

I set the unsettling thought aside as I turned the handle on the front door and stepped inside. A shiver went down my spine, thanks to the office's arctic-like thermostat setting. Roger was known to like his office cold in the summer and hot in the winter, so he could get comfortable quickly when coming in from the field.

"Hello. Anybody here?" Despite the overhead lights being on, the office appeared deserted. I had a mission to accomplish, so I wasn't leaving until I talked to someone.

Light came from under an office door near the back of the building. I knocked on the hardwood surface and waited. A moment later, heavy footfalls confirmed someone was on the other side.

The door swung open. "Is it a deal or not?" With a cell phone clamped between his shoulder and his ear, Roger made eye contact with me. "I'll call you back." He shoved the phone into his pocket.

"Sorry for coming to see you without an appointment. Do you have a few minutes?" I gave him my sweetest smile, the kind I gave Diane when I wanted extra whipped cream with my hot chocolate.

He crossed his arms. "If it's about the alleged screwed-up mulch delivery, talk to the police. That wasn't our fault."

"I know it wasn't. I'm sorry your truck was stolen. And I'm sorry your company's been dragged into this mess."

"Yes, well, thank you. A phone call would have been sufficient, though." He leaned on the door frame, as if he was relaxing, but still had his arms crossed.

"I was hoping I could talk to you about Georgie. I understand he used to work for you."

With a snort, Roger went to his desk and motioned me into a chair across from him. He put his feet on the corner of the desk while he laced his hands behind his head. His work boots were spotless, though the treads were worn from use.

"The mayor warned me you'd be paying me a visit." He cracked a half-smile. "I believe he referred to you as playing amateur Nancy Drew."

"I'd like to think of myself more along the lines of Veronica Mars." A chuckle escaped me. "I just want to find out what happened to Georgie, and—"

"And in the process, clear your name. I know. He told me." He put his feet down and placed his tanned forearms on the desk. "I don't know if I should talk to you about this. When Officer Wilkerson took my statement about the truck, she told me to talk to her if I thought of anything."

I sensed he was stalling, that he wanted to get rid of me without revealing what he knew about Georgie. I could appreciate his dilemma. I wasn't leaving without that information, though.

"Please, Roger. I know you don't know me well, but I've always been straight with you, right?"

"I guess that's true." He picked up a pen and doodled on his desk calendar. "How do I know you didn't do it? Do you have an alibi?"

I didn't, and thanks to the mayor, he probably knew that. Still, I needed him to come around. It was time to play the only card in my deck.

"Nope. Such is my life, the only one who can vouch for me is a cat. I have a question about the truck that was stolen. Does it have a manual or an automatic transmission?"

"You were there. You should know."

"I'm not much of a truck person." I forced a smile, even though I was almost at the point that I wanted to pop the uncooperative jerk on the head.

"It's a two thousand seven model with a six-speed, manual transmission. It's easy to drive. Even you could do it."

I spread my arms wide. "I haven't owned a car in over a decade. I get around on a bike. I have to use a step stool to reach the top shelves in my apartment. Do I look big enough to drive one of those behemoths?"

It was a bluff. My parents insisted that my siblings and I learn to drive a manual transmission. The skill had come in handy on a European vacation a few years ago. On top of that, my ability to operate a stick allowed me to drive the Porsche 911 Sloane had inherited from Thornwell.

Roger didn't need to know any of that, though.

After a second of dead silence, he burst out laughing. "You've got me there." Roger shook his head. "All right, you win. What do you want to know?"

"Tell me about Georgie's time as your employee."

"The man had a silver tongue. I knew about his checkered past, the drinking, the way he treated women, including you. Standing you up on the night of your senior prom." He shook his head. "What kind of knucklehead does that?"

I looked away as the curse of small-town life raised its ugly head again. In a matter of days, news of your personal business could spread from one end of town to the other like wildfire, especially if it involved heartache and scandal. Shoot, even Roger knew Georgie had asked me to senior prom and then blew me off the night of the dance. If he knew, there probably wasn't a person alive in Rushing Creek who didn't know.

"I'm sorry I brought that up. It's a night you want to forget, I'd imagine."

"It's in the past." I took a deep breath and tried to tell myself that memories of that utterly humiliating incident didn't hurt anymore. I couldn't do it. "You were telling me about Georgie as your employee."

"Right. He convinced me that if I hired him, he'd toe the line. He did, for a few months. After that, he was the definition of mediocrity. He did just enough to not get fired. Then he got Lori pregnant, and I couldn't fire him. I couldn't do that to her. Until..."

He grimaced, got up, and went to a window that overlooked the work area of Parke Landscaping. I didn't want to overplay my hand, so I stayed seated and kept my mouth shut.

From my vantage point, massive piles of mulch in colors from black to red to tan formed a wooden mountain range. The equally impressive mounds of stone, from pea gravel to road stone, were out of sight, as was the garage that housed the company's vehicles. I needed to get a look at that area to see if I could puzzle out how the murderer stole the truck.

"Until what?"

"I keep forgetting you lived out of town for so long." He picked up a dart and threw it at a dartboard hanging on the wall behind me. "Until Georgie wrecked one of my trucks making a delivery. God, what a mess."

He unlocked a filing cabinet and pulled out a manila folder as thick as a hardbound copy of *War and Peace*. "This is my Georgie Alonso accident file."

I jumped when the file landed on the desk with a deafening *thunk*.

"He takes up the rest of that drawer, by the way." He flipped open the folder as he sat back down. "Long story short, Georgie normally didn't drive the big trucks. I didn't trust him. Then one day I had a guy call in, so I assigned Georgie to take a load of fill dirt to a customer. He took a bend in the road too fast, mowed down a guardrail, and wrapped the thing around a tree. I could have forgiven him, until the drug test came back."

"It was positive, I take it." I knew the story but wanted to hear Roger's version of it.

He gave a quick nod. "The truck was totaled. Even after insurance, I still had a ten-thousand-dollar gap I had to cover for a new rig. The towing company billed me for the accident cleanup, and I ended up losing the customer."

"That must have cost you quite a lot."

"That's just the start of it. Then he filed a worker's compensation retaliation lawsuit. Said I fired him because he hurt his back in the accident. I've lost track of how much money that punk cost me over the years. And now this."

"This?" I assumed he meant Georgie's murder, but I wanted to be sure.

"The truck hasn't been released by the police yet. Roberson said it's evidence."

"If you don't mind me saying, you don't seem broken up about Georgie losing his life." I made a mental note to move Roger up on my suspect list when I got home.

"This community, and Lori especially, is better off without him. He caused enough damage around here. I'm sorry someone died but not sorry that person was Georgie."

Make that the top of my suspect list.

Chapter Eight

The chat with Roger left me unsettled as I pedaled home. On the one hand, the man had the ideal profile to be a prime suspect. There was no doubt Georgie had cost Roger tens of thousands of dollars, if not more. Then there was the question of whether Georgie received anything from his lawsuit. If so, that could be thousands more. I'd have to look into that.

On the other hand, if he had something to hide, why would he have been so open with me? Georgie couldn't harm him now. It didn't fit.

Unless there was another piece to the puzzle.

I waved to Maybelle Schuman, a retired schoolteacher who now served as the unofficial town gossip, as I rolled through the downtown area. She was the key cog in the Rushing Creek rumor mill, even if her information was sometimes less than reliable. If anybody had unsavory intel on Georgie, it was Maybelle.

That was for another day, though. I picked up the pace so I could get home and update my notes as soon as possible. Roger had given me a lot of information, and I didn't want to forget anything.

A little while later, while I was cooking some stir fry, there was a knock at my front door. It was Luke.

"Asian. Excellent." He rubbed his hands and strode toward the kitchen.

"Hey. Don't you have a fiancée to go home to?" Despite my admonishment, I set out two plates while he moved the wok from the stove to the dining table.

"Sloane's out for a run. She had a personal best during her race Monday, so she wants to keep the momentum going by increasing her training." He poured us a couple of glasses of water and took a seat.

We chatted about the Labor Day Festival while we ate. As director of Rushing Creek's Parks Department, Luke had worked all day, making sure the downtown area and the town's parks stayed clean and picked up. He'd heard about my fleece going missing and wanted to know if it had turned up.

"No. My guess is some kid stole it. Hopefully someone who needs it will put it to good use."

He wiped his chin with a napkin. "You're a better person than me. And it's not like you're rolling in dough right now."

Ah, yes. The Money issue. Or, to be accurate, Luke's Concern That Allie Didn't Have Enough Money to Get By issue. Since practically the day I returned to Rushing Creek, he'd tried to talk me into taking a part-time job so I'd have a steady source of income until the agency started to make money.

I told him back then I'd taken care of myself for over a decade and hadn't lost that ability just because I'd moved home. As I let him take the last chunk of chicken from the stir fry, I rebuffed him again.

"Have it your way. In other news, I've got some intel on Georgie. You should get your notebook." Intrigued, I fetched it while Luke cleared the kitchen table.

He held his tongue until we were both seated and I had opened the notebook to a new page.

"I was talking about Georgie with my crew today. While we were talking, one of the guys mentioned a rumor that Georgie had a life insurance policy. Supposedly, it's worth half a million, maybe a million bucks. If it exists, that is."

I sucked in a breath. One million dollars. Questions raced through my mind all at once, jockeying for position, like traffic streaming into the Lincoln Tunnel at rush hour.

"That's some serious cash. Any idea who the beneficiary is?"

He shook his head. "Like I said, it's only a rumor. There's nothing in his employee file about life insurance other than a simple ten-thousand-dollar death benefit the city gives each of us employees. His little girl's the beneficiary of that one."

While Luke talked, I jotted down the names of people in Georgie's family. Any recipient of a windfall of that magnitude would join Roger Parke at the top of my suspect list.

Revenge and money. Two of the classic motivating factors when it came to committing murder. God, I was getting way too knowledgeable on the subject.

"If we assume it's true, my first thought is that Brittany would be the beneficiary. Next, Lori, even though they never got married. Last would be his parents." I tapped my pen on the page. "I think it's safe to rule Brittany out. God, the poor kid."

"Yeah. At five, she's probably just old enough that she'll remember this all her life."

I closed my eyes. To be five and lose a parent was something I couldn't imagine. I was twenty-nine when Dad passed away, and that had been hard enough. At that moment, it didn't matter that Georgie was a lazy schemer. What mattered was that a little girl would grow up without her father. It was heartbreaking.

And more motivation to make sure Georgie, Brittany, and Lori received justice.

"Looks like I need to pay Lori a visit. Think she'll talk to me?"

"Depends on if she has anything to hide." He drained the last of his water. "We haven't talked very often, but she always asks about you. She thought it was cool you were living in New York."

"I can't deny it had its moments."

Luke accepted my offer to stick around for a beer, and we adjourned to the patio for a drink.

The patio was really just my landing for the fire-escape stairway, but it was big enough for two chairs and a small group of vegetable plants. The view wasn't anything to write home about, but the vibe reminded me of New York and brought back good memories.

I could have spent all evening kicking back with my bro, but after an hour, he took off to spend the rest of the evening with Sloane. Back inside, I was a ball of nervous energy, so I rooted the toy onion ring out from behind the couch and batted it back and forth with Ursi.

The toy had just slid under the coffee table when there were two sharp knocks on the front door. This time Matt was my visitor. He was in his indigo Rushing Creek Police Department uniform and was chomping on a piece of gum.

This wasn't a social call.

To lighten the mood, I peeked into the hall after I welcomed him into the apartment. "You're by yourself. I'll take that as a good sign."

"Thought I'd save you the embarrassment of a perp walk." His stone-faced expression morphed into a grin when I sucked in a breath. "Sorry. Couldn't pass up the opportunity."

I closed the door, then slapped him on the arm. "Very funny. Since you're not here to arrest me, what brings you by?"

"I've got news on the case I thought I'd share with you." He wandered around the apartment for a few moments, at one point getting down on one knee to scratch Ursi between the ears. "Your place looks great. I like what you've done with it."

"Thanks." My cheeks warmed at the compliment. The apartment was in a dismal condition when I rented it. That made the rent dirt cheap, so I didn't have to live at Mom's house until the agency started generating enough income to pay the bills.

To put it mildly, the place had been a wreck.

Renee Gomez, the woman who ran the bookstore on the floor below me, owned the building. For years, she'd used my apartment to store overflow used-book inventory. When I asked if she'd be interested in renting the space, she initially said no, claiming she had no place to store the boxes upon boxes of paperbacks and hardbacks.

I might be small in stature, but when I really want something, I can be as relentless as Javert in *Les Misérables* and as impossible to stop as the winds of change in *A Tale of Two Cities*.

And I wanted that apartment.

Maybe it was because it reminded me of my apartment in New York. Or it could have been because it was located a staircase away from my favorite business in town—Renee's Gently Used Books. It didn't matter. Once I laid eyes on the hardwood floors, the crown molding, and the ten-foot ceilings, I had to have it.

She burst out laughing when I went back and offered to move her inventory to the basement. The laughter came to an end when I sweetened the offer by promising to group the books by author's last name.

Within an hour of the offer, we had a deal.

The moment I signed the lease, my eyes filled with tears of joy. I'd proven I could come home again. My choice to leave the security as a literary agent with a large New York firm for the uncertainty of owning my agency in my hometown had been the right one. I wrote the deposit check with a smile.

The moment I opened the door to my apartment, my eyes filled with tears of despair. I had a ton of work ahead of me. Everything was covered with a thick film of dust. Cobwebs had taken up residence in the corners of every window, their tiny strands causing me to break out in goose bumps. Fortunately, there was no peeling wallpaper, only paint in god-awful shades of pink and pea-soup green that looked like it had been applied in 1975.

The first week after signing the lease was the worst. After a backbreaking weekend lugging the books downstairs and putting them in order, I spent my days scrubbing, buffing, and painting. I spent my nights doing agenting work. I slept on an inflatable mattress, too stubborn to even spend a few days living with family members.

By the time the last piece of furniture was finally moved in, my fingers were red and chapped from the weeks of exposure to paint and cleaning compounds. Every time I blew my nose, black gunk filled the tissue. And every time I raised my arm, my elbow rocked me with a white-hot jolt of pain.

But I was happy.

The hardwood floors, which Matt refinished, shone like new. The black-and-white checkerboard tiles in the kitchen and bathroom, which Luke regrouted and polished, made me want to get down on my hands and knees and play a game of chess. The new roman blinds, courtesy of Sloane and Rachel, added a touch of elegance and unity to the apartment.

In the end, Ursi was the one who convinced me I'd made the right choice in living quarters. The moment I let her out of her cat carrier, she took one look to the left, another to the right, and went straight to an end table I'd positioned below one of the windows. With unparalleled grace, she leapt onto the table, surveyed her surroundings, then turned her attention to what she could see through the window.

I let out a chuckle as Matt chatted with Ursi, who was sitting on that same perch today. The only difference between now and then was that now a seat cushion was fastened to the table to make her napping more comfortable.

"So, about this news?" I was prepared for it to be bad. Hopefully, it wouldn't be devastating.

"The preliminary autopsy report came back." He opened his notebook and cleared his throat. "Georgie's death was ruled as smothering by mechanical obstruction. Basically, the weight of the mulch stopped him from being able to breathe."

"Good Lord." I grabbed the arm of a chair to steady myself, then lowered into it. "He was buried alive. That's horrible. Did he, you know, suffer?"

"Toxicology reports haven't all come back yet, but there was alcohol in his system. There's something else." He took a spot on the couch across from me. "We finished clearing away the mulch pile earlier today."

"Why do I get the feeling you're not going to tell me I can resume work at the park tomorrow morning?"

Despite the fact Matt was my ex-brother-in-law, a man who had cheated on my sister, I'd forgiven him and come to respect him. He had his flaws, as we all did, but he was trying to be a good father to his children, a good ex-husband to my sister, and a good police chief to the people of Rushing

Creek. He truly cared about the community and took his job seriously. That seriousness was coming through loud and clear.

"We found some things at the bottom of the pile—an empty bottle of bourbon, a set of bolt cutters, and a padlock that had been cut open."

He stared at me, no doubt looking for a reaction to help gauge my innocence or lack thereof, but also to see if I could make sense of the information he shared.

"Okay. It sounds like whoever did this got Georgie drunk enough that he either passed out or was too out of it to do anything when the mulch was dumped on him."

"Agreed. Go on."

"And if there's any way to connect the lock with Parke Landscaping, it would be reasonable to assume the killer used the bolt cutters to get through Parke's gate."

"My assessment as well. Anything else?" He jotted down something in his notebook.

I thought for a moment until a question popped into my head. "Why are you talking to me about this? I thought I was a suspect."

"You were until we got a look at the lock and the bolt cutters. You're strong, Allie, but I don't think you're strong enough to have cut that lock."

"Oh, I see." I jumped to my feet. "You don't think I could have done it just because I'm a girl, huh? Well, that's sexist of you. I…"

With a mixture of relief and embarrassment at what Matt was implying, I stopped and returned to my seat. I was in the clear. That was the important thing.

"God, I'm such a dork. I should thank you for sharing this with me. Do you want me to come to the station and try a simulation or something to confirm whether or not I can cut the lock?"

"You know," he snapped his fingers, "that's a good idea. That way we can objectively rule you out. Or at least we can rule out any thought that you did it alone."

"Close enough." I let out a long sigh of relief. This was tangible progress on the case that didn't involve more fingers being pointed at me. "Are there fingerprints on the things you found?"

"We'll get the results in a few days, but I'm not hopeful. The Parke Landscaping truck came back clean. I'm releasing it to Roger tomorrow."

I drummed my fingers on my thigh. There was something just out of reach. Then it hit me. "This wasn't an accident, or a prank gone wrong, was it? Whoever did it made sure no fingerprints were left behind. It was planned."

Matt nodded as he popped another piece of gum into his mouth. It was regular spearmint. Evidently his stress level was low at the moment.

"If it was unplanned, a crime of passion, I'd feel comfortable assuming that someone would eventually blab about it. The fact this was premeditated changes the equation." He went to the window to scratch Ursi again. "I know you're looking into this, Allie. What can you tell me?"

I told him everything I'd learned, except for the information about Tommy. There was no way I was going to break Mom's confidence to a police officer. That could get us both in another kind of trouble, and I didn't have time for that. Besides, I didn't know how Matt would react to having his promotion put under the microscope again.

No, if I was going to take a close look at the dangerous Officer Tommy Abbott, I was going to do it alone.

Chapter Nine

First thing the next morning, I called Jeanette and asked if she could arrange a time for me to talk to Tommy Abbott. I had a hard time believing a police officer would murder someone, but his temper had already demonstrated that he wasn't immune to acts of violence.

While I waited for her response, I got to work editing a new client's manuscript. It was a lighthearted, humorous action adventure and was the perfect medicine on a stress-filled morning.

The story had made me laugh out loud three times, a sure-fire good sign, when I received a text message. Jeanette and Tommy were having lunch at the pub. She suggested I stop to say hi on my way to see my sister. I laughed again. Having a sneaky friend sure came in handy.

A little while later, I pulled up in front of the pub. A bright yellow bike rack had been installed. Instead of boring parallel bars between which one could insert a front tire, this structure resembled a massive corkscrew that had been placed on its side. It was six feet from end to end and came up to my waist. There was room for at least a dozen bikes.

Slipping my bike between the rack's circular tubing was a snap, and I was able to fasten my lock in such a way to make my wheels much less vulnerable to theft. It was encouraging to see my town becoming more bike-friendly. Hopefully, more people would spend time on two wheels instead of four when they saw they had safe places to store their rides.

Despite my distrustful nature, at heart I was an optimist. My hope for the bike racks was proof.

Since it was Wednesday, and I'd be meeting with my sibs later to check in about Mom, I made my visit with Rachel quick. She raised an eyebrow when I told her the real reason for my surprise visit.

"You're getting underhanded." She put a hand over her heart. "My goody-two-shoes little sister is growing up and spreading her wings. I know how I can help. Go have your lunch. I'll see you in a bit."

Surprised by Rachel's compliment, I made my way toward Jeanette and Tommy. It wasn't that my sister was always mean to me. On the contrary, when Dad passed away, we came to terms with how awful our relationship was growing up, and we'd been working on being good sisters ever since. Still, with Dad gone less than a year, receiving kind words from her was taking some getting used to.

Jeanette saw me and waved me over. This was going to make my visit seem even more coincidental. Hopefully, that would be a good thing.

"Hi, guys. Mind if I join you?" Without waiting for an answer, I dropped into the booth next to Tommy, blocking him in.

A moment after I joined them, a server brought their lunches. He was having a patty melt. She was having a turkey club on rye.

Jeanette slid her plate in my direction. "Have some fries. There's no way I can eat all these."

While they ate their sandwiches and I ate most of Jeanette's fries, we chatted about the usual things Rushing Creek locals talked about—the tourists who drove too fast, the teens who were out too late getting into trouble, and how long it would be before Ozzy Metcalf, the difficult owner of Ye Olde Woodworker, drove his newest neighbor, Scents and Soaps owner Shirley Price, to a new location.

Our consensus was the speeding tourists, and the traffic citations they paid, were good for the local economy. The teenage misbehavior wouldn't subside until it got too cold to socialize out of doors late at night. Shirley was tougher than her hippie exterior suggested, and Ozzy's attempts to run her out would prove fruitless.

When the conversation started to lag, I told them I was visiting the police station later for my strength demonstration. "Chief Roberson said if I can't cut the lock, that should rule out any theories that I killed Georgie alone." I took a sip of my ice water and waited for a reaction from Tommy.

It didn't take long.

"Between the three of us, I want to find out who did it so I can give that person a medal." He wadded up a paper napkin and dropped it on his plate. Agitation emanated from him. "Sorry. I didn't mean that. I won't miss him, though."

"You didn't get along?" It was a cautious way to broach the subject. Too cautious, perhaps, but better than overplaying my hand.

"You could say that. I should be going before I say something I'll regret." He reached for his Rushing Creek PD baseball cap at the same time Rachel appeared with two dishes, each laden with a slice of apple pie topped with a scoop of ice cream.

"I don't do this often enough, but these are on the house." She placed one dish in front of Tommy, the other in front of Jeanette. "A little thank-you from all of us at the pub. Enjoy." With a smile, she spun on her heel and walked away.

Well done, sis. Impeccable timing. I made a mental note to thank her. And reimburse her.

Tommy and Jeanette looked at each other with wide eyes and open mouths. After a moment's hesitation, in unison, they picked up their forks and dove into the dessert.

I took a moment to enjoy their collective surprise as they enjoyed the homemade pie and locally sourced vanilla ice cream. Regardless of the manipulative steps I'd taken, they deserved treats like this. Sure, Rushing Creek wasn't a hotbed of crime, but it didn't change the fact that every day they put their lives on the line for the community.

Rachel had done well.

When Tommy was about halfway through his pie, I made another go at him. "For what it's worth, I get why you didn't like him. When I was a senior, he asked me to prom. We were in the same government class and I'd helped him study a couple of times. I didn't think anyone was going to ask me, so I was over the moon when good-looking bad boy Georgie Alonso asked me to go. Things didn't work out like I'd planned."

"What happened?" He put down his fork and wiped his mouth. His attention was entirely directed at me.

"There I was in a full-length lace and chiffon gown. We had dinner reservations at seven. It got to be six-thirty, when he'd promised to pick me up, then seven-thirty, then eight—and still no Georgie."

I took a deep breath and closed my eyes. Even over a decade later, the memory was still a kick to my solar plexus.

"I don't remember when the humiliation overtook me and I broke down in tears, but Mom was there and held me while I cried my eyes out. Eventually, she helped me upstairs and got me out of my dress and into bed. Then she popped a bowl of popcorn, and we ate it together while we watched *Adventures in Babysitting*.

"The next day I found out Georgie went with a bunch of other kids who blew off the prom and spent the night partying at the state park. When I saw him at school, first he acted like he didn't remember asking me. Then he made a big deal of laughing at me. I was humiliated all over again. Except for when my dad died, it was the worst time in my life."

"Wow. That's bad." Tommy traced a figure eight on his plate with his spoon and scooped the last bit of ice cream into his mouth. "Since we're sharing, everyone knows we got in a fight a few years back. People think it's because he thought I was hassling him over a public intoxication thing. They're wrong."

"What was the reason?" Jeanette's quiet tone had a calming effect to it. She was skilled at dealing with agitated citizens.

"I caught him hitting on my wife. That was bad enough. What made it worse was that Lori was six months pregnant at the time. He tried to make a move on her at Lori's baby shower."

"Ewww." Jeanette and I said it at the same time.

I was filled with a combination of revulsion, sympathy, and anger. Revulsion at Georgie, who I thought couldn't sink lower than what he'd done to me. Sympathy for Tommy, whom I'd manipulated into revealing a painful, personal secret. Anger at myself for putting the man in this position.

"I'm sorry." I drained the rest of my water. "I'm sorry I brought it up. I didn't know."

"It's okay." He drummed his fingers on the table. "You'll keep this between us, won't you? I was working the night Georgie was killed. I don't want to give people a reason to think I did it."

When he was satisfied with Jeanette's promise to keep his secret, he shook hands with us and headed out. I thanked my lucky stars he didn't wait for me to make the same promise.

"What do you think? Raises more questions than it answers, doesn't it?" Jeanette took a bite of her pie.

"That's putting it mildly." I evaluated the likelihood of Tommy committing the crime. Revenge would have been his motive. His job would have provided him the means. Working the night of the crime would have given him the opportunity. Which led to a question.

"I haven't heard anybody mention Georgie's car. Have you guys found anything helpful in it?"

"Um, no." She took a drink as she stabbed piecrust crumbs with her fork. "It's missing."

"What do you mean? Did someone steal it? It was impounded as evidence, right?"

"No. Nobody stole it. We can't find it." Her aggravation at making the admission was palpable.

After seconds of uncomfortable silence, I took a drink of water while I thought this through. A man murdered. A dump truck stolen. A car missing. No solid leads. It was a bleak picture. Made it easy to understand Jeanette's frustration.

"That would explain my conversation with Matt last night." I told her about the question-and-answer session with the police chief.

"Let's take this outside." My friend dropped some bills on the table and marched toward the exit, with me practically running to keep up. When we reached her cruiser, she motioned me to get in.

"Here's what I know, which isn't a lot since I'm off the case. We have an approximate time Georgie left Hoosiers. We have the approximate time Tommy last saw him. We know when you found him and how he died. We're still investigating, but there's more we don't know. Don't take this the wrong way, but you being cleared sets the investigation back." She forced a smile.

The admission hurt, but it was understandable. It called to mind the frosty relationship I had, and probably would always have, with Jax Michaels, given the accusations I had directed at him regarding Thornwell's murder.

"Sorry to complicate things." I made sure my tone was light. "Has anybody talked to Lori?"

"No. She's not ready yet. At least, that's what she says. She's a sympathetic figure since she's a single mom now, and given who her father is, Matt doesn't want to lean on her."

"At some point, he'll have to talk to her, won't he?" I told her about the insurance policy rumor Luke had shared with me. "A big insurance check in exchange for a loser boyfriend seems like a pretty big motive."

Jeanette let out a long sigh and rubbed her eyes. She, like the rest of the department, no doubt, was under a lot of pressure, and the stress was showing.

"I think he's hoping something will break and he won't have to."

My smartwatch went off. I was due at the police station for my strength demonstration.

"I gotta go." I gave Jeanette a hug. "I'll tell you one thing. If Matt won't talk to Lori, I will."

A little while later, I pulled open the door to the Rushing Creek Police Department with authority. A wave of confidence was building as my snooping picked up steam. My heart went out to Tommy, but his spot on the suspect list couldn't be denied. As the cool air from the HVAC system washed over me, I added Lori to the list. Connections with City Hall be damned. If she had killed her boyfriend, she deserved to have the despicable deed uncovered.

For a second, I debated making a detour to the mayor's office. It was in the section of the municipal building adjacent to the police department. I could claim I was dropping by to discuss the park's construction progress and try to turn the conversation toward Lori. I decided against it. First things first. If he was available after the demonstration, I'd try then.

With my course of action plotted, I stepped inside. An electronic *ding dong* sounded as the door swung closed behind me. The police department's lobby area was deserted. I figured Matt and whoever else was on duty were getting the demo ready, so I went to push open the swinging gate and practically cut myself in two.

The gate didn't budge. My momentum carried me headfirst over the barrier as my knees banged against it with a sound like two gunshots. My arms spun like pinwheels in a stiff wind, and I cracked both elbows on the tile floor. My feet eventually followed the rest of me over the barrier, and I finished my tumble on my back.

It was probably the most insane way anyone in the history of Rushing Creek, Indiana, had ever gotten past that gate.

I concentrated on the fluorescent lights directly above me while I waited for the spots in front of my eyes to go away. As the ringing in my ears subsided, heavy footfalls alerted me to the arrival of helpers and impending massive embarrassment at my predicament.

"Allie? What in God's name happened?" Matt got down on one knee and did a quick physical assessment. Satisfied I hadn't suffered any serious medical trauma, he helped me to my feet.

"Did you"—his gaze went from me to the gate and back to me; he pointed at the offending piece of office furniture—"fall over that?"

Behind him, an officer covered his mouth to stifle a laugh.

My knees stung, my elbows ached, and my cheeks were burning. The discomfort and embarrassment combined to light a fire of indignation inside of me. I was here to prove my innocence, not be the butt of jokes.

"Why is that thing locked? That's a safety hazard. I could have been killed."

The officer who'd been trying not to laugh moved around me and flipped a switch on the gate. It was Pete Naughton. In his forties, Officer Naughton was known for his patience with the public and his easy smile. He wasn't smiling anymore. "Sorry about that, ma'am. With the murder investigation going on, we're increasing security."

"Ma'am?" I squeezed my eyes shut. My utter humiliation was complete. After a moment to gather my thoughts, I opened my eyes and glared at the officer. "It's Ms., as in Ms. Allie Cobb."

I turned my attention to Matt. "Chief Roberson, as we agreed, I'm here for the strength test. Are your preparations complete?"

"They are. If you'll follow us." He turned on his heel and walked down the hall. He appeared to be treating this exercise seriously. I made a mental note to thank him for that.

Halfway down the hall, we turned left into a conference room. A rectangular table large enough to seat twelve had been pushed against the far wall. A bolt cutter lay on the polished surface. In a corner of the room, three chairs had been chained together. A heavy-duty padlock held the chain in place.

A video camera on a tripod had been placed ten feet from the chairs. Officer Naughton took his position behind the camera.

Matt handed the bolt cutter to me. The tool was about three feet long and ended in an intimidating set of silver jaws. The black rubber handles made it easy to maintain a grip, which was good since the contraption was heavy and unwieldy.

I looked at the lock. There was no way I was even going to make a scratch on it. I shook my head. *My freedom's on the line.* I needed to give it my best effort.

Matt took a few minutes to explain how the demonstration would go. Once he gave the signal for the camera to start rolling, he would make a short introductory statement for evidentiary purposes. Then I was to state my name, confirm that I was appearing voluntarily, and attest that I was going to execute the demonstration to the best of my ability.

To keep calm once we were live, I closed my eyes while Matt recited his lines. Once he was finished, I stepped into the camera's field of vision. Harkening back to my days on the Rushing Creek High School Debate Club, I looked into the camera and spoke in an unhurried, clear tone.

My approach toward the lock was a little unsteady as I wasn't sure how to actually cut it open. With a grunt I hoped the camera's audio recorder didn't catch, I hoisted the cutter in the air. It took some effort to open it far enough to fit around the lock's U-shaped piece of metal, which some research had told me was called a shackle.

Once I was confident in the cutter's position, I squeezed the handles with all my might. A surge of adrenaline coursed through my system when the jaws began to burrow into the shackle.

I took a breath and squeezed again. And yet again, but the jaws refused to budge. I even opened the jaws and tried to slam them closed, hoping the tiny extra amount of momentum would finish the job.

When my final effort at cutting the lock was unsuccessful, Matt stepped between the camera and me and spoke a few words to conclude the demonstration. Then he asked Officer Naughton to give us a few minutes alone.

He gave the shackle a close examination, speaking into a digital voice recorder as he did so. At one point, he used a ruler to determine how deep of a cut I'd put into the metal bar.

"Nice work, Allie. You made it a third of the way through."

"Does that mean I aced the test?" With the demonstration over, the adrenaline I'd been running on since I took my tumble was running out. I slumped into a chair and massaged my elbows. A warm bubble bath was in my near future.

"It was more of a pass-fail proposition." He pulled up a seat next to me. "You cut that lock a lot deeper than I expected."

"You'd be surprised how strong I can be when I'm angry. Don't mess with She Hulk Allie Cobb." I growled as I flexed my arm muscles like body builders do.

Matt laughed. "I'll remember that. Before you go, I want you to know I don't think you killed Georgie. I know this little dog and pony show"—he waved toward the lock that was still hanging from the chain—"doesn't officially put you in the clear. But you're innocent as far as I'm concerned. You always were. It's not in your nature."

"I appreciate the vote of confidence." It was true. Despite the fact that I *was* innocent of murdering Georgie, it made me feel good to hear Matt say it. "What now?"

"We get you out of here. Your elbows are already starting to bruise. I don't want anyone claiming your fall affected how you did in the demonstration."

As we walked down the hall, I promised to keep Matt apprised of anything I learned. Before I could ask him to do the same, he leapt ahead of me and held open the gate.

I smiled and shook his hand. "Thank you, Chief. Let me know if I can be of any further assistance."

With the demonstration behind me, I swung by the mayor's office. The receptionist, who still hadn't warmed up to me after I had pulled a fast one on her to gain access to the mayor almost a year ago, told me he was out for the afternoon. When I asked if she could tell me where I might find him, she said she didn't know and wouldn't tell me if she knew.

With a bow, I asked her to please let the mayor know I stopped by and wished her a good afternoon. There was no point in further antagonizing the woman. I had more constructive things to do.

As I stepped into the bright afternoon sunshine, the gears in my mind were turning. I had three suspects—Roger, Tommy, and Lori. They each had the motive, means, and opportunity to kill Georgie. Despite the aches and pains in my knees and elbows, I had no doubts I was headed in the right direction until a question brought me to a halt.

Who did I go after first?

Chapter Ten

Allie Cobb's newest rule of investigation—when your body hurts, and you've got a lot on your mind, go to Soaps and Scents to get some personal care items.

I loved the businesses in Rushing Creek. Like me, most of them were small operations. Unlike me, they depended on the Rushing Creek community for much of their income. For that reason, I went to great lengths to patronize as many of them as I could.

It was easy to support Soaps and Scents. The owner, Shirley Price, had the most awesome vibe that combined equal parts hippie, Wiccan, and scientist. She dressed like she'd just returned from the Woodstock festival, all the way down to her ever-present Birkenstocks. She celebrated the traditional American holidays but had an additional devotion to the summer and winter solstices. Her fragrance of choice, patchouli oil, completed the picture.

Appearances could deceive the unwary, though. Just because she had a wardrobe and belief system that was out of the norm, she was no airhead, like a lot of intolerant people wanted to believe. She could talk at length about the science of essential oils, mindfulness, and alternative medicines. And whenever someone wanted to doubt her bona fides, she could pull out her chemical engineering degree.

Shirley was the real deal.

My bergamot oil supply was running low, and I was in major need of the calming effect it had on me. I figured I'd get a bottle to use in my diffuser, along with a bar of bergamot and Earl Grey soap I'd been dying to try. Then I'd have a long, relaxing bath in my claw-foot tub.

The gentle jingle of wind chimes welcomed me as I entered the store. Before I got too far, I took a deep breath and reveled in the day's featured scent. It was peppermint, one of my favorites.

According to Shirley, peppermint oil could be used in a variety of ways, including as an energy booster. On a couple of occasions, when I was up late editing and didn't want to resort to a cup of coffee, I'd rubbed a couple of drops of peppermint oil on my temples. The boost to my alertness level had amazed me and turned me into a true devotee of Shirley's products and advice.

She was also a kind soul who never had a cross word for anybody, even the disagreeable Ozzy Metcalf. In the fifteen months since Shirley had opened her store next door to Ozzy's woodworking shop, the man had alternated between passive-aggressive behavior and complete boorishness.

Ozzy was anywhere between sixty and seventy-five, depending on who I talked to. He'd never been known to be teddy-bear friendly, but the gray-haired, bespectacled artisan had been a valuable member of the Rushing Creek business community for over forty years. He donated to local causes and every year taught a class on basic woodworking with the Rushing Creek Library. His work was stunning, too. The man was a true artist.

His artistic brilliance didn't make his boorish behavior toward Shirley acceptable, though. Things boiled over when he lodged a complaint against Shirley, alleging that the scents emanating from her store created air pollution and a public nuisance.

When I heard about the dispute, I made it my personal quest to ensure that Shirley emerged the victor. I don't know why the issue mattered so much to me. Maybe it was because Shirley had been so nice after Dad died. Maybe it was because her products had truly made a positive difference in my life. Whatever the reason, I hired a lawyer to represent Shirley and paid the legal bills.

"Allie." Shirley enveloped me in a tight hug, even lifting me off the ground for a moment. "All hail the conquering hero, the Kickboxing Crusader."

"Oh, please." I rolled my eyes. "What's with the over-the-top greeting?"

"This came in the mail today." She handed a me piece of paper. It was a letter on official City of Rushing Creek letterhead.

I read the letter once, then a second time. It was short, only three paragraphs, but what it lacked in length, it more than made up in significance.

"Yeah, baby." I hugged her back and then read it aloud. Our antics caught the attention of two women in the shop, who gave us nasty looks, but I didn't care. It was from the Rushing Creek Zoning Commission and said Soaps and Scents wasn't breaking any laws or violating any local rules. Ozzy's complaint had been dismissed.

"Couldn't have done it without you. I was so worried I was going to have to move the shop. You have no idea how much of a relief it is to have this off my shoulders."

"Glad I could help." And I was. I'd spent my whole life as the underdog. When I was a teenager, I promised myself I wouldn't sit idly by if I saw an injustice being done to someone. Ozzy's complaint was such an injustice. It felt good to prevail.

It felt better to make a difference.

"As a token of my gratitude, I have something for you." She went behind the sales counter. When she returned, she was holding a brown paper bag and sporting an ear-to-ear smile. "Enjoy."

The bag contained a collection of spearmint-scented items—body lotion, bubble bath, shampoo, and lip balm. My eyes clouded over, and I had to swallow twice to get rid of the lump that had formed in my throat.

"There's something else." Shirley leaned toward me. "As a peace offering, I asked Ozzy to meet me for breakfast to see if we can reach a compromise on our differences. He said yes. We're going to talk Monday."

"That's great, but you shouldn't have to do that." I pointed at the letter. "Not after getting that."

"Which is why I want to. One of the things I've learned in my years on this Earth is the value in offering to share control when you have it. Ozzy and I have never really talked to each other, so this is the perfect opportunity to build a bridge where none had existed."

I shook my head. The woman had a graciousness about her I could only hope to attain someday.

Shirley asked me to stick around and have a cup of herbal tea after she took care of the other customers. With a wink, she said it would be our victory celebration. Given the way my knees were beginning to ache, I gave an emphatic yes and took a seat behind the counter.

An hour later, I left Soaps and Scents with a light heart and a tranquil soul. While I loved my apartment, my coffee, and my kitty cat, there was a certain magic to sitting in Soaps and Scents, sipping a warm cup of chamomile tea, and chatting with Shirley.

We'd focused on pleasant things, like Sloane and Luke's wedding and plans for the Fall Festival. They were topics that were important, but not heavy. It was the kind of conversation I needed to have with people more often.

At a languid pace, I made my way back to the pub for my weekly dinner with the sibs. The afternoon sun warmed me but didn't leave me sweat-drenched. September really was an ideal time to live in Rushing Creek. It had all the benefits of good weather without the summer vacation crowds. The Boulevard still got congested on the weekends, but it was a small inconvenience. That was Rushing Creek in a nutshell. It was a pleasant place to call home, and the problems tended to be small.

Except for murder.

I brushed the morbid reminder aside as I arrived back at the pub and put the gifts from Shirley in my bike's saddlebag. I was making headway on the case and saw a path forward, but it needed to wait.

Now, it was time to unwind with my sibs while we checked in with each other about Mom.

As usual, I arrived before Luke. Rachel wouldn't take a break until he was on the scene, so I took our usual corner booth and tried to catch up on work e-mails. I'd reduced the unopened items in my inbox by half when a hairy hand got in the way of my phone.

"Enough of work, sis. Time to focus on your family." Luke took the seat across from me as I put my phone down on the table.

He was right. Not that I liked to admit it, but I often got so immersed in a project I let it consume me. I'd stopped counting the times I stayed up all night editing a story while forgetting to eat and feed Ursi. This was one of those times. Between work and the investigation, I was on my way to becoming overwhelmed. I needed to step back and put my sibs and Mom at the forefront.

We were chatting about a new housing addition being built west of town when Rachel joined us with the traditional Cobb meeting dinner—a plate of deluxe nachos. All conversation ceased for a few minutes while we dug into the six-inch-high mountain of cheese and salsa-laden tortilla goodness.

"I can't stay long. The twins have their first soccer practice tonight." She took a drink from her tumbler of water. Her children, Tristan and Theresa, were six and keeping her busier than ever now that they were in school.

Thankfully, there wasn't much to discuss this week. When there wasn't much to talk about, that was a sign Mom was doing well.

I talked about my time spent with her on Sunday, leaving out details related to the case, of course. Luke reported he'd dropped by her house Monday evening with some pork burgers from the Labor Day fest and they'd spent a few hours hanging out in the backyard. He also said Sloane was planning a new training route so she could go past Mom's house twice a week. Rachel didn't have anything to report.

"Sorry, guys. Between the kids' schedules and Matt working sixteen-hour days right now, I'm maxed out." Her sigh as she stared at the ceiling spoke volumes. My sister never sighed. She'd once said a sigh was a sign of weakness. That was a trait she didn't want in her life.

For the first time in ages, I reached across the table and gave my sister's hand a comforting squeeze. We locked gazes for a few seconds, then she squeezed back. A ghost of a smile appeared as she did so. And then, like a cool breeze on a summer night, it was gone.

No words were spoken, but it didn't matter. It was another quiet breakthrough. We'd had a handful of them over the last year, and each one sent a charge through me. The massive wall we'd built between us growing up was tumbling to the ground, brick by brick, with each of these quiet moments.

It gave me hope. Hope that if my sister and I could make things right between us, then anything was possible.

"Sounds to me," Luke said through a mouthful of nachos, "like things are good. Let me know when you get the kids' game schedule. I don't know diddly about soccer, but I'd love to watch 'em play."

"Same here." I knew a little about soccer from my days at Indiana University. One of my roommates dated a guy on the men's soccer team. The team was a national power, so it was fun going to the matches. Watching my niece and nephew would be way different, but I had no doubt seeing them run up and down the pitch would be a lot of fun.

"Thanks, guys." Her eyes misted over. "I'll do that. We could have our own little Cobb family cheer block."

As she dipped a tortilla chip into some sour cream, she asked for a report on my chat with Jeanette and Tommy. I told them what I'd learned, while admitting I wasn't proud of the way I'd learned it.

"Yeah, but if Tommy's the killer, you got some really valuable information." Luke wiped a salsa-laden finger on his napkin.

"And if he isn't the killer, then you tricked a man into talking about a painful part of his past. Hope that doesn't come back to bite you."

My sis was right. I'd never been one who believed the ends justified the means. I couldn't start behaving that way now. I pledged to avoid using underhanded investigation tactics in the future and shifted the conversation by telling them my next step was to visit Lori.

"She's a nice girl." Rachel's phone buzzed. "I need to go. Don't be a jerk to her, okay?" With her purse in one hand and her phone in the other, she made for the door, stopping only long enough to have a word with one of the staff.

Luke popped a slice of jalapeño pepper into his mouth. "She doesn't know about the insurance policy, does she?"

I shook my head. "Haven't had the chance to tell her."

"Yes." He slapped the tabletop. "For once I know something Rachel doesn't."

"Really?" I gave him the side eye. "I'm trying to catch a murderer, and you're happy with knowing something our sister doesn't? You're horrible." I threw a wadded-up napkin at him.

"I know my place in the world. For example, you concentrate on finding Georgie's killer, and I'll concentrate on getting your park finished on time." He pulled the plate of nachos from the center of the table to right in front of him. "Mind if I finish these?"

* * * *

My bike ride home from the pub wasn't long, only five blocks, but as I cranked the pedals, I felt like I was taking a victory lap at the Indianapolis Motor Speedway. I'd made progress on the case, helped Shirley win her dispute with Ozzy, and had another breakthrough moment with Rachel. All in all, it amounted to what Dad had called a red-letter day.

With my bike over my shoulder, I scaled the flight of steps to my apartment with less discomfort than I expected. Maybe it was the endorphin release from the ride, but as I unlocked the door and rolled the bike to its designated parking spot, I promised Ursi we'd go for a walk after dinner.

Normally, when I arrived home, my kitty wound her way through my legs and then trotted straight to her food bowl. This time, she did neither. Instead, her attention was focused on a card on the floor. She'd pushed it partway under a floor mat and was struggling to get it back out.

I left her to her fun while I went to the bathroom to unload my goodies from Shirley and to wash my face and hands. Once word had gotten out that a literary agent was living in town, I'd started finding random items slipped through my mail slot two or three times a week. I'd received everything from business cards to ten-page writing samples.

One time, a misguided soul managed to slip a three-hundred-page manuscript page by page through the gap between the floor and the door. It took me ten minutes to track down all the pages, which Ursi had playfully distributed throughout the entire apartment during the time between the delivery and my arrival home. That was a less than ideal afternoon.

Evidently, some folks thought bypassing e-mail or regular mail would be a way to get my attention. They were right, but that attention consisted of annoyance more than anything. Ursi's piece of mail could wait.

By the time I got back to her, she was on her side with her front legs halfway under the mat.

"What have you got this time, girl?" When I pushed the mat aside with my foot, she pounced on the piece of paper.

Upon closer inspection, Ursi's plaything wasn't paper. It was a credit-card-shaped piece of plastic. I picked it up and ran my thumb across the blank surface. Curious at who would lay out the extra cash for a plastic business card, I turned it over.

It took a few seconds to make sense of the printing and photograph. It wasn't a business card. It was an ID card.

"Holy samolie!" In shock, I let the card fall from my hands.

It was Georgie Alonso's Rushing Creek work ID.

Chapter Eleven

My hands were trembling as though I was caught in an earthquake. My eyes were cloudy from the panicky tears I was trying to blink away, with little success. My heart was racing as if I was sprinting down a dark alley with a mugger mere inches behind me.

How did a dead man's ID end up in my apartment? With the question repeating itself over and over, like a record with a scratch in it, I called Matt.

"I'll be there in five minutes. Don't touch anything." He cut the connection before I could ask him what his second sentence meant.

To keep from hyperventilating, I closed my eyes and counted backward from one hundred in Spanish. The concentration needed to execute the task pushed other concerns out of my mind, so by the time Matt arrived, my heart rate had slowed from an all-out gallop to a trot.

It jetted right back to a gallop when Tommy followed Matt into the apartment.

The police chief guided me to the couch, while the officer unsnapped his gun holster. Once Matt had me seated, Tommy searched the apartment.

"Nobody else is here except Ursi." My voice was uneven, but at least my hands had stopped shaking.

"Standard police procedure. We want to make sure you're safe." He sat next to me and took out his notebook. "Tell me what happened. Start from when you arrived back here."

I took a deep breath and recounted all I could remember. Since there wasn't much to the story, it didn't take long, and I finished at the same time Tommy joined us from his search.

"Nothing, Chief. No signs of forced entry, either." He slipped on a pair of exam gloves and deposited the ID card in a clear-plastic evidence bag.

"Check across the hall and then downstairs. I want to know if anybody saw or heard anything unusual." He held out his hand. "I'll take custody of that while you talk to people. I have a few questions for Ms. Cobb."

When we were alone, Matt cleared his throat. "Not gonna lie. This doesn't help you."

"Oh my God. Seriously?" I pounded my knees with my fists. "Earlier this afternoon you said I was in the clear, and now because of this stupid ID card you think I killed Georgie?"

"No, I don't. Please try to calm down so we—"

"Calm down?" I let out a high-pitched laugh that was filled with alarm. "When has anyone ever, in the history of the civilized world, calmed down when asked to calm down? It's obvious someone's trying to set me up."

"I understand you're upset." He scratched his chin. "Let's think this through. Obviously, if you were the murderer, and I'm not saying you are, and you had Georgie's ID, you wouldn't tell anybody you had it. Especially the police."

With his words offering me reassurance, I unclenched my fists. "Do you want to search my apartment to make sure I don't have anything else of his?"

"No need, but thanks for the offer. We did an inventory of Georgie's personal effects. His wallet, his driver's license, all of those things were accounted for." He scribbled down a note. "I'm going to ask around to find out where Georgie kept this. It's possible someone found it and they're playing a horrible practical joke on you."

"Or the killer took this from Georgie the night of the murder with the idea of planting it on whoever found the body."

"And since you found the body, you were put under suspicion. Let's say when an arrest wasn't made, the killer used this," he tapped the evidence bag with his pencil, "to draw attention back to you. That doesn't make sense, though. The only way for the ID's whereabouts to become known would be for you to tell someone."

"Unless I was expected to try to hide it. Then someone could make an anonymous tip." I swallowed. The picture forming in my mind wasn't a pretty one. "That would have looked bad."

"Really bad." Matt put his hand on my shoulder. "No offense."

"None taken. I know what you mean." Boy, did I ever.

To give myself time to think, I went to the kitchen to get us each a glass of water. While the second glass was filling, something important fell into place.

"Trying to set me up was a bad move. Anybody who knows me knows I wouldn't hide the ID. I'd call you."

Matt took a long drink of the water I gave him. "Good point. That tells us the perp doesn't know you, or at least doesn't know you well."

"That's a lot of people in this town." *Including my main suspects.* I took a sip of my drink. The cold water tasted as good as Matt's affirmation of my conclusion felt. It was reassuring to know he was, beyond a doubt, on my side.

"What do we do next, Chief?"

"I check in with Tommy to see how his interviews are going. The way this town's rumor mill turns, word is probably already out that you called this in, so I'm not expecting any anonymous tips." He headed for the door.

"What can I do?" I was in such a jumbled-up state, I needed to do something, anything, to contribute to the case. To let Matt know how much his belief in me meant.

"Keep the lines of communication with me open. If this was part of the murderer's plan, it backfired. It's a mistake. My gut tells me he'll make more."

Ursi was winding her way around my legs again, so I picked her up and scratched her back. I used the time to debate whether to bring up my suspicions about Tommy. When she licked my hand, I took it as a sign to go for it.

"So, about Tommy." Suddenly, I was tongue-tied.

"What about him? Do you need to talk to him before we go?" He reached for his radio.

"No. I was wondering if you guys were doing okay working this case together. You know, with this being such a high-pressure deal and the history you guys have."

God, talk about being a two-time loser. First, I was totally chickening out asking about Tommy. Then I was doing a horrible job of covering up for my lie. Sometimes, I could be so pathetic.

Matt clenched his jaw and stared out the window as he took his sweet time opening a piece of gum. I held my breath as he chewed. "I suppose you were going to bring the subject up at some point. Tommy and I are fine. He's a good cop. I trust him with my life. Any rumors you've heard about problems between him and me are flat-out wrong. Got it?"

"Got it." The forcefulness of his defense of Tommy pushed me back a step. *I hope you're right, Matt.* "You know how vicious rumors can be." I forced a laugh.

"The same could be said for you." He shook the bag containing Georgie's ID. "Hang tough."

* * * *

I like to think I'm good at a lot of things, but if there's one thing I know beyond the shadow of a doubt I'm good at, it's hanging tough. As I got out of bed the next morning, I picked up Ursi and gave her a little squeeze. Then I kissed her on her little orange-and-black nose.

"We'll get through this, girl. You and me. And then we're going to finish building Dad and Thornwell's park and have a grand opening celebration like this town's never seen."

She looked at me. Her big, golden eyes seemed to see deep into my soul. Like she was assessing me to make sure I was telling the truth. Then she put a paw on my cheek and licked my chin.

In my effort to not laugh at my kitty's surprising display of affection, I loosened my grip on her, and she leapt from my arms, landed on the bed, and vaulted to the floor with the grace of an Olympic gymnast. As I wiped my chin, the last I saw of her was her tail, held majestically high in the air, as she turned the corner and sauntered to the kitchen for her morning meal.

While I ate breakfast, I checked work e-mails. I was halfway through my bowl of oatmeal with raisins and walnuts when an e-mail from an editor stopped me mid-chew. It was an offer of publication for the first author I'd signed after moving to Rushing Creek. The novel was a mystery, set in England during World War I. I'd had high hopes for the story and took the offer as another sign the tide was turning in my favor.

I called my client, crossing my fingers she'd pick up. The excitement rendered me speechless for a second when she answered. I gave her the good news, along with some details about the offer, the publishing house, and the editor who'd made the offer.

After answering a few questions, I recommended she take a few days to think things over. In the interim, I'd inform the other editors who were considering the manuscript that we had an offer. If any of them wanted to make an offer, I needed to know within two days.

She agreed to my suggestion, so after a few minutes, I ended the call with a light heart. My next task was to revise the spreadsheet I kept on each manuscript when it was out on query. I updated the spreadsheet, then sent e-mails to the editors who hadn't yet responded to let them know we had an offer and what our response deadline was.

Still in the full glow of the exhilaration an offer always brought, I gave Ursi an extra kitty treat and headed out the door. My first stop was downstairs to chat with Renee Gomez. I figured while we visited, I could be on the lookout for any new books I couldn't live without.

Stepping into Renee's Gently Used Books was like crossing the threshold into another universe. Music from some obscure artist was always on the sound system. Most of the time, Renee played something on her turntable, as she was a vinyl aficionado. Other times, she played a rarity from the store's massive used compact disc collection. The only time she resorted to the radio was when she could get the blues show broadcast by the public radio station out of Bloomington. Today, I recognized the musician. It was Chuck Mangione, the jazz performer who had had a top-ten pop hit back in the seventies.

Renee greeted me by lifting a stoneware coffee mug inscribed with the letter R and saluting.

"What's the word, boss?" Boss was my affectionate nickname for Renee. I gave it to her when she handed me the list of things I'd have to do before she'd lease the apartment to me. It was also a nod to the fact that she lived in the apartment across from me and, to a certain degree, kept tabs on me.

"Today's word is interrogation." She poured coffee into a ceramic mug with a purple capital A on it.

I accepted it with a thank-you when she joined me by the front window.

With her shoulder-length, jet-black hair, deep brown eyes, and six-foot height, Renee was striking. When you added the fact that she was dressed from head to toe in black, the image was borderline intimidating. It was a false image of the woman, though. She smiled easily, had a fabulously dry sense of humor, and loved to chat, especially about books.

"How'd your conversation with Officer Abbott go?" There was no point in beating around the bush. Besides, I wanted to save my delicate approach for the next person I was visiting.

"He was fine, even if he got a little abrasive at times. It's the reason for his visit that has me concerned." She took a sip of her coffee, her lime-green fingernails a stark contrast to her dark outfit. "I hate the thought of someone creeping around my building. It makes me so angry."

"Did you see anyone who seemed out of place yesterday?"

"No. We had two tour bus groups come through. It was wall-to-wall customers most of the day." She wandered toward the cash register, stationed near the entrance. "I was either ringing sales or answering questions."

I pointed to a small camera hanging above her. "What about that?"

"The footage is saved to an SD memory card. I gave it to Officer Abbott. He's not going to find anything helpful, I'm afraid. Whoever left that ID card probably walked in, dashed upstairs, and was back out the door in no time."

I took a long drink of the dark and aromatic coffee to give me time to mull over the situation. While I did so, Renee kept tapping on the counter with her index finger. Her nervous activity was worrying since, as the old saying went, she was the type of person who was normally as cool as the other side of the pillow.

Then it hit me.

"Your apartment wasn't messed with, was it?" Until that moment, it hadn't occurred to me somebody else might have been victimized.

"Not that I know of. Officer Abbott looked around and told me to let him know if I noticed anything out of place. Thankfully, I didn't have to call him." She let out a long, ragged breath.

"I'm sorry. I'm sure we'll catch the killer soon."

Renee was a good person, a kind person, and didn't need the additional stress my situation was putting on her shoulders. The sooner the murderer was behind bars, the better. For all of us.

I gave her a hug and went across the hall to the Sock Shoppe, a store that sold practically every style of sock under the sun. If you wanted knee-high stockings with rainbow horizontal stripes, the Sock Shoppe had you covered. More of a fan of white anklets made from recycled materials? They had those, too.

It didn't stop there. The store also carried caps and scarves featuring the colors and logos of college and professional teams like the Indiana Pacers and the Chicago Cubs. It even carried a few items decorated with the Indy 500 logo. Despite my less-than-ideal situation, it was a fun store to visit.

A display filled with pet-themed socks caught my attention, especially an adorable pair of fuzzy, sky-blue socks with cat-paw prints. After promising myself I could come back to get them later, I checked with the manager, a guy named Mike Crump, to see if there had been any reports of unusual activity the previous day. He said he already told the police everything he knew. When he asked why I was asking, I told him that since I lived upstairs, I was trying to help the police.

That was me—Allie Cobb, selfless public servant. Good Lord, at times it seemed like I could I weave a tale of fiction as creatively as my authors.

Fortunately, Mike and I didn't know each other beyond friendly waves going into and out of the building. I was counting on that lack of familiarity to keep him from asking any more questions. He was a nice enough guy, but I had places to be and didn't want to get drawn into a conversation that might take me who knew how long to end.

With no surveillance cameras in the store and no more information to be gleaned, I thanked him for his time and promised I'd be back later for the cat socks.

My next stop had me as jumpy as a grasshopper halfway there. I was headed for First National Bank.

Lori Cannon's place of employment.

I was a customer of the bank and visited once a week to make deposits, to transfer funds, things like that. I could have done my banking from the comfort of my couch, but going to the bank was another way to get fresh air and exercise. It was also a good way make contact with people in town. Like Lori.

My athletic shoes squeaked on the polished marble floor as I walked toward Lori's teller station. I thanked the karma gods there were no other customers to eavesdrop on our conversation. Assuming she would talk to me.

"Hi, Allie. Welcome to First National Bank. How can I help you today?" She smiled, but it didn't reach her eyes.

"Just need to make a withdrawal." I scribbled out the information on a bank slip. "I'm so sorry about Georgie. How are you doing?"

"I don't know." She shrugged. "Still in shock. Brittany keeps asking when her daddy's coming home." Her eyes got watery, and she sucked in a long breath.

I recalled Luke pointing out Brittany during last year's Fall Festival. She was an adorable little ginger with freckles just like her mother. Georgie may have been a louse, but no child should have to live through the nightmare of learning her father had been murdered.

"Would you like to talk about it? Over lunch, maybe?" Part of me was disgusted at my manipulative behavior. The other part reminded me that a man was dead and Lori had a lot to gain from his demise.

I couldn't remember if Lori had an interest in drama. Maybe she was putting on a show. Maybe she was an innocent victim of this horrible crime. It didn't matter. She had information. I needed information. End of story.

"That'd be nice. My break is at one."

"I'll meet you at the Brown County Diner at five after."

Chapter Twelve

How did one tell a woman she was a prime suspect in her boyfriend's murder without getting a bowl of steaming vegetable soup thrown in one's face? As Lori sat across from me, I pondered that issue, mindful that my time to question her was running short.

"Thanks again for meeting with me. I don't think I'd be able to function if I was in your position." I took a sip of my iced tea, hoping my open-ended statement would get her talking.

"Yeah, well, I guess I'm not surprised. Dad always told me Georgie was no good, that he'd come to a bad end." She twirled her spoon around in her soup. "I guess he was right."

"This isn't your fault. Someone did this to him."

"I know, but you know how Georgie was. He promised me he was going to change. That he was going to get me a ring and we'd finally get married. A pipe dream, I know, but I loved him, and I thought I could change him. God knows I tried."

Angela brought us our main courses, a Cobb salad for me, a chicken sandwich for Lori. She placed a hand on Lori's shoulder and gave it a little squeeze. Lori looked at her and simply nodded. Sometimes, words weren't necessary.

While I made steady progress on my salad, Lori plowed through her sandwich like she hadn't seen a meal in days. It made me wonder whether grieving people lost their appetites or turned to food for comfort in such a traumatic time.

Or whether her grief was an act.

"Are you and Brittany going to be okay? Over the long run, I mean."

"No worries on that end." She barked out a laugh that had more venom than mirth in it. "Sorry, Allie. It's not you. It's practically everyone else in town."

"What do you mean?" I was pretty sure I knew what she meant, but this was no time for guesswork. I might not get another crack at her in such a trusting mood.

She leaned toward me. "Georgie had a life insurance policy. A big one. It was worth a million dollars."

I let out a low whistle. Rumors confirmed.

"I didn't know anything about it until yesterday when I got a call from the city's HR department. They told me it was taken out the week after he started working at the Parks Department. I still haven't seen the policy. And now people are saying I killed him for the money. Why would I do that?"

Why, indeed. "You know how some people can be. I love Rushing Creek but could totally do without all of the gossip."

With one suspicion confirmed, it was time to change tactics.

"Do you know of anyone who would have wanted to hurt Georgie? Or if he was in any kind of trouble?"

Lori stared out the window, tracing a circle on the tabletop with her index finger as she did so.

"Dad told me you were playing private eye again. He said you should leave crime investigation to the professionals."

"Well, I'm a believer that crime doesn't pay." I kept my voice light, hoping some levity would bring forth whatever she was holding onto.

"Oh, yeah. The Kickboxing Crusader." She mimicked a karate chop at me and laughed. "No offense, but that nickname is pretty dumb."

"I'm not a fan of it either, but Sloane loves it, so I'm stuck with it." I winked. "Don't tell her I said that."

"I'm glad you were able to help her out. She's always nice when she comes in the bank. The two of you were always nice to me in school. I haven't forgotten that." She took a drink of her lemonade, then looked out the diner's picture window. "There was one thing. Georgie had a gambling problem."

"What kind of problem?" This was news. Nobody had mentioned gambling to me.

"He liked to bet on sports, but he was terrible at it. Between you and me, most of his paycheck went to cover his gambling debts. He told me he was one lucky hit from getting rich." She shook her head. "And like everything else, that lucky hit never came."

I'd read manuscripts about people who ran gambling operations. They were ruthless. Could someone have killed Georgie over an unpaid debt? I couldn't rule it out.

"Do know where he gambled? Did he mention any names?"

"You might try Hoosiers. Lord knows he spent enough time there."

"I'll do that. And I promise that if I find anything out, I'll let the police know and let the professionals handle it. That ought to make your dad happy, right?"

She laughed. This one carried genuine happiness. "Let's hope so. Thanks for lunch, Allie. I feel better."

"You and Brittany are going to be okay." I reached across the table and took Lori's hand in mine. "I promise."

"You're the best, Allie. I'm so glad you came home." She gave me her cell number and invited me to visit and meet Brittany. When I said she could count on it, she gave me a big smile, then returned to work, leaving me with my thoughts and a full glass of iced tea.

As I sipped the tea and checked work e-mail, the angel of good choices who was perched on my right shoulder started beating me over the head with my case notebook and berating me for my duplicitous behavior. She said I was doomed to eternal damnation for lying and taking advantage of a young, single mother, who was now likely to raise her daughter alone.

Meanwhile, the demon of not-so-good choices danced an Irish jig on my left shoulder, lit a cigar, and said through a cloud of smoke that Lori was the one who was taking advantage of people's naïveté. She asked the angel of good choices who was the one about to cash in on an insurance windfall while getting rid of a total loser boyfriend in the deal.

Which version of Lori was the accurate one? I wanted more than everything to believe her. I'd been the victim of Georgie's games and knew all too well the pain he caused people without giving it another thought. And my experiences were nothing compared to what he'd done to Lori. Of that, I had no doubt.

On the other hand, just because she said she didn't know about the insurance policy didn't make it true. If she did know, it gave her one million reasons to get rid of a problem and start anew. It wouldn't be enough to live on forever, but it would cover college for Brittany and a new start for Lori, with plenty to spare.

A woman could start over with a clean slate with an insurance settlement like that. Especially if she was smart.

Lori was smart.

By the time I finished another glass of tea and updated my case notebook, it was almost time for the diner to close for the day. When Angela brought me the bill, she placed something else on the table.

"Very nice." It was a bumper sticker inscribed with a simple MILLER FOR MAYOR slogan. The lettering was in bright blue on a white field. It was simple, easy to read, and classy. At least as classy as a bumper sticker could get.

"It's for you. You can put it on one of your bike's saddlebags." She took the spot across from me and pulled a wad of bills from a pocket of her apron. "You don't mind if I count my tips, do you? I figure I can do that while you tell me what intel you pried out of Lori."

I threw up my hands in frustration. "Come on. Can't I have lunch with someone I knew from my high school days?"

"Of course you can." She organized the bills into piles of ones, fives, and tens. "But how many of those old friends just had their boyfriend murdered?"

After counting each pile, she wrote the totals on a piece of paper. She folded her hands and gave me a long look. "You're sailing in dangerous waters, Allie. You need to be careful."

Angela's message came across loud and clear. If I messed with the mayor's daughter, I messed with the mayor. Sure, Larry was powerful and, thanks to his office, had his fingers in all aspects of Rushing Creek life. He could make one's life difficult, and Angela was looking out for me. I appreciated that.

What Angela didn't know was that I had dirt on Larry that nobody else had. It was information I'd come across while investigating Thornwell's death. Back then, Larry and I had reached a truce when I made him aware I was privy to his secrets. In fact, it was that truce which had led to the decent relationship I currently had with the man. We'd managed to set aside our mutual distrust for the benefit of our community and, in doing so, forged a solid partnership.

"I appreciate it, but I've got it covered. I don't see having lunch with Lori causing me any trouble."

Angela raised an eyebrow. "Are you sure? You've changed a lot in the years you were gone. The same could be said for Lori."

"What do you mean?" I trusted Angela like she was a member of my family. If she had something to say, I'd be foolish not to listen to her.

"Working in a place like this, you see and hear a lot of people. I know what Lori put up with, especially after Brittany was born. I also know she's patient and she's astute. What happened to Georgie had to take a lot of planning. As in years' worth."

My demon of not-so-good choices was snapping her fingers and telling Angela, "Preach it, sister." Meanwhile, my angel of good choices had curled up in a ball and covered her ears.

I closed my eyes for a moment and told the angel of good choices that it was time for her to make a graceful exit. There was simply too much circumstantial evidence to give Lori the benefit of the doubt. I wasn't ready to convict her, though.

"Assuming you're right, how do you account for the lock that was cut open at Parke Landscaping?" I told Angela about my attempt to cut through a similar lock at the police station.

"That's easy. She got Georgie to do it."

I threw other questions at Angela, like could Lori drive a stick shift, did she leave Brittany home alone while she carried out her plan, and did she really know about the insurance policy?

My friend had answers to every question. Some were less plausible than others, but none of the answers crossed the line into the realm of impossibility. I had to hand it to Angela, she had all the bases covered.

"You've put a lot of thought into this. Shall I turn my private eye gig over to you?"

Angela rolled her eyes. "Please. I'll stick to running for public office. That's frightening enough. Seriously, though, Georgie's murder has me worried. I'm sure Chief Roberson and his team are doing all they can, but the way they dragged you in for questioning made me mad. I want to help you and this town at the same time. So, yes, I have put a lot of thought into this."

I drummed my fingers on the linoleum tabletop while I let Angela's words sink in. She was right. I needed to set personal histories aside and follow the facts, regardless of where they took me. The facts were pieces to a puzzle. I needed to gather more pieces before I could put them together. To do that, I needed to keep my eyes and ears open to all possibilities and give them equal consideration.

"I'll be careful. I promise." A clock hanging above the grill chimed three times. Closing time. "Any other advice?"

She pulled a blue-and-white pin about the size of a quarter out of another apron pocket and fastened it to the collar of my shirt. "Yes. Vote Angela Miller for mayor."

Leaving the diner, I took a moment to soak in the scene on the Boulevard. With the sun out in all its glory and not a cloud to be seen, the day had turned into one of those glorious late-summer ones when the air carried a hint of the aroma of ripe apples, the grass was still soft and green beneath one's feet, and I could spend all day out on a hike without breaking a humidity-induced sweat.

I had to get back to my office to do some work that paid the bills, but given the weather, I opted for a walk to decompress. With a goal of thirty minutes of brisk walking in mind, I popped in my earbuds and got moving.

A scorching tune full of mighty guitar riffs by blues artist Samantha Fish had me setting a fast pace five minutes into my walk when someone shouted my name loud enough for me to hear over one of Samantha's guitar solos.

With reluctance, I slipped the earbuds into my pocket. I hated stopping when I was on a roll, but I didn't want to be rude. Especially when the person calling to me was Maybelle Schuman. It was time for some gossip.

"Gorgeous afternoon, isn't it?" I took a seat beside the elderly woman. From our vantage point on a wooden bench in front of the Rushing Creek General Store, we had a clear view of the Boulevard as it ran north and south through the middle of town.

I wasn't in the mood to talk, so after exchanging pleasantries and the usual family updates, I kept my mouth shut. If there was something on her mind, and I had no doubt there was, I was going to make her broach the subject.

"I hear you're impersonating Miss Marple over the awful incident involving the Alonso boy."

"More or less." While Miss Jane Marple was an amazing amateur detective, being compared to an elderly Englishwoman, regardless of her status as a genius in fictional literature, didn't sit well with me. I was only thirty, after all.

It was her reference to Georgie as a boy that grated on my nerves, though, like a pebble lodged in a shoe that wouldn't come out. In my book, calling someone a boy implied a young, innocent male. Georgie was neither young nor innocent at the time of his death.

"You're hiding your grief well." She patted my leg. "It must be hard, losing him so suddenly. I want you to know I'm here if you want to talk."

I furrowed my eyebrows. Despite my vow to keep quiet, my curiosity got the best of me.

"I'm not hiding anything. What are you talking about?"

"It's just this, dear." She looked around, then leaned in close to me, as if she was going to give me the combination to the safe at the bank. "People are saying Lori killed Georgie."

"Okay." What was so secret about that? Shoot, it was the same thing Angela had told me.

"Oh, honey." She scooted right next to me. "They're saying she killed him because he was romantically involved with you. People remember the torch he carried for you when the two of you were in high school, after all."

"I…" The shock of the outlandish accusation rendered me speechless. Anyone with even the vaguest recollection of our high school years would know the rumor was crazier than the thought of me reading *War and Peace* again. Once was way more than enough.

On top of that, it was downright spiteful toward Lori. No, this wasn't simple rumor. This was an example of someone intentionally hurting Lori and leaving me in the cross fire.

"Me and Georgie? Together? You can't be serious."

When she nodded, I burst out laughing. It was a gut buster that left me doubled over, howling at the utter absurdity of the rumor, to the point that tears began streaming down my face. It took me two or three minutes before I got myself under control enough to look at Maybelle.

Her clenched jaw and eyes that had narrowed to mere slits told me she wasn't happy with me.

"Oh, come on." I wiped both tear-streaked cheeks with the sleeve of my shirt. "You don't believe that, do you?" I gave her a quick recap of my nightmarish prom night. "After someone did that to you, would you ever become involved with them?"

"Of course not. I mean, of course I don't believe the rumors, either. I was simply trying to be a friend and let you know what other people are saying."

"I know, and I appreciate it." There was no doubt in my mind that Maybelle was, in fact, among the *other* people spreading the awful rumor. I was better off playing her game, though. With her connections around town, she could be a formidable enemy if I got on her bad side.

"So, you weren't… involved with him, then?" Maybelle's cheeks had pinked up now that the conversation had veered out of her control.

Her discomfort made me happy. It wasn't that I disliked the woman. I liked her. What I didn't like was the way she thrived on gossip and rumors.

"No, I wasn't. I do intend to find his killer, though." I got to my feet. "Even though I didn't like the man, he didn't deserve to have his life taken from him. Whoever did that needs to pay."

I said good-bye and turned on my heel. Perhaps it was an overly dramatic exit, but it was true. I was going to find Georgie's killer. Justice needed to be served. For Brittany, if for nobody else.

Chapter Thirteen

Still fuming over the insane rumor Maybelle shared with me, I race-walked home, arriving at my door in record time. I took a few minutes to cool off by snuggling with Ursi. My fuzzy friend wasn't the most tolerant fur baby, but she had an amazing sixth sense of knowing when I needed her warm black-and-orange body close to me. This was one of those times, so she let me hold her and even rewarded me with loud purring as I scratched under her chin.

After that, I spent the rest of the day editing a client's manuscript. It was a young adult novel set in a steampunk world in which the teen-aged heroine was investigating her parents' disappearance. The tale pulled me into the world like I was living there. It was the perfect escape from the drama of my day.

By the time I finished editing, it was past one in the morning, so it wasn't surprising I was awoken the next morning by a fuzz face pawing at my nose.

"All right, all right." I brushed her paw away as she let out a *meow* to let me know it was about time I got her breakfast. It was fascinating how put upon Ursi could sound with a single vocalization. It was a skill I envied.

The clock on the microwave indicated it was almost nine. As I poured Ursi a bowl of dry cat food and placed it by her kitty water fountain, I let out a contented sigh. A full eight hours of sleep with no nightmares. That was the right way to start the day.

I scrolled through e-mails while the coffee maker gurgled its way to a full pot. I was about to fill my mug when an unexpected e-mail caught my eye. It was from the author who had received the publication offer.

She'd accepted.

I let out a *whoop* and danced the Electric Slide on my way to the kitchen counter. In celebration, I tossed a kitty treat to Ursi, threw together a breakfast burrito, and got out my mega-large coffee mug. It was a bright yellow ceramic piece of art adorned with the words SUPER AGENT and a logo that evoked Superman's *S*. I only used the mug on special occasions.

This was one such occasion.

"The Cobb Literary Agency is going to have another published author. High five, Ursi." I held out my palm, but she walked away after giving it a sniff. "You'll thank me tonight when I give you some of your favorite chicken."

Feeling as tall as the mythical Paul Bunyan, I acknowledged my author's e-mail, then shot off another one to the editor, letting her know the offer was accepted. Almost in the blink of an eye, the editor promised to deliver a proposed contract in a month or so.

My mug was still half full when I finished my e-mails letting editors who hadn't responded to my offer notice know that the manuscript was no longer available. Intent on enjoying the moment of success, I spent the rest of the morning working in the sunshine on the patio.

When the bells of the clock tower in the county courthouse rang eleven times, I closed my laptop and headed indoors. It was time to pay a visit to Willie Hammond at Hoosiers.

Despite my small physical stature, I had enough self-confidence that few people scared me. As luck would have it, Willie was one of them. He was a harder version of his brother, Al, as though he'd been forged in the fires of Mount Doom and battle-tested on the shores of Normandy.

While they were both massive, Al was like a cross between Santa Claus and Hagrid from the Harry Potter books. Al had shaggy hair and an easy smile and was quick with a joke that more often than not was about the round belly that hung over his belt. He was generous to a fault and gave to every youth and civic organization that approached him for a donation.

Willie, on the hand, looked like an NFL linebacker. With a shaved head and chiseled physique, he cut an intimidating figure. Add in his salt-and-pepper goatee, and he was known to make cocky kids trying to get into Hoosiers with fake IDs run away in fear. Those who knew him said he had a dry wit and keen intellect and loved to debate military history.

I didn't know Willie, so I couldn't comment about his wit and brainpower. What I did know, from my few encounters with Willie, was that he lacked patience and didn't care for small talk.

With trembling fingers, I slipped my case notebook into my purse. I'd never been frightened of interviewing a witness before. Of course, I'd never interviewed someone who ran a bar and a gambling ring and could probably break me in half with one arm tied behind his back. That was when I reminded myself there was a first time for everything.

I gave Ursi a kiss on the head as I made my way out the door. "Wish me luck, girl. Here goes nothing."

As a bar for the Rushing Creek locals, Hoosiers didn't mess around with a fancy menu or drinks with cutesy names to attract business. The place served uncomplicated pub fare like burgers and sandwiches with fries or coleslaw on the side. There was always fresh popcorn that folks raved about, though some said it was on the salty side to entice customers into ordering more drinks.

As I settled onto a barstool and munched on a bowl of popcorn the bartender placed in front of me, I had to admit, the snack smelled heavenly and tasted even better. I looked around to get a feel for my surroundings, hoping they'd give me a glimpse inside the owner's head.

The building was split into two large rooms—the bar area, where I was sitting, and a dining area. A set of folding French doors provided access between the two rooms and gave the establishment an old-world English pub feel. With the doors open, the melody of an unfamiliar country song drifted my way from a jukebox that was beyond my field of vision. The dining area had dark green carpeting, which transitioned to the hardwood floor in the bar area.

On the walls, art deco–style wall sconces provided indirect lighting while exuding a touch of class I didn't expect. The bar, a solid wooden structure that was long enough to seat twenty, was bathed in a warm glow by can lights from above. The bar back featured intricate wooden carvings with a beveled mirror, engraved with an elegant script *H*, smack-dab in the center.

Hoping to ingratiate myself with Willie, I scanned a menu. I figured if I was going to question him, the least I could do was have lunch while I was doing it.

Picking out something to eat wasn't hard. The grilled ham and cheese with coleslaw was calling my name. The tough part was picking out something to drink. While the food section of the menu took up one page, the drinks section took up three pages. One page was dedicated to beer, another to hard liquor, and the third to wine.

"I make most of my money selling alcohol. Thus, the unparalleled variety," a low, gravelly voice came from in front of me. "What can I get you, Miss Cobb?"

Though I'd not heard the voice in a long time, there was no doubt to whom it belonged. I lifted my gaze from the menu to the mountain of a man who had, with the stealth of a cat, taken up station a mere meter from me. I swallowed. Willie wore a black polo shirt that was straining at the seams, due to his huge biceps. His hands, which were placed on the bar on either side of me, were the hands of a giant. A gaudy ring circled the third finger of each hand. One ring sparkled with what appeared to be dozens of tiny diamonds. The other featured a red stone so large it bordered on gauche. He would have made an ideal Corleone brother.

He wore a smile, but his eyes told a different story. I sensed he knew why I was sitting on one of his barstools and he didn't care for it.

I gave him my food order and confessed I was having trouble deciding what to drink. When I told him I wasn't a fan of beer, he knocked twice on the surface of the bar.

"I know just the thing for a lady of your upbringing." He went to the far end of the bar and returned with a bottle of wine. "Rushing Creek Winery's latest pinot grigio. You used to work there, did you not?"

"I did. How'd you know that?"

He ignored my question, poured two glasses, and handed one to me. With a nod, he lifted his glass and clinked it against mine. Then he swirled the wine in his glass, gave it a long sniff, and drank, swirling the wine around his mouth before he swallowed.

"Not bad. A touch heavy on the green apple, but I like the hint of honeysuckle. What's your impression?"

I'd spent my summers during my college years as a server at Rushing Creek Winery. In that time, I'd developed a decent wine palate. I also never saw Willie Hammond visit the winery. As I swirled the yellow-hued drink, then inhaled the subtle fruity bouquet, my gut told me to be on my toes around this man.

With my eyes on him, I took a small drink and rolled it across my tongue and around my mouth. Willie was right. The apple did border on overpowering, but it didn't ruin the taste.

"I agree with your assessment, but you might consider serving it slightly more chilled. That would help bring out the other flavors."

He scratched his goatee and took another drink. After a moment, he raised his eyebrows.

"Point taken. I enjoy a good bottle of wine, but my clientele, not so much." He handed my food order to the bartender with instructions to turn the wine cooler temperature down two degrees. "May I join you? I figure it will make it easier for you to ask your questions."

"I…well, yes." I took out my notebook and tried to get my reeling mind in order while he made his way from behind the bar. A wine aficionado who also ran a gambling ring. The contrast had me feeling like I was stuck on a balance beam trying make my way from one end to the other using only one foot.

He cracked his knuckles as he slid onto the barstool next to me. "I heard you've been asking questions about the untimely death of Georgie Alonso. By your lovely presence before me, I assume you believe I can be of service. How so?"

"I wanted to talk to you about Georgie. I understand he was a regular customer." Since Lori had confirmed the rumor that Georgie spent almost every weeknight at Hoosiers, I was curious about how Willie would respond.

"Regular is such an imprecise term. If you're asking did I roll out the red carpet when he graced my establishment like he was royalty or did I simply welcome him with a wave and a friendly greeting like I do with all my customers with whom I'm on a first-name basis—"

"Spare me the evasive wordplay. It's beneath you." I didn't have the time or the inclination to screw around with this man. The sooner I got my answers and made for the exit, the better.

"As you wish." He took a drink of his wine, then studied the glass as the bartender placed my lunch before me. "Please eat. The ham and cheese are both locally sourced, which makes a stunningly fresh experience for the palate."

I took a bite and almost melted into the wood of the barstool. The cheese was milky and flavorful, while the ham had a touch of smokiness to it I didn't expect. The bread was toasted to perfection, too, crunchy on the outside but still soft in the middle.

"This is amazing." I ate three bites before I could force myself to put down the sandwich. "About Georgie, though, was he here the night he was killed?"

"Alas, he was, as I told Chief Roberson the other day." Willie drained his glass and refilled it. "Surely you don't think anyone connected to my establishment had anything to do with the heinous act."

It wasn't a question. I took the statement as a challenge. "I don't know. Is there a reason for me to suspect someone who works here?"

"None that I know of." He used his thumb to spin the diamond-encrusted ring around his finger. Was it a sign of nerves, what poker players called a tell?

I made a mental note to ask Al about it while I ate some coleslaw. When my sandwich was half gone, I went on the offensive.

"What if he owed somebody money? Gambling losses, for instance."

"I'm afraid you've lost me, Ms. Cobb. The only gambling that goes on here is the annual pool we run around the college basketball tournament. Half the money from that goes to the youth sports league." The ring was spinning as fast as a toy top. Interesting.

"Perhaps I can point you in the right direction." I leaned toward him and lowered my voice. "Georgie had gambling debts. Big debts. Debts he ran up in this very place."

"What do you want me to say? If the occasional twenty passes from one person to another over a ball game, what am I supposed to do? It's a free country, and this is a place for adults, not children." He paused to let the insult hit its intended target.

I let the barb bounce off me with a grin and another bite of the sandwich. The man was a cool customer, and much more genteel than I'd expected. I couldn't escape the feeling he'd be right at home in a three-piece suit working for a mob boss in a big city.

"That's true. Adults *are* responsible for their actions. I suppose you wouldn't object to me relaying your sentiments to Lori Cannon. You know, the woman now responsible for raising Georgie's darling little daughter all by herself." I shook my head and finished off my wine. "Of course, I couldn't tell Lori and expect her to keep information like that to herself. That wouldn't be fair. Maybe I could ask her to keep it between her and her parents."

Willie stared at me for a moment, then let out a long, loud laugh that caused the half-dozen customers in the room to turn their heads in our direction.

"Bravo, Miss Cobb." He gave my hand a friendly pat. "Your reputation doesn't do you justice. Duplicitousness suits you, though I don't know whether your mother would consider that a compliment."

"I prefer to think of it as a dogged desire for the truth."

"Indeed. To that end, I say this: Yes, I have been known to take the occasional bet on a sporting event, including from Georgie. I make my living running a neighborhood grill, though. Not as a sports bookie."

"So, he didn't run up gambling debts with you?"

Willie started spinning the ring again as he stared at his empty wineglass. I sensed a crack in his confident, urbane façade.

"Not with me, no. The bets I handled for him were small-time things. Over time, he wanted to raise the stakes beyond what I deal with, so I referred him to a colleague."

"That's all you have to say? You nurtured a growing gambling addiction and fed him to bigger sharks when the water got too deep?" I made no attempt to hide the disgust in my voice. Until now, I'd wanted to keep things as cordial as possible, hoping Lori's claim was wrong. With it confirmed, I no longer cared about decorum.

He clenched his fists. "I resent the accusation I fed anybody's alleged gambling addiction. As I said before, this is an establishment for adults. Customers are expected to take responsibility for their actions."

"That's a convenient attitude." I had him. It was time for the kill. "One might conclude that attitude contributed to Georgie's death if he was murdered for an inability to pay off his gambling debts. Not unlike a drug dealer who starts selling someone marijuana before progressing to more powerful, and addictive, drugs."

"That is enough." He slapped the bar so hard I was practically startled out of my seat. "I agreed to speak to you out of a civic duty to help locate a man's murderer, not to have my name dragged through the mud."

"Is that a denial or not? If you have nothing to hide, why play so coy?"

"Was Georgie Alonso killed because of gambling debts? I don't know. I've neither seen nor heard anything to support that supposition." He hauled himself from the barstool. "If you'll excuse me, I have things to do."

"Just one more question, please."

"Good afternoon, Miss Cobb. Your lunch is on the house. Please give my regards to your sister the next time you see her." Without so much as a look over his shoulder, he stomped into an office near the far end of the bar and closed the door.

Shoot. In my excitement at gaining an advantage over the man, I'd overplayed my hand. Now I'd have to leave without asking the key question.

Who was with Georgie at Hoosiers the night he was killed?

Chapter Fourteen

I left Hoosiers with mixed emotions. For all intents and purposes, I got Willie to admit Georgie was at the bar the night of the murder. I also got him to confirm Lori's claim that Georgie had run up serious gambling debts. That was good.

On the other side of the coin, I didn't know any of the big-time gamblers' names. More importantly, I'd failed to get names of people who saw Georgie that final night. That wasn't so good.

As I jotted down notes on a bench in front of the store that sold custom leather goods, I wanted to kick myself.

Willie and his staff had given Matt a list of customers at Hoosiers that night, of that I had no doubt. My dilemma was how to get my hands on the list. I could ask Jeanette, or maybe even Matt, but whether they'd give me a copy was another matter. Man, this election-season drama was annoying.

Another missed opportunity was my failure to ask Willie directly if he'd killed Georgie. Sure, it was a long shot, but, with his admitted ties to gambling, I couldn't rule it out.

I made a mental note to ask Al, in a tactful way, if his brother could be the killer. After all, Willie looked strong enough to cut through the lock. And I recalled Al talking one time about the truck with the manual transmission that he and Willie drove when their parents owned the restaurant.

As I was writing down another observation about Willie, a wave of shame passed through me. I lowered my head until my chin touched my breastbone. Asking a lifelong family friend if his brother was capable of taking another's life. Yeah, that would go over really well.

With a sinking feeling in my belly, I headed home. My visit with Willie had provided a couple of pieces to the puzzle, but I had no idea where they went.

Patience, Allie. You'll figure this out.

Trudging up the steps to the apartment, I hoped I was right.

After an afternoon of agent work and an evening watching my guilty pleasure, *Rugrats*, with Ursi on my lap and a glass of wine, I woke up the next morning calm and relaxed. In the past, when I was struggling with an editing job or having a hard time negotiating a contract, I stepped away from the project for a while.

The break typically might not last long, but the time away gave my brain a chance to subconsciously process the troublesome task. Inevitably, when I returned to it, with fresh eyes and a clear mind, it was easier, and often more enjoyable, to finish the work.

While I waited for my coffee to brew, I hummed the *Rugrats* theme song. My friends Tommy, Chuckie, Angelica, and the rest always had played an admirable part in giving me a much-needed break.

Of course, I was also happy because Brent was coming into town for the weekend. I'd warned him I needed to talk about the case, and he'd agreed to be my sounding board.

The thought of him listening to me, letting me think out loud, and offering objective input made me smile, despite the chilly, drizzly weather. We planned on going for a walk and taking Ursi and Sammy with us. While our furry companions weren't the best of friends, they got along well enough that the four of us could hang out without worrying about Sammy chasing Ursi under a bed or up a tree.

It was the damage an unsupervised Sammy could do to the rest of the apartment that worried me. One time, Brent and I had come home from a dinner date to find Sammy had knocked over a plant and pulled all of the toilet paper off its roll. From that date forward, the energetic canine was allowed to be in my apartment only when Brent or I were around to supervise.

Unless it was raining buckets when Brent and Sammy arrived, we'd go outside. Damp sidewalks didn't bother Ursi. In fact, she enjoyed drinking from downspouts whenever I let her. Sure, we were an odd foursome, a six-five man with a shaggy golden retriever and a five-one woman with a smallish tortoiseshell cat, but our differences made life interesting.

Our differences also made us happy.

Well, it made Brent, Sammy, and me happy. It was always tough to tell when it came to Ursi.

To prepare for our walk, I popped over to the deli down the street and picked up fresh bread and cold cuts. There was a park across the street from the library that Brent was fond of, so I figured we'd take a stadium blanket and have a picnic in the park. While we ate, Sammy could romp around in the grass and Ursi could nap.

Then we could visit the library and say hi to our old friend Vicky Napier, the woman who ran it. Vicky would probably scold us for bringing pets into her library, but I was certain that, after a minute, she'd give in and let us stay for a short visit. We were friends, after all. It was going to be fabulous.

I was slicing the loaf of multigrain bread for our sandwiches when my phone went off. My shoulders drooped when the name on the screen wasn't Brent.

"I hope you've got good news for me, Chief." Maybe I was getting delusional, but it seemed like the only time Matt called was to deliver bad news.

"Depends on what you consider good. It's Friday. That's good, right?"

He was stalling. That wasn't promising. I told him to stop the delay tactics.

"The report came back on the items we found at the bottom of the mulch pile. The only fingerprints we found belonged to Georgie."

My mind accelerated into a full sprint. If the only prints were Georgie's, did that mean he was the one who both cut the lock and drank the bottle of bourbon? That he was alone?

No. That didn't make sense. If he was alone, there was no possible way he could have suffocated himself under ten thousand pounds of mulch.

The questions came in a torrent. Were Georgie's prints somehow placed on the items before he died? If not, did he really cut the lock and drink the whole bottle of liquor?

The bottle. I snapped my fingers as a ray of hope cut a path through the flood of questions.

"What about DNA? Did the lab test for it around the mouth of the bottle? If Georgie shared the bottle with someone, maybe there are traces of it."

"Hmm." Matt was silent for a few excruciating minutes as he flipped through pieces of paper. "The lab still has the bottle. I'll ask them to check. It'll take a few weeks to get those results."

I let out a sigh of relief.

"The problem is Larry. He's leaning on me to come up with enough evidence to make an arrest. I don't know if I can hold him off long enough to get DNA results."

And there it was. Matt didn't need to spell it out for me. I was back at the top of the official suspect list, assuming I'd ever been removed from it.

"I know what you're thinking, Allie. The answer is no. I still don't think you did it."

"Is that because of the rumor that Lori killed him when she found out I was having an affair with him?" It was a pointless, spiteful question, but it was out of my mouth before I realized what I'd said.

"Yeah, I heard that rumor, probably from the same person you did." He chuckled. "I have to admit, with news of this insurance policy, Lori isn't lacking in the motivation category."

We discussed the case for a few minutes, then Matt said he needed to go. I asked him for a list of the witnesses at Hoosiers the night Georgie was killed. After some hedging, he said he'd see if he could get me the information.

"Believe me, Allie. I'll be as relieved as anyone to get this case solved. Let me know if you learn anything. Even if it doesn't seem important."

I promised to do exactly that, and we said our good-byes.

While the situation was far from ideal, the phone call had been enlightening, and it helped that it came before Brent arrived. While the puzzle pieces were still coming together at a glacial pace, the framework of a plausible theory was beginning to form.

A little while later, a knock at the door, followed by an emphatic *woof,* sent Ursi scrambling off the couch and into the bedroom to hide. I set my notebook aside and went to the door.

"Who is it?" Even though I knew it was Brent and Sammy, it was fun to feign ignorance and hear an inevitably unique and often-entertaining response.

"Your knight in shining armor and his faithful companion, here to free you from the bonds of literary drudgery and boredom." Brent's response was followed by another *woof,* then a sneeze, probably from Sammy. I adored the dog, but her sneezes could flatten a house.

Literary drudgery, huh? "I'm in the middle of editing a scorching-hot romance, so I don't need to be freed right now. Can you come back later, after I cool down?"

"You wound us, fair maiden. We have traveled many miles, over hill and dale, to sit at the feet of you and your feline counterpart. Will you not grant us an audience?"

"What's in it for me?"

"I brought chocolate."

I had the door open a split second later. While coffee was necessary for me to make it from day to day, chocolate was often key to making each day worth living.

Brent wrapped me in a hug as Sammy nosed her way through the door to hunt for Ursi. "The whole *Don Quixote*-inspired knight greeting thing didn't work for you, huh?"

"I would have led with the chocolate." I got up on my tiptoes and kissed his cheek. "In the future, always lead with chocolate."

While Sammy padded from room to room searching for Ursi, Brent and I got comfortable on the couch to chat. We typically talked on the phone or via Skype two or three times per week, but there was no substitute for in-person conversation.

His current genealogy installation project was nearing completion. As opposed to his project in Rushing Creek, which included two computer stations at a single library, this one involved three library branches and six stations.

"Everything's in place. We go live next Tuesday. I'll spend Monday testing all the systems and worrying, so I'm ready to forget about work for a few days." He stretched out his long legs and propped his feet on the coffee table. "You hanging in there okay?"

I brought Brent up to date on the events of the past couple of days. Even though I'd talked to a handful of people about the case, it was a huge help to confide in him.

He let me talk without interruption, and I must have gone on for fifteen minutes straight. That was one of the things I really liked about Brent. He was a fabulous listener. He made eye contact and nodded while holding my hand. When I was finished, he was quiet for a minute while he stared at the clock.

"Man, I miss a little, I miss a lot. By that look in your eye, you have a plan of action?"

"I have a theory." I got to my feet. "I'll tell you about it on our walk."

With our pets leashed, we made our way downstairs and out into a gray, damp afternoon. Brent had a stadium blanket and other picnic supplies in a backpack slung over his shoulder. I had the sandwiches and snacks in a tote hanging from my shoulder. Ursi took a moment to step onto the sidewalk, as if she was waiting for a flock of paparazzi to descend on her, but Sammy greeted the outdoors with joy, straining his leash as he dashed this way and that to sniff at everything within reach.

Once Sammy settled down, Ursi made a light step onto the sidewalk and glided along the concrete surface with her head held high and her tail pointed upward.

"I guess she's too cool to be seen having fun outside," Brent said as we followed my cat's lead.

"She has her reputation as the famous Rushing Creek Walking Cat, after all. She probably doesn't want to be seen by one of her fans doing something as lowbrow as playing in the water." Brent and I shared a laugh as, at that very moment, Ursi stopped to take a drink from a puddle.

Back in May, Kim Frye had asked if she could do a profile of us since she'd never seen a cat out for a walk on a leash. I agreed, figuring what the heck, every bit of publicity would be good for the agency, even if only locals read the article.

I had no idea how popular a feature about a cat whose owner took her out for regular walks would be in southern Indiana. It appeared in the digital edition of the *Brown County Beacon* on a Thursday. Within a week, it had been shared hundreds of times, liked a few thousand times on Facebook, and had a link tweeted halfway across the globe.

Ursi had become a celebrity. For pretty much the entire month of June, whenever we went for a walk, someone stopped us and asked to take a selfie with the famous feline. Fortunately for all parties involved, she was used to people and crowds from our time in New York and was patient with people. Of course, it helped that I learned giving her a treat immediately after a visit with a fan made her much more amenable to her newfound fame.

Sammy joined Ursi at the puddle, and once both were sufficiently hydrated, we continued our walk in a comfortable silence. The rain had turned into a light mist that was cool on my skin. It also deadened nearby sounds to create the illusion that we had the world to ourselves.

We were stopped at a crosswalk when Brent broke the silence. "Do you want to tell me your theory?"

I took a deep breath. "I'm convinced Georgie's murder was planned. There are way too many pieces in play for it to be a random act."

"Why do you say that?" Brent's tone was encouraging. As opposed to when we were in the apartment and I wanted to unburden myself, he now knew I wanted someone to respond to my ideas, to get me to think.

"First off, there's the mulch pile. Whoever did this had to know the mulch was scheduled for delivery that Friday morning. Because of that, the murderer also had to be familiar with the routine at Parke Landscaping."

"Why does that matter?"

As we crossed the Boulevard, I explained that when Roger Parke had morning deliveries, he loaded up his trucks the night before. That way he could get the materials dropped off immediately, which gave him time to fit in an extra delivery during the day.

"You think the murderer knew how to find Georgie and knew there would be trucks loaded with mulch at the landscaper. And knew where to find the keys." Brent lengthened his stride. It was a sign he was getting excited. It was gratifying that we were on the same page, but it also made it hard for Ursi and me to keep up with him and the long-legged Sammy.

"Exactly." I went over my lock demonstration to support my belief that someone strong would have had to cut the lock. "I'm not saying a woman couldn't have cut that lock, but I think it was more likely a man."

We arrived at the park and set aside our discussion while we laid out our picnic. The minute Brent had the blanket in position, Ursi claimed a corner and began licking her front legs. Sammy, the good boy that she was, sat patiently while Brent screwed a leash stake into the ground and attached both leashes to it. Our pets weren't the type to run off and get in trouble, but the last thing I wanted was for Ursi to dash off after a bird or Sammy to chase a squirrel and make us go look for them.

Thanks to the damp conditions, we had the park to ourselves, which let us debate the issue without fear of being overheard. While we ate, we discussed the insurance policy. It was a fact I couldn't reconcile with the others.

"The insurance proceeds turn Lori into a suspect." In my notebook, I drew a circle around her name and connected it to a dollar sign to represent the insurance cash. "But there's no way she could have cut that lock from Parke's gate herself."

"She could have convinced Georgie to do it, right?"

"Sure." I got up and made a few loops around the blanket. Luke said it was weird, but my habit of walking while I was thinking proved to be helpful quite often.

After more discussion, we agreed Roger and Lori were credible, if not perfect, suspects. They had reasons to want Georgie gone for good, even if their motives were vastly different. When you combined the dump truck, the bottle, and the mulch, they both had the means to do it. They knew Georgie's habits, so they had the opportunity to get him alone to commit the murder.

Our conversation then turned to Tommy Abbott. As soon as I finished my analysis, Brent jumped to his feet, eliciting a yowl in protest from Ursi, who'd been napping.

"He's gotta be the one. He's a cop, so he'd be able to keep tabs on Georgie. He's got plenty going on in the revenge column. As a city employee, I'd bet he had access to information about the mulch delivery, and he wouldn't need any help with the lock issue, like Lori would."

The theory had merit, but I was reluctant to mention it to Matt. It was one thing to accuse a member of the community of a murder. It was something entirely different to accuse an officer of the law.

"I need more than circumstantial evidence before I go to Chief Roberson about one of his own. That's one accusation I can't afford to be wrong about."

Brent dug a plastic grocery bag out of his backpack and used it to clean up a dropping Sammy left. As he headed toward a trash can in the corner of the park, I scratched Ursi behind the ears and thanked her for using a litter box.

"What about the ID?" Brent sat down next to me and crossed his legs. "Seems to me only someone with inside info would know to plant it on you. Plus, he'd have to have access to the body. A cop would have that more than the other two, especially if he's trying to frame you."

I recounted my conversation with Matt about the ID card. "The chief thinks it was an attempt to frame me. An attempt that failed epically." I brushed a few blades of grass from my shoe. "I don't see a cop making that kind of mistake. Someone else, though…"

Brent crossed his arms. "Okay. If it's not the cop, who do you think it is?"

"If we assume it was either Roger or Lori, Lori would be the more likely one." I shook my head and looked at the slate-gray sky, blinking back tears as a devastating scenario hit me.

Lori Cannon, the sweet girl I was kind to in high school, murdered her boyfriend and tried to pin it on me.

Chapter Fifteen

The next day was a big one. Actually, it was huge, all nineteen buildings of Rockefeller Center huge.

Sloane and I were heading to Indianapolis for a final fitting of her wedding dress. While we were gone, Luke and Brent were going to work on the house. Then, when we returned, we were going to grill on the back porch and spend a fun evening hanging out.

To be honest, we could have found a dress in Columbus or Bloomington, both of which were closer than Indy. Shoot, with Slone's newfound wealth, she could afford to hire a dressmaker from New York to create a one-of-a-kind wedding gown.

Making the trip to the state capitol gave us an excuse to spend the day together, though. Between the increased training and travel that came from her ever-improving race results and my growing client list, spending quality time together wasn't easy. With Luke and Brent in the picture, carving out time for just the two of us was more challenging than the five-thousand-piece puzzles Mom was doing now that she was home alone most evenings.

After a cup of coffee, I filled Ursi's food bowl and promised her an extra kitty treat when I got home. She was still on the bed, curled up in a black-and-orange ball. Yesterday's adventure had left her as worn-out as my battered paperback copy of *A Christmas Carol*, which I had read every December since I turned thirteen. A quiet day alone would do her good.

I hopped on my bike and pedaled at a languid pace to Luke's house. Old habits die hard, so it was going to take me a while to think of it as Sloane's house. Luke and Brent's remodeling plans for the day would help me remember, in no uncertain terms, the change in status, though.

As I rolled to a stop in front of the house, Brent was carrying drop cloths from his truck to the house. He gave me a kiss as I leaned my bike against the house.

"Is that the best kiss you can give the woman, librarian?" Sloane was at the front door, with her hand on her hip. She was grinning from ear to ear, having caught us in the act. "You're lucky to be dating a superhero, dude. The least you can do is act like it."

"Superhero? Yeah, if the superhero's Mighty Mouse." My cheeks grew hot as Luke's voice drifted out of house, to be followed by the man himself, who put his arms around his fiancée, eliciting a giggle from her in the process.

Luke's jab was harmless. He'd teased me about my tiny stature for years and always followed up his digs by complimenting me about my smarts. In the world of big brothers, he was a keeper.

He took the drop cloths from Brent. "I want to say you can do way better than this bean pole, Allie, but since he's helping me make my fiancée happy, I'm not going to say that."

Brent scratched his chin. "I should probably take offense, but I know it's his way of showing he's scared of being shown up in the handyman department by a mild-mannered librarian. Just because I like tweed, have a degree in library science, and make my money setting up genealogy departments in libraries doesn't mean I don't know my way around construction tools."

To prove his point, Brent fetched a nail gun and circular saw from the toolbox in his truck and struck a pose like he was a bandit from a Zane Gray novel brandishing a pair of six-shooters. "Say hello to my not-so-little friends."

Sloane snorted. "Promise us neither of you will end up in the emergency room."

"And when we return, you'll have all of your fingers and toes, and dinner will be ready." I gave her a high five. "Come on, girlfriend. Let's get going so the alleged manly men can get to work."

We piled into her Subaru in high spirits. The clouds and rain from Friday had cleared out, so we had blue skies and perfect conditions for driving and shopping. I let out a little *whoop* as Ed Sheeran's latest single started playing. The day was off to a fabulous start, and I couldn't wait for it to get better.

Our first stop was Big Al's Diner for a hearty breakfast before we hit the road. After the week I'd had, I was in the mood for comfort food. Sloane was good with the idea since I offered to buy.

Al was at the grill and gave us a salute with his spatula as we took our seats at the counter. While we perused the menu, he poured me a mug of coffee and brought Sloane a cup of hot water and a bag of green tea.

"Morning, ladies. What will you have?" Al leaned across the counter and lowered his voice. "I heard you paid my brother a visit the other day." He straightened up. "And lived to tell about it."

I tried to give Al the evil eye while Sloane laughed. "I'll have the western omelet scrambler with an English muffin, please. And yes, I had lunch with your brother. He even paid for it."

"My brother picking up the tab. It's a shock to my system." He put his hand over his heart and put his arm out to the side in a humorously bad imitation of a heart attack. "He either wants something from you or he's afraid of you."

"You don't mess with the Kickboxing Crusader." Sloane's gaze never left the menu. "I'll have the Belgian waffle with strawberry jam, an order of mixed fruit, and for my protein, a side of turkey bacon."

Al scribbled down her order as he complimented her on her recent race results.

Sloane's eyes went wide, and her cheeks pinked up at the kind words. "I didn't know you followed trail running."

"I don't." He gave her a friendly punch to her upper arm. "But I get a kick out of seeing how well you're doing. It's a treat to have a professional athlete from Rushing Creek."

A waitress rang a bell to signal an order was in. "Gotta get back to work. Let me know when you're finished with breakfast. We'll talk then."

As soon as Al was out of earshot, Sloane nudged me with her elbow. "Okay, give me the scoop. Have you solved the mystery yet?"

"Come on. This is your special day. Let's not spend it talking about unpleasant things. When's your next race?"

My effort at redirection worked. While we waited for our orders, she told me in animated tones about her run coming up in three weeks.

"It's the national championship. I'm entered in the twenty-one-kilometer distance. If I win my age group, I get a free entry to the world championship." She went on to tell me about her training plan leading up to the race, as well as her strategy.

To hear Sloane talking about such prestigious events in an excited but matter-of-fact tone made my heart want to burst for joy. She'd been through so much pain and suffering for so much of her life, culminating in her father's murder. It was gratifying beyond all measure to see her, finally, pursue her dream full-time. And see it come to fruition.

It wasn't until Al put our plates in front of us that I was able to get a word in edgewise.

"That will be amazing if you can pull off a win. Do you think you can do that? Not to be a Debbie Downer, but it'll be your first national championship. I imagine the competition will be ultra-tough."

"It will be." Sloane munched on a slice of her turkey bacon. "That's what makes it so exciting. My mind-set's changed. When I first thought about entering, I wondered if I could even compete with the best. Now, as my finishing times keep getting better, I know I can. I can compete, and I can win."

I scooped up a mouthful of omelet and let it melt in my mouth while I got my head around her response. Less than a year ago, my bestie was on the verge of walking away from her dream, like so many people who were forced, or thought they were forced, to choose between a lifelong passion and the realities of everyday living.

For those folks, the need for a steady paycheck had overcome the desire to travel halfway across the country to participate in an event with other athletes or artists. For Sloane, the path to following her dream had been cleared, but she hadn't just followed the path. She took hold of the opportunity like her life depended on it and sprinted down the path at full speed.

"Pretty cool to see us both actually living out the dreams we talked about when we were younger, huh?"

"Yeah, it is." She chuckled. "And it wouldn't have happened without the fearless exploits of the Kickboxing Crusader."

"Ugh. You had to go and ruin my appetite. Some best friend you are." Despite my admonishment, I couldn't keep from grinning, which led both of us to giggling like we were twelve.

We spent the rest of breakfast getting caught up on the usual things like family news and town gossip. The most interesting piece of news was Sloan's report that Ozzy had met Shirley over breakfast at the Brown County Diner. Evidently, they'd spent over an hour together and were smiling when they left. Sloane had run into Maybelle, who gave her the full sequence of events, up through this morning.

"According to Maybelle, Ozzy and Shirley had a drink at Hoosiers last night. How's that for a plot twist?"

"Interesting. I'll have to pay Shirley a visit and see what I can find out." I was inclined to discount the story, given its source, but wasn't in the mood to be disagreeable. Besides, if it was true, that would be welcome news to have them getting along.

When we paid the bill, Al told us to meet him by his truck behind the restaurant. As we walked down the sidewalk toward the back parking lot, Sloane tapped me on the shoulder.

"Do you know what Al's truck looks like?" It was a valid question.

When I lived in New York, the most common vehicle was a yellow cab. Here in rural southern Indiana, the vehicle of choice, by a mile, was the pickup truck. It wasn't a stretch to estimate that for every car in Rushing Creek, there was a truck. If you didn't own one, the odds were better than ninety percent your significant other did.

We reached the end of the building and came to a stop at the edge of a parking lot. Of the dozen vehicles in the lot, seven were trucks. Even though I'd never laid eyes on Al's, there was no doubt in my mind which one belonged to him.

At the far end of the lot, a massive vehicle gleamed in the sunlight. The shine of its glossy black paint was exceeded only by the near-blinding reflection of the chrome bumpers and trim. It was the largest truck in the lot, taking up the better part of two spaces. To eliminate any doubt about its owner, the truck had a vanity license plate on the front that read BIG AL.

I looked at Sloane.

She crossed her arms like she was deep in thought. "Let's roll the dice and try the big, black one."

I adored my bestie's penchant for silliness.

Al came out of the back of the building as we were halfway across the parking lot. With a long, loping stride, he came alongside me.

"A beautiful day in the making, don't you think, ladies?" He stretched his arms above his head as he placed a foot on the truck's front bumper. "It's always good to take a few minutes to get away from the grill. So, what's up?"

While I gathered my thoughts, I rolled a pebble back and forth with my shoe. Al and Willie weren't close, but I didn't want to insult my friend by unfairly disparaging his brother. I guessed it was time to test the adage about blood being thicker than water.

"The other day was the first time I've talked to your brother in a long time. He wasn't what I expected." I crossed my fingers in the hope I'd used a sufficient amount of tact in my opening.

Al rolled his eyes. "I get that a lot from people. Was it his attempt to sound like a big-city lawyer or his shirt that's two sizes too small?"

"Both, actually." When Al laughed, I joined him. It broke the tension in my gut. "Where did he learn to talk that way? For a while, it was like I was having a conversation with one of my college professors."

"He's talked that way for years. It's his way of trying to sound smarter than me. You didn't want to talk to me about my brother's odd habits, though."

I glanced at Sloane. She knew what I wanted to ask. We'd discussed it on the drive to the restaurant.

After a moment's hesitation, she put her hand on my forearm. "Go ahead, Allie. He needs to hear this."

"Do you think your brother could have anything to do with Georgie Alonso's murder?" In for a dime, in for a dollar, as the saying went.

Al took a multi-tool from his pocket and ran the knife under his fingernails. He was deliberate in his movements, with the assurance of one who had wielded a knife professionally for years. No word was spoken until he'd cleaned all ten digits and put the tool back in his pocket.

"Willie's no devil. Some could make an argument he's no angel, either. That said, he's employed a lot of people over the years. He's been a good corporate citizen."

Not the strongest endorsement of a sibling ever.

"About your question." He looked up as a cloud floated in front of the sun, casting us in shadow. "When it comes to business, he can be unforgiving. His hard-nosed approach is one of the reasons we went our separate ways. If Georgie got himself on Willie's bad side, that wouldn't be good. My brother's not a murderer, though, if that's what you're asking."

"Actually, I was thinking more in terms of Willie's business associates. He told me Georgie liked to gamble, more than he wanted to handle, so he referred Georgie to some bigger-time gamblers he knows."

"That I believe. Willie likes to play the horses, and he's not above taking small bets on ball games. I even place a few bets with him on big events." He leaned close to us. "Don't tell anyone, but our dad was an accomplished poker player. It wasn't unusual for him to spend a few days in Vegas, come home, and put his winnings right into the restaurant."

Sloane let out a long whistle. Her surprise matched mine. Al's father was known for attending church every Sunday and organizing the annual Thanksgiving meal for the less fortunate. The thought of him sitting at a poker table made my brain freeze up, like a computer that wouldn't function when a faulty command was entered.

I shook my head to set aside the image. It was yet another secret about my hometown and its citizens. Someday, I'd have to write a book about them all.

"Do you know any of his gambling contacts? I'd like to talk to them about Georgie." It was way more forward than I wanted to be, but Al's time was short, and I couldn't take a chance on wasting it with niceties.

He scratched his forearm as he gave first Sloane, then me, a long, penetrating look. "I might. But I'm not going to give that information to either of you. Those men are dangerous. Let me make some discreet inquiries."

He had me where he wanted, so I agreed.

I had more one question before we left, though. "Are those men so dangerous they would kill someone?"

Al put one arm around me and the other around Sloane. "Aye. Dangerous enough to kill. And then some."

Chapter Sixteen

Al's words left Sloane and me shaken up, so the first part of the drive to Indy was quiet. As we headed north out of town, we passed through a wooded area. Wildflowers along the side of the road were bursting with every color of the rainbow. Behind them, trees stood silent and tall, their brown bark and green leaves a muted complement to the exuberance of the purple, yellow, and red of the flowers.

Sloane finally broke the silence while we were at a four-way stop, waiting for a trio of Canada geese to cross the road. Such was life in rural Indiana.

"Pretty crazy what Al had to say about his brother, huh?" She laid on the horn in a futile attempt to get the geese to pick up their snail-like pace.

"And then some. Do you know Willie very well?"

Thornwell had been a regular at Hoosiers until he quit drinking a short time before he died. Sloane had told me too many times to count about getting a call from the bartender saying her father was too drunk to drive and was demanding his daughter come and take him home.

"Not really. Too many bad, Dad-related memories, so I steered clear of the place. Willie was nice enough to me when we crossed paths, though. God knows he should have been nice, with all the money Dad spent there."

Ouch. I hadn't meant to reopen old wounds. Today was supposed to be a day for and about Sloane. I wanted her smiling and laughing, not frowning and sharing memories from the days of her dad's alcohol abuse. It was time to take control of the conversation with some good news I'd been holding onto until I could share it in person.

"But you and your dad had good days, especially when he was writing again, right?"

That got a nod and a small smile out of her. I was on the right track.

"Speaking of which, I got an e-mail yesterday from a film studio. They want to know if there's any interest in selling the film rights to *The Endless River*."

"Are you kidding me?" Sloane pulled over onto the shoulder of the road. "What are they offering? When do they want to film? Can I be in it? Can I read the script? When do I—"

"Hold on, girl." Her excitement-induced barrage of questions had me laughing. "Let's not get ahead of ourselves. At this point, all they want to know is if you'd be interested in entertaining an offer."

"Well, duh. Of course I'm interested." She turned down the radio. "I mean, is there any reason I shouldn't be?"

"Maybe. Get us back on the road."

Once we got moving again, I took her through a basic course in how a book became a movie. I wanted her to be aware of two important points. Once she sold the rights to the film, she'd most likely lose all control over the finished product. It was also possible the film might not get made if sufficient financial backing couldn't be arranged.

"The important thing to keep in mind is you have options. If you're interested, we can ask for more information. If you get to a point that you want to stop, we'll stop. You don't have to agree to anything if you don't want to."

"What do you think I should do?"

It was tough giving Sloane advice on an issue like this because she was the only client I had who wasn't an author. Technically, I was the literary agent for the estate of Thornwell Winchester, so my job was to ensure that the best interests of the estate were represented. As Thornwell's only child, she was the sole representative of the estate, so all decisions regarding her father's affairs were left to her.

For all practical purposes, she was my client on all matters related to Thornwell's books. Because of that relationship, and the fact that we were lifelong friends, I had a close-up view of her finances. Only a handful of people knew it, but my bestie was the wealthiest person in Rushing Creek.

The simple fact was Sloane didn't need the money from selling the film rights to *The Endless River* or any of her father's novels. Between her inheritance and the income from the books, she was set for life, provided she stayed smart with her investments.

It was no secret Thornwell didn't want his stories adapted for the screen. Like the best-selling mystery author Sue Grafton, the man simply didn't want Hollywood to get its hands on his work.

Sloane wasn't Thornwell, though, so any decision on this topic was hers. I needed to make sure any decision was made with her best interests first.

"I think you should listen to what they have to say. Interest in your dad's work will never be higher than now. That could put you in a strong negotiating position. Especially since you can always say thanks, but no thanks."

She said she'd think about it and let me know what she decided in a few days. It was the response I wanted to hear. Sloane didn't lack intelligence, by any means, but sometimes she had a childlike naïveté when dealing with people. She wanted to trust those with whom she crossed paths. It was an honorable approach to life.

It was an approach I was incapable of taking in my own life.

As a general principle, I didn't trust people. My siblings liked to say it was because I watched too many *Scooby-Doo* episodes and read too many Boxcar Children books when I was young. They thought my exposure to all that mystery and suspicion at an impressionable age had destroyed any belief I might have in the basic goodness of people.

I let them believe it. It was easier than the truth, in which my distrust of humankind stemmed from the unkind and sometimes cruel treatment I had received from kids in town while I was growing up.

In elementary school, kids had liked to make fun of me because I got straight As and preferred books to video games. Things got worse in middle school. Too many times to count, I had my books knocked out of my hands by mean girls in retribution for refusing to let them copy my homework.

Then there were the taunting comments. The most hurtful words from the boys were reminders of how Rachel was so much prettier than me. The girls' go-to insult was calling me Alexander, saying that since I looked like a boy, with my flat chest and short haircut, I must really be a boy.

Mom and Dad gave me as much support as they could, but they also insisted I learn to stand up for myself. They believed that if they came to my rescue too often, I'd become too reliant on them. Hindsight proved they were right, but at the time, the self-reliance they were teaching me often left me feeling alone, like an outsider, in the town where I'd spent my entire life.

On the other hand, they propped me up time and again by telling me I could go wherever I wanted and do whatever I wanted. With encouragement like that, it was no wonder I took off for the bright lights of a faraway city the first chance I got.

Not everybody was cruel, of course. I had Sloane and a few other friends, but over the years, the slights, the put-downs, and the heartless behavior from others wore me down. I'd become convinced there was no place for me in Rushing Creek. That distrust, that feeling of being marginalized was cemented when Georgie humiliated me on prom night.

By the time I graduated from high school, I was over Rushing Creek. Eighteen years of being different from the other kids had taken its toll, and I was ready to put my hometown in my rearview mirror.

In time, I got over the anger and resentment that, like undetected cancer cells, had grown within me. I realized couldn't change the past any more than I could change those who had wronged me. What I could change was how I lived my own life. And I realized that I had to let go of the negativity of my youth.

It took a long time, over a decade, but eventually I came to terms with my past and found there was a lot I could learn from it. Among the most important lessons was the understanding that, while I still didn't trust people in general, that was okay because that was part of my nature. Thanks to that understanding, I learned to value the individual relationships I built, and to not worry about what others, who didn't know me, thought of Allie Cobb.

My less than trusting outlook on the human race was a key reason I was so thankful to have Sloane in my life. She brought the clean light of dawn to the twilight of my worldview. She found the joy in simple things I often missed. She also reminded me that growing up in an emotionally abusive home and retaining her belief in the goodness of people was a lesson in faith and perseverance. If you worked hard enough, eventually you would be rewarded.

For years, I tried to deny my prove-it-to-me nature. It wasn't any fun being the killjoy in the room, after all. As I got older, I accepted it and put it to good use. Being a skeptic during my years in New York came in handy as too many people to count thought they could take advantage of a tiny, single woman from the Midwest.

Now that I was investigating the second murder in my hometown within a year, for better or worse, that personality trait was coming in handy again.

As we made our way through the rolling hills and farmlands of south-central Indiana, I took advantage of a break in the conversation to mull over Al's revelations.

The information clouded the picture in a most unwelcome way. I had been ready to turn my full attention toward Lori, but now I wasn't so sure. If only I could get my hands on the list of witnesses at Hoosiers the night Georgie died, I could ask those folks if they saw him that night with anyone who seemed out of place.

Despite Matt's promise to see what he could do, I wasn't counting on him to get the list to me. He couldn't take that chance.

The list was a long shot, but it was still a puzzle piece I needed to fit somewhere, so as the soybean and corn fields gave way to the subdivisions on the outskirts of Indianapolis, I sent Jeanette a text. Since she wasn't on the case, nobody would expect her to have access to the witness list, right?

After a few more turns that left me with a feeling we were in a maze, Sloane guided the car into a strip-mall parking lot. The center store, Wendy's Bridal Boutique, was our destination. There was an open spot right in front of the store, but we motored right past it.

"Before you start whining, after that breakfast, we need to get some steps in." She finally settled on a spot at the far end of the parking lot. The closest car was forty feet away.

"Won't have to worry about anyone dinging your bumper." I let out a low growl as I got out of the car.

"Shush. It's a glorious day, and you know the exercise is good for you." She stuck her tongue out at me, turned on her heel, and headed for the store.

I was short of breath by the time I caught up to her, a mere five feet from the boutique's door.

"You need to get your heart rate up more often, Allie. Strolling around downtown Rushing Creek isn't getting the job done. I need to put you on a training plan." With an evil grin, she gave me a light tap with her elbow and opened the door.

"I do *not* need a training plan. You've got six inches on me. I have to work way harder than you to travel the same distance." I elbowed her back. "Especially when you're being mean and walking fast on purpose."

We went back and forth with our mutual teasing until a tall African-American woman with a name tag that read CLARICE emerged from the back of the shop. She spread her arms wide in welcome. "Ms. Winchester, it's so good to see you again."

We exchanged greetings after she gave Sloane a warm hug.

"Ready to see your dress?"

She led us past rows of breathtaking gowns in varying shades of white to a door labeled SALON TWO in elegant script. "I think you're going to love it. Shall we?"

With her eyes as wide as teacup saucers and a smile that went from one ear to another, Sloane nodded. She radiated a level of happiness that brought a tear to my eye. Her eagerness, as Clarice opened the door, sent a shiver down my spine.

With floor-to-ceiling mirrors on three walls and a raised dais in the middle of the room, the salon seemed more spacious than my apartment. Sloane's dress shimmered with the white light of a thousand stars as it hung on a mannequin in the center of the dais.

"Oh, my Lord," she said in a breathless tone as she stepped up to the dress and ran her fingers along a silken sleeve. "It's perfect."

"Well, we do aim to please." Clarice stepped behind the dress and unzipped it. "Allie, why don't you help Ms. Winchester get into her gown. I'll be right outside. When you're ready, let me know, and then we'll see if any adjustments need to be made."

Sloane chattered away nonstop as I helped her into the gown. It was an over-the-shoulder style that accentuated both her incredible level of fitness and her tan. She was so busy going on about how thrilled she was with the fit of the gown, she didn't seem to notice when I put her hair into a messy updo and went to get Clarice.

While the women discussed the gown's fit, I settled into a comfortable wingback chair and checked my phone. There was a text from Jeanette with a list of names. I took my latest investigative tool from my purse. It was a pocket-sized notebook, not unlike the ones Matt used. There was no substitute for my full-sized case notebook, but this little one fit in my purse and hopefully would come in handy by allowing me to jot things down on the fly. As Sloane admired herself in the mirrors, I transferred the list into the notebook.

I was thankful the list wasn't long, only fifteen names. Half of the names were familiar. Luke or Rachel could give me details on the ones I didn't recognize. Five were guys who hung out with Georgie back in high school. I put stars next to them. If anybody knew about the dead man's secrets, like gambling contacts, long-term cronies would be high on the list.

My musings about the list of names were interrupted when Sloane called my name.

"Allie." Her hands were on her hips. "For the third time, what do you think of the fit?"

Busted. Unlike the bride-to-be, I wasn't a fast runner. I was a fast thinker, though.

"Like you were born to wear that dress." She smiled, so I added icing to the cake. "Luke won't be able to take his eyes off of you."

Her cheeks pinked at the mention of her fiancé. "You really think so? You don't think it's too tight or revealing, do you?"

"Can you breathe in it?"

She nodded.

"Can you move in it?"

She stepped off the dais with no problems and glided around the room twice. Granted, she was barefoot instead of wearing the four-inch heels she was planning on for the wedding, but her movements were fluid.

"One final question. Can you do the hokey pokey in it?"

Sloane opened her mouth in confusion for a moment, then let out a laugh.

"Let's find out." She raised her arms and turned in a little circle while weaving from side to side. When she completed the circle, she clapped three times, just like she'd be doing it on the dance floor in a few weeks.

When Clarice and I applauded, Sloane rewarded us with a curtsy.

As she stepped back onto the dais, I slipped the notebook into my purse. I'd vowed today was to be all about my bestie, after all.

"It's time to celebrate," I said when we were back in the car. "How about some frozen yogurt before we head home. My treat."

Sloane had asked for two minor alterations, which Clarice had assured her would be no problem. We'd left the store in high spirits and with an appointment to pick up her gown the Tuesday before the wedding.

"Not until you make a final decision on your dress." She turned right as we exited the parking lot, instead of left, which was the way to get home. "Which we are going to do right now."

"Do we really have to?" I made every effort to sound like a whiny eleven-year-old.

I wasn't a dress woman. It wasn't that I disliked dresses. On the contrary, I totally appreciated them, especially when they were being worn by the right person.

I wasn't the right person.

The last time I'd worn a dress was when Rachel and Matt got married. The most recent time before that was the disastrous prom night. Given the results of both of those events, I believed dresses weren't meant to be part of Allie Cobb's life.

Sloane had laughed in a good-natured way when I asked if I could wear a tuxedo as her maid of honor. She knew about my aversion to dresses, so she let me complain all the way to a nearby department store.

Keeping my grumblings to myself, I followed her through the store's rotating doors, past the fragrance section, and across the fine jewelry aisles until she stopped in the dress section of the women's department. She went straight to a salesperson and exchanged a few words before the woman stepped away.

Sloane put her arm around me. "Close your eyes. I picked out your dress."

A minute later she told me to open them.

The saleswoman was standing before me, holding a lovely sage-green dress. It was about knee-length, rather than the full-length model I thought she wanted me to wear. The bigger surprise was I didn't hate it.

The A-line cut was clean, which I liked. It had a single-shoulder neckline and a slightly angled, asymmetrically draped waistband that ended with a gathered skirt that was soft to the touch. Elegant, but simple.

"I think I like it." My fingers had a barely perceptible tremble as I took the dress from the saleswoman and let her guide me toward a fitting room.

A few minutes later, my head still spinning from my positive reaction to the dress, I was staring at myself in a mirror, a beaming Sloane at my side.

"You look hot." She fluffed my hair, which was an accomplishment since I kept it in a short bob. "The color of the dress brings out your eyes. We'll get you a nice pair of heels and some sparkly earrings and you'll be the most beautiful woman at the wedding. Next to me, of course."

I took Sloane's hand and did a little twirl. I did look pretty darn good.

The day couldn't get any better. It was like a dream. If only dreams didn't have to come to an end.

Chapter Seventeen

My incredible Saturday had left me as tired as Scarlett O'Hara after she escaped Atlanta the night it burned, so I responded to my alarm going off Sunday morning by hitting the snooze button and hiding under a pillow.

When the alarm went off again, I got up, but not without complaining to Ursi that it wasn't fair she never had to go to Sunday Mass. My kitty expressed her empathy by standing up, stretching her front legs as far as they could go in front of her, then curling up and going back to sleep.

It wasn't that I dreaded going to Mass. On the contrary, I enjoyed spending a few hours every Sunday morning with Mom. It also served as a good reminder that there was a big world out there, populated with people whose needs were far greater than mine. It was a time to be humble, to be mindful that every day I had the opportunity to be of service to others, even in small ways, and I should be thankful to be in that position.

It was also a great opportunity for people watching.

Brent had begged off going to church with me, claiming he and Luke had one more project on the house and they wanted to get it knocked out first thing. While that may have been true, I knew the real reason. He wasn't much of a churchgoer. To make up for it, he'd promised to meet me at the apartment after Mom and I had breakfast. He had something special planned for our afternoon.

As I walked into church with Mom, I put Brent's promise out of my mind. I was interested in seeing if anyone on the list Jeanette sent me was also attending Mass. On the drive home from Indianapolis, Sloane had given me physical descriptions of those I didn't know, so I kept my eyes peeled as we took a seat and waited for the service to begin.

I'd just feigned a need to scratch the back of my neck to see who was seated behind us when Mom cleared her throat.

"What is with you this morning? You're acting like you've got ants in your pants." As if I was eight all over again, she put her hand on my shoulder to stop my fidgeting, and I settled down.

I hadn't gone to church all my life without learning how to spy on people without getting caught, though. Putting my long-dormant church observation skills to work, by the time Mass ended, I'd located five people on the list.

It was a pleasant morning weather-wise, so I was hoping people would congregate outside the church entrance to catch up on the latest news. It would provide an ideal opportunity to strike up a conversation with one or two of my new persons of interest.

My plans were thwarted when someone tapped me on the shoulder mere seconds after I stepped outside. It was Lori.

Instinct kicked in, and I gave her a hug as we said hello. It was a good thing. Even if she was at the top of my suspect list, she didn't need to know I didn't trust her. To keep the charade going, I bent over and introduced myself to Brittany.

"Mommy says you're a secret agent who makes books."

I grinned. She wasn't too far off the mark for a five-year-old. "Kind of. I help people who write books."

"Can you help find my daddy? I want him to come home."

My eyes got watery. No child should ever have to ask a question like that. After blinking the tears away, I glanced at Lori. Her face was flushed, whether from embarrassment or guilt, I couldn't tell.

"I told her about our chat the other day," Lori said. "You know how kids can be with their imaginations."

"Some really smart people are working very hard to find out what happened to your dad. It's their job. Your job"—I tapped the little girl on the tip of her nose, which brought forth a giggle—"is to be a good girl for your mom. Do you think you can do that for me?"

"Okay." Brittany tugged on Lori's pants leg. "Can I go say hi to Doctor Cobb?" Without waiting for an answer, she left us, heading in the direction of my mother.

"Sorry about that." Lori let out a nervous laugh. "I did want to talk to you about something, if you have a minute."

"What's up?" I guided Lori to a spot under a sugar maple tree, where we could have some privacy while keeping an eye on Brittany.

"It's about Georgie. Do you know why Roger Parke fired him?"

"It's my understanding he failed a drug test after his accident." Which was the final straw, according to Roger, but I didn't think mentioning that would be helpful.

"That's what he wants everyone to think." She crossed her arms. "That's not the real reason, though. The real reason is Georgie got hurt in the accident. When he filed a workers' compensation claim, Roger went through the roof."

"So, you're saying Roger fired Georgie for filing an injury claim."

"Yes, so Georgie got a lawyer and sued Roger. Firing someone for filing a workers' compensation claim is illegal. The case took forever, but they finally settled a few weeks ago."

"Let me guess. Georgie was due a settlement payment and Roger wasn't happy about it." The plot was getting thicker. "Do you mind me asking how much the settlement was for?"

"Twenty-five thousand dollars. I should have told you about it when we had lunch, but it slipped my mind. My memory's not very sharp right now."

I'll bet it's not, especially if you're hiding something, Lori. "Did Georgie receive the settlement payment before," I shrugged, "you know." Despite my suspicions of her, I couldn't bring myself to use the word *murder* with Lori.

"I don't know. He promised to take whatever he got from the lawsuit and put it into a college fund for Brittany. That would make a nice nest egg for her, know what I mean?"

"I do." Mom and Brittany were walking our way, hand in hand. If there was more Lori wanted to tell me, it would have to be another time. "I'll look into it."

Mom took Lori in an embrace as they exchanged a few words. I couldn't hear what was being said, but the way Lori was nodding, it made me think Mom was imparting some motherly advice sprinkled with medical guidance on taking care of herself.

That was Mom, always ready to lend a hand.

By the time we said our good-byes, the crowd had dispersed, and I'd missed my chance at cornering anyone on my persons of interest list. While that development disappointed me, Lori's information was intriguing. And it led to a whole new list of questions.

Did Roger have insurance coverage to pay the settlement, or did he have to pay it out of his own pocket? Had the check been cut? Did Georgie receive the funds? If so, where were they? And last, but not least, was there a way I could get a look at Georgie's bank records?

"Brittany's such a cutie, isn't she?" With a smile, Mom was watching Lori load her daughter into her car, a nondescript silver four-door. As they pulled away, she waved to them. "I'm worried about her. Both of them, actually."

I was in total agreement with Mom's concerns about Brittany. At some point, Lori was going to have to tell the little girl her daddy wasn't coming back. A chill went through me as I imagined myself in Lori's position. That had to be a parent's worst nightmare.

To me, Lori's well-being was a different matter, at least until she was cleared. From what I knew, she hadn't met that test. Her alibi consisted of being home in bed all night. It was an alibi Brittany was too young to verify.

"What has you worried about Lori?" I got into the passenger seat of Mom's car as she started the engine. We were headed to the Brown County Diner for a late breakfast.

"Psychological trauma. I know what kind of man Georgie was, so I have no doubt Lori will be better off without him. Still, a life-changing event like this could have devastating consequences down the road. I'm talking depression, anxiety. Not to mention the daily challenges of being a single parent."

We stopped at an intersection. There was no traffic, so the car crept forward as Mom eased off the brake. I put my hand on her arm to stop her.

"What if Lori did it?"

"Did what, dear?" Apparently oblivious to my implication, she tried a second time. I shifted the car into PARK and maneuvered her so she was looking at me.

"What if Lori killed Georgie?" I gave her an abbreviated rundown of the situation, including my suspicions of Lori being driven by the life insurance payout. "Think about it. Lori's smart, and you just said she was better off without him."

Mom let out a long sigh and rubbed her arms as if she'd just had a chill. "I don't know. Just because I said she was better off without Georgie doesn't mean I think she's capable of murder."

"Do you accept that it's a possibility?" When she gave me an almost imperceptible nod, I let go of her. Satisfied with Mom's acceptance of my premise, even if it was made with reluctance, I allowed us to resume our drive to the diner.

"You have better suspects than Lori, I hope." We turned a corner, and the diner came into view. Mom's belief in Lori's innocence wasn't surprising. Her compassion led her to believe in the best in people.

That was one key difference between my mother and me. Like Sloane, she trusted people and wanted to give them the benefit of the doubt. For me, trust had to be earned.

"I don't know about better. I've got other suspects, though." The diner was packed, a common occurrence on Sunday morning, so I gave the hostess my name, and we took a seat on an empty bench in front of the restaurant.

While we waited to be called, I took Mom through a point-by-point analysis of my suspicions about Tommy Abbott, Roger Parke, Lori, and the gamblers associated with Willie Hammond.

"A police officer, two well-respected members of the business community, and the mayor's daughter. You sure you don't want to implicate the pope while you're at it?"

Despite the joking nature of the comment, Mom's concern about my suspect list wasn't lost on me, even if I wanted to quibble with her inclusion of Willie among the well-respected members of the business community. What mattered was I was pointing a finger at people who had a lot of friends in Rushing Creek. If I was going to accuse one of these folks of murder, I was going to have to make sure my case was locked down tighter than the vault at my bank.

Another issue came to mind as we rose to our feet in response to the hostess calling our names and passed a MILLER FOR MAYOR sign in the window. Would Matt support me if I had anything less than smoking gun–type evidence?

To a certain degree, he was in as much of a fix as I was. Thanks to the election, the pressure he was under to make an arrest, which was tremendous to begin with, kept increasing, like the fluid in an old-fashioned thermometer measuring the temperature of a sick patient with a high fever.

He couldn't make just any arrest, though. Charging the wrong person would prove to be disastrous to the accused, to his career, and to the community. No. Just like me, Matt's evidence had to be more ironclad than an aircraft carrier.

I kept that thought close to my heart as reassurance he wouldn't come knocking on my door to read me my rights anytime soon. I also used it as motivation to keep digging, to find Georgie's killer, so I wouldn't have to worry about that frightening development.

Angela arrived at our table with a smile and a carafe of coffee. She knew us well enough to fill our cups without asking.

"Any news on the investigation, Allie?" She pulled a pen and pad out of her apron to take our orders.

"Still looking for clues." I ordered a Belgian waffle with blueberries.

Mom ordered a bowl of mixed fruit and a bagel with strawberry jam. "I'd also like a MILLER FOR MAYOR button like the one you're wearing."

With wide eyes, Angela pulled a button from her apron pocket and handed it to Mom. I clapped as Mom pinned it on her blouse.

"To what do I owe your endorsement? You've always kept your politics close to the vest." Since Mom and Angela had known each other for decades, I figured the answer was obvious. Mom wanted to vote for a friend.

"Walter thought it was important to maintain an appearance of political neutrality. He was afraid I'd lose patients if people knew I voted for this candidate instead of that candidate. Now that he's gone, I've decided life's too short to be quiet about matters that are important to me."

Mom took Angela's hand. "You're vital to this town. You own a business here. You've raised a family here. You know everybody. I can think of no better person to lead Rushing Creek than you."

Angela gave Mom a hug, then headed to the kitchen to submit our orders. The scene left me speechless. It was the first time I'd heard Mom discuss politics of any level in public.

"Oh, don't act so surprised." She poured some creamer into her coffee.

"But you and Dad always voted for Larry."

"That's because he never ran against Angela. I've been maneuvering behind the scenes for years to get her to run for office. It's about time she said yes."

I reached for a sweetener packet but missed. The shocking revelation had me as off balance as a tightrope walker in a tornado. When Mom sighed, I shrugged. "Wow. I don't know what else to say. Do you have any other secrets I should know about?"

"Some may be bigger, some may be smaller, but we all have our secrets." She took a drink of her coffee. "Like the meetings you, Luke, and Rachel have every Wednesday to check up on me, for example."

I sat back and stared at Mom as she stirred her coffee. Her grin made it seem like we'd been talking about the colorful new bike racks the mayor was having installed around town.

"How long have you known?" The way I whispered the question, one would have thought she'd busted me for cheating on my taxes or, worse, turning down the corner of a page in a book instead of using a bookmark.

"Long enough. Long enough to be upset at what I perceived as a betrayal. That you kids didn't think I was capable of taking care of myself."

"Mom, we—"

"Long enough for that anger to morph into self-doubt and worry that maybe you were right."

She paused while Angela served us our breakfasts.

"Long enough to get past the anger and self-doubt and come to the realization the three of you have your hearts in the right place."

"I'm sorry, Mom. We never meant to hurt you. We wanted to be helpful without… interfering, I guess."

"I know. I also know I haven't been myself since your father died. I spent my entire adult life with him. I miss him every day. I don't think I'll ever get past that, and I don't want to. But you know what?"

I shook my head.

"Every day I'm getting a little better at living without him. I'm not going to lie. Some days are better than others, but I'm adjusting. And getting better at remembering where I left my keys." She winked.

"I'll tell them you're wise to us and we don't need to meet anymore."

"You most certainly will not. I've seen how your weekly meetings have brought the three of you closer together, especially you and Rachel. It's also nice to have your brother taking care of things around the house. Let your meetings run their course. We'll keep this our little secret."

"Deal." As our discussion turned to more pleasant topics, like the twins' latest antics, a weight was lifted from my shoulders.

Mom was going to be okay.

For months, I'd looked forward to the day I'd be able to say it. Now that the day had arrived, I was happy, feeling like anything was possible. It was a great feeling.

It made me wonder, though. Did everybody in town have something they were trying to hide? If so, were any of those secrets related to Georgie's murder?

Chapter Eighteen

To get my mind off the case, Brent's surprise was a trip to the state park Sunday afternoon. We spent hours hiking the trails with Sammy by our side. After the relatively modest space of Luke and Sloane's backyard, the dog was in heaven as she romped along rocky ridges, through bubbling streams, and across wide-open green meadows. A few squirrels and a cardinal didn't appear to appreciate Sammy's desire to play with them, but his exuberance made Brent and me laugh.

By the time we returned to Brent's truck, Sammy was exhausted, so we enjoyed a delectable dinner on the patio of the park's restaurant while the dog snoozed at Brent's feet. From time to time, Brent would slip a morsel of his meat loaf to his canine companion, who managed to eat what he was given without ever seeming to wake up.

I chose a more dignified route with my grilled salmon and set aside some of it, along with the leftover dinner rolls, to take home. My only question was which would be gone first, Ursi's fish or my rolls.

Brent had to be at work early on Monday, so after escorting me into my apartment and giving me a memorable kiss good night, he hit the road. Once I was alone with only my kitty to keep me company, a nervous energy bloomed inside me. Even though I'd hiked over five miles, I couldn't keep still. While Ursi munched on the fish I brought her, I found myself walking the same route through the apartment over and over again.

Lucky for me, the culprit was easy enough to identify. I was suffering from information overload. Between Lori, Mom, and Brent, I'd been on the receiving end of so much input today, on top of the stress from the case, that my brain was struggling to process it all. The way to get past my climbing-the-walls state was to drive myself to exhaustion. The way to do that was an extended session with the kickboxing bag.

"Time to get sweaty, girl."

Ursi was too busy finishing her dinner to acknowledge my invitation.

I changed into workout clothes, filled a water bottle, dialed up Linkin Park on my playlist, and set the timer for a ninety-minute workout. I started out easy with some stretching, then moved to footwork exercises. At the ten-minute mark, I added punching and kicking to the mix. Even though the music made it impossible for me to hear the *bam, bam, bam* as my gloved fists and shoes punished the bag, the concussive force as leather hit leather reverberated up my arms and legs, which added fuel to the workout.

When the timer hit the forty-five-minute mark, my arms were weary from the punching, my hips and thighs were tired from the kicking, and my vision was blurry from sweat, but my brain was slowing down. During the second half of the workout, I reached "the zone," that glorious state when one's body, mind, and spirit merged and all my thoughts, all my movements centered on the red bag before me.

There was still snap to my kicks and pop to my punches when the buzzer went off to signal the end of the ninety-minute session. I gave the bag a final one-two-three punch combination, followed by a roundhouse kick and lifted my arms in the air in victory.

"Yes. I am the champion."

Ursi seemed impressed as she ran circles around me as I doused my face with the remaining contents of the water bottle. She even accompanied me as I shuffled to the fridge to get more water. I leaned on the appliance's cool metal surface as the bottle filled and laughed as her rough tongue licked at my sweaty ankles.

"You're weird, but I love you." I gave her fresh water with an ice cube, then took a few laps around the apartment that were interspersed with stretches for my cool-down exercises. After that, I went to the patio to relax.

Sometime later, I woke up, still on the patio, with a crick in my neck. I found the water bottle under my chair. It was empty. I let out a laugh since I had no memory of finishing it.

Since I was covered in dried sweat, I took a shower, humming a bouncy Sara Bareilles tune as I got clean. It had been quite a day, and I was pleased to have it end on a positive note. Ursi opened one eye, yawned, and went back to sleep as I slipped into bed. The last thing I remembered before falling into a deep, dreamless slumber was hearing myself murmur the phrase "Mission accomplished."

* * * *

Between the hiking and the workout, head-to-toe sore muscles made it a challenge to get moving on Monday, but I had the clear head I was after. While I showered, I put my day in order. The top priority was to get on the phone with editors. Then I'd catch up on e-mails. When that was finished, I'd update the agency website.

I wouldn't even think about the case until I put in a full day of agenting. Being an amateur sleuth wasn't making me any money, after all.

My phone calls didn't yield any offers but were promising, nonetheless. One editor told me she loved the manuscript and would be presenting it at her acquisitions meeting later in the week. A manuscript going to an acquisitions meeting was a huge step, indicating serious interest. While it didn't guarantee that an offer to buy the manuscript would be made, the odds were good.

When the phone calls were complete, I updated the spreadsheet I used to track manuscripts that were out on query. I always got a sense of accomplishment when I updated the document. It had grown so much since I took the reins at the Cobb Literary Agency. It wasn't that long ago that the only book on the spreadsheet was Thornwell's *The Endless River*. Now, there were nine, and two more were almost ready to be added to the list.

Feeling good about my morning's progress, I put Ursi in her harness and went for a walk on my lunch break. The streets of Rushing Creek were quiet. The weekend tourists had checked out the day before, and we wouldn't see a new wave until Thursday.

I didn't have a specific destination in mind, which was good since a new bike rack being installed in front of Creekside Chocolates caught my attention. Kim Frye from the *Beacon* was taking pictures of the mayor, who was seated on a black cruiser-style bike, yet wearing a dress shirt and tie. Diane, who had placed her hands on the rack, was standing next to him.

They were sharing a laugh when Ursi and I arrived on the scene.

"And here is one of our most prominent bicyclists." Larry stepped off his bike and came to shake my hand. "She's a big influence in our effort to make Rushing Creek more bike-friendly with the installation of bike racks like this one."

"Really?" His comment caught me completely off guard. Sure, it was common knowledge that I didn't own a car, but I'd never asked for the installation of bike racks. I was happy about it, but I couldn't claim the idea.

"Yes. I first noticed you riding your bike back in the spring and having to lock it around telephone poles. I thought why not put a few bike racks around town? The response has been positive, and it even inspired me to get this beauty." He returned to his bike and put on his helmet. "It's a great way to get around town, and I've even lost a few pounds. Well, I've got an appointment back at the office. See you all soon."

Kim had to get going too, leaving me with a wide-eyed Diane, who was running a cloth over the candy-apple-red rack, and a disinterested Ursi, who was leaning against one of bars that anchored the rack to the sidewalk while she groomed herself.

"What do you think?" Diane stuffed the cloth into her hip pocket and gazed at the rack with a rapturous smile.

"That you've finally met your soul mate."

She threw the cloth at me. "I've been asking for one of these since the first one went up in front of the municipal building. Do you have any idea how much this will help business, especially with the high schoolers?"

I shook my head. Diane, who was as thorough and methodical as a brain surgeon when it came to business decisions, probably had a three-inch-high stack of paper in her office on the subject.

"Some research indicates a five to ten percent boost in traffic when one of these is installed in front of a business. So far, the evidence around town is anecdotal, but they seem to be having a positive effect. Your sister told me at a Chamber of Commerce meeting that her bike rack is completely full on the weekends, and she's noticed a corresponding boost in sales."

"Wow. Maybe I should look into getting one installed in front of the bookstore." My alarm went off, signaling my hour break for lunch was over. "I gotta get back to work. I'll stop by soon for some hot chocolate and to catch up." I gave her a hug. "If I can get through the overflow crowd, that is."

On our way home, we stopped by the bookstore to tell Renee about Diane's bike rack. She promised to get on the phone with the mayor to ask for one that very afternoon.

I had to give Larry credit. Installing bike racks around town was a great idea. It was a tourist-friendly move. It showed young people they were welcome downtown. And if it meant more and better places where I could lock my bike, who was I to argue?

My chat with Renee was the final straw for Ursi, who had curled up in a ball at my feet, so I carried her upstairs and placed her on her favorite couch cushion. She rewarded me by licking my hand and giving me a soft *meow* before tucking her nose under a paw. Within a minute she was snoring, a sign she was in a deep sleep.

My webmistress skills were improving at a glacial pace, but they were getting better, so it took only a couple of hours until I had the agency website updated to my satisfaction. I posted news of the update on the private agency social media loop and turned my attention to a three-chapter submission from an author interested in working with me.

The submission was good. Technically, it was rock-solid, with only four grammatical errors. The story had an interesting hook, and the characters were unique. There was only a solitary problem.

I didn't love it.

In my role as an agent, I couldn't represent a manuscript in good conscience if I didn't adore it to the point where I would fight tooth and nail to see it get published. If I was going to invest my time in a story, I had to believe in it with all my heart.

I liked the submission, but *like* didn't make the cut. So, with a tinge of disappointment, I sent the author an e-mail letting him know I wouldn't be able to offer representation on the manuscript. I added a line at the end of the e-mail to let him know I'd be interested in seeing other material he might have in the future.

One never knew what the next big hit might be in this business that was so dependent on subjective tastes and ever-changing trends. Maybe his next project would knock my socks off. I truly hoped so, because I believed in authors and the stories they want to tell.

With a feeling of accomplishment, I shut down my computer, then spun my office chair around in a three-hundred-sixty-degree circle a few times to celebrate an uber-productive day. I almost fell to the floor when I got out of the chair but steadied myself by leaning on the desk while Ursi gave me a long look to say she didn't approve of my youthful behavior.

"Not everybody can be dignified all the time like you, missy. Remember that while I make your dinner. Come on."

The word *dinner* registered, as she practically jumped in the air while executing her own one-hundred-eighty-degree turn and trotted off to the kitchen.

While we ate, I plotted out my plan to make my night as productive as my day. Lori's confirmation of the lawsuit settlement was troubling. I reviewed the notes from my conversation with Roger, but didn't find anything regarding a specific settlement amount. As I closed my notebook, I was certain of one thing.

I didn't trust Roger.

To be honest, I didn't trust any of the suspects, but there was one way to rule Roger in or out. It would have to be done after dark.

When the clock on my phone flipped to ten, I gave Ursi a kiss and slipped out of the apartment via the patio and descended the escape ladder. It was a five-foot drop from the bottom of the ladder to the concrete walkway beneath, but I landed with a minimum of fuss or, more importantly, noise.

Going out the front door would probably have been safer, but I didn't want to take the chance of bumping into Renee in the hall between our apartments or someone seeing me in front of the building. It was probably paranoia, but given the stakes of my adventure, the risk of a broken ankle seemed like a better alternative to running into someone.

I was in a tiny courtyard that ran the width of the building and was eight feet deep. Six-foot-tall privacy fencing enclosed the courtyard, providing seclusion from the alley on the other side of the wooden structure. Green outdoor carpeting had been laid to give the impression of an urban oasis.

A gas grill was stationed in one corner of the courtyard, next to a stack of plastic lawn chairs. Every month, weather permitting, Renee invited her tenants to join her in the courtyard for a cookout. It was always a pleasant few hours and brought back fond memories from my New York days.

The focus of my attention this evening wasn't the grill or the chairs. It was my bike. Normally, I kept it inside, on the landing, just outside my front door. If it was muddy or if I'd just washed it, I left it in the courtyard, locked to a drain pipe.

Earlier in the evening, I'd taken it to the courtyard under the pretense of giving it a good cleaning. Now, as I guided the bike through the gate and into the alley, I was entering ninja mode.

My nocturnal adventure had begun.

It was a bad idea to ride a bike at night without lights or reflectors. Then again, what I was about to do was worse. It was an I-could-get-caught-and-spend-time-in-jail level of bad idea, but it was a risk I was willing to take. Being content with talking to people and hoping they'd be honest had left me going in circles. It was time to go on the offensive.

As I pedaled through town on my way to Parke Landscaping, I rehearsed my plan. It should take less than an hour to pull off. It was foolish, dumb, and insane, but if I pulled it off, I'd have Georgie's killer in my sights.

Rushing Creek was the type of community where they rolled up the sidewalks at night, so I was confident I'd make it to Parke Landscaping's gravel drive without being seen. I let out a long breath in relief as I turned off the road. My confidence had been justified.

Step one accomplished.

When I made it to the gate, I stashed my bike among the nearby trees and took a few minutes to get my breathing under control. From my wooded vantage point, the coast was clear. A few security lights mounted on telephone poles were on, but the place appeared deserted.

I counted to ten and then made my move. A quick climb over the gate was followed by a sprint to the building's back door. Still no signs of life beyond an owl hooting in the distance. I was in luck. The door's only lock was in the doorknob. That would save me time.

Now for the hard part.

Once I had gloves on, I pulled a thin, metal device, a hook pick, from my pocket and inserted it into the keyhole. During my early days in New York, I had a bad habit of locking myself out of my apartment. The locksmith bills were expensive and embarrassing, so I talked a friend into teaching me how to pick a lock.

After a few lessons, I became quite adept at picking locks. While it had gotten me out of a tight spot more times than I cared to admit over the years, it was a skill I kept to myself. Not even Sloane knew about my criminal talents.

With the patience of a bomb defuser, I maneuvered the pick and worked the doorknob, holding my breath to help me feel the pins come into alignment. It was a quality lock, but no match for my skills. I had the door open in three minutes. With no lights or sirens going off.

Step two accomplished.

Once inside, I used a tiny penlight to guide me to Roger's office. I had the hook pick at the ready, but his office door was unlocked. Roger appeared to be a trusting soul, like most folks in Rushing Creek. I started to ponder the drawbacks of my distrustful nature but shelved the topic for examination another day. There were more pressing matters at hand.

I thanked St. Nicholas, the patron saint of repentant thieves, that I remembered the filing cabinet from which Roger had taken documents on my last visit. My luck was holding as the top drawer opened without so much as a whisper.

The drawer was full, so it took a while to flip through the files. I wanted to linger over a few documents, but time wasn't on my side. With nothing related to a workplace injury lawsuit, I went to the drawer that was second from the top.

My fingers were well-oiled machines as I flipped through the files, which were labeled in a large, easy-to-read font. I was near the back of the drawer when I hit pay dirt. A manila folder containing two inches worth of documents was labeled ALONSO, G—WORK COMP CLAIM."

Step three accomplished.

With my heart racing, I placed the file on Roger's desk and checked my watch. I'd only been in the building fifteen minutes. *Plenty of time.* I scanned the pages. They confirmed what Roger and Lori had told me. Georgie was fired for failing a drug test taken after the accident. He then filed a lawsuit alleging that the drug test was flawed and that he was terminated by the company to avoid paying for injuries sustained in the accident.

So far, so good.

My heart began beating even faster when I turned to a letter that included the words "Settlement Offer" in the page's header. I was about halfway down the page when the lights came on.

"Hold it right there." The tone of Roger's voice was cold, hard, and angry. But that wasn't what frightened me. What frightened me was the blood-chilling sound that followed the command.

It was the metallic click of a bullet being loaded into the firing chamber of a gun.

Chapter Nineteen

I raised my head at a glacial pace until I made eye contact with Roger. With my heart jackhammering against my breast bone and my brow dripping with a cold sweat, I stepped away from the desk and raised my hands.

Roger's eyes went wide. He let out a blistering string of curse words hot enough to melt iron. With the gun pointed at me, he went to the desk and spun the file around so he could see what I'd been reading.

"You need to tell me how you got in here and what you're doing. Right now. Or I'm calling the police."

"Lori told me you guys settled the lawsuit and made a settlement payment to Georgie, which you failed to mention when we talked." I jabbed my finger at him. It wasn't the best move to make in the direction of someone who was pointing a gun at my chest, but I wanted to put him on the defensive. "Since you weren't straight with me, I had no choice but to find out for myself."

"By breaking into my business? Christ, you're a bigger nutcase than Mayor Cannon says you are." His voice was still hard enough to crush rock, but he lowered the gun.

"Yeah, well." I shrugged. "The mayor and I don't see eye to eye on a lot of things. What matters is that file definitively clears you of any suspicion."

"Why should I be under suspicion?" He narrowed his eyes as he raised the gun again. "What do you know that I don't?"

"That your insurance carrier paid the termination retaliation settlement." I pointed at the file. "That a check was cut before Georgie was killed. Which eliminates any incentive for you to knock him off to avoid making that payment."

He flipped through some of the papers in the file. "For argument's sake, why should any of what you just said matter?"

Good. I had him talking, which, combined with the lack of sirens, seemed to indicate he hadn't called the police yet.

"Because Chief Roberson wants someone collared. The sooner the better." I really meant the mayor, but what with Roger and Larry's friendship, I thought it better to place responsibility on someone else.

"Since I found the body, they brought me in for questioning, thinking maybe I'd done it. Evidence they've found since then has ruled me out, so the police will have to cast a wider net. Do you really want to risk being caught in that net, and even mentioned as a possible suspect? What would that do to your business?"

He chewed on his lip. "Everyone knows I didn't kill Alonso. How'd you get in here, anyway? I could have you jailed for breaking and entering."

"The back door was unlocked, but that's not important." I went to the page identifying the date the check was cut. The longer I kept him thinking about why I was in his office instead of how I got into his office, the better off I'd be. I hoped.

"What's important is this." I tapped my index finger on the photocopy of the check. "This was put in the mail three days before Georgie was murdered. Lori says she hasn't seen it, so where is it? Did he deposit it? If so, where? Did he spend it? If so, what on?"

"Just like the old saying, follow the money."

"Exactly. Don't you see? You could tell the police about this. I have no idea where the trail will lead, but people will know you gave them this tip. Georgie may have been a loser, but his daughter will still have to grow up knowing her father was murdered. This information could help catch his killer. And bring Brittany justice."

I was laying it on thick, but I didn't want to take the chance of underselling my hand. I still had to figure out a way to get out of here, after all.

"You know I hated Georgie, right? The man stole from me. He stole from me when he crashed that truck, and he stole again when he filed that lawsuit. I didn't want to settle, but the insurance company did. They were holding the purse strings. What choice did I have?"

He thumped his fist on the desktop. "That punk was stoned when he drove my truck. I should have had him thrown in jail. And yet he had the nerve to sue me. How do you think that makes me feel? I was the victim, and he was the one who got paid. What kind of justice is that?"

"An utter lack thereof." Since insurance paid the settlement, my sympathy for Roger was muted somewhat. But having been on the receiving end of Georgie's shenanigans, I understood Roger's frustration.

"You've got that right." He sighed and dropped into his chair behind the desk.

"Which is why this is about doing the right thing. Don't think of it as doing something for Georgie. Think of it as doing something for Brittany. She's a victim, too."

"Maybe you're right. I'll think about it." He waved the gun at me. "After you tell me how you broke in."

My shoulders sagged. Well, it was foolish to think he'd let me waltz out the door with nothing more than a wave good-bye. I'd concocted a story, and I needed to stick to it.

"I told you. The back door was unlocked. Come see for yourself."

He waved the gun toward the door. "You first."

I kept my mouth shut as we walked through the building. There was no way I was going to risk complicating things by saying something that might come back to bite me. On our way, Roger told me to stop while he checked the windows.

Every window was locked.

When we reached the back door, he flipped on the lights and bent over to get a close look at the thumb turn, the component in the center of the doorknob. The edges of the thumb turn were oriented vertically, indicating the door was unlocked.

With the lights on, my attention was drawn to the top of the door frame, where a sensor was mounted. God, I was such a dummy. There must have been a keypad up front that I failed to notice.

I'd tripped a silent alarm system when I opened the door. The alarm company must have called Roger, and he came to investigate. I wiped a bead of sweat from my brow as I envisioned how the scene would have played out had the police arrived on the scene instead of Roger. Talk about a close call.

"I'll be damned." Roger opened the door and rotated the thumb turn ninety degrees until it was oriented horizontally. As he did so, the bolt glided out of its housing. He rotated the thumb turn back, and the bolt slid back until it was flush with the door's edge.

"I would have sworn this door was locked when I left." He gave the exterior doorknob a close examination as he dug a set of keys out of his pocket.

We were nearing the moment of truth. If I'd damaged the locking pins, Roger's key wouldn't work. If it worked, but in an abnormal fashion, it would raise suspicion. While he was busy with the door, I slipped the pick inside my jeans in case he asked me to empty my pockets.

I held my breath as he inserted the key in the lock. It went in effortlessly, like an ice skater across a pristine, frozen lake. He turned the key, and the bolt came right out. No muss, no fuss. He tried it three more times before throwing up his hands.

"Fine, you win. Somebody must have left it unlocked when they went out for a smoke break or something." He leaned against the door frame and crossed his arms. "I've got another question for you. How did you know to pay my office a visit the night it just happened to be unlocked?"

"Luck? Fate? I don't have an explanation." Again, I needed to keep my story simple. "All I can tell you is that after mulling over my conversation with Lori, I had to do something. I know it was a rash decision, and, for that, I apologize."

He let out a little *hmpf* and closed the door. With a dramatic flourish, he switched the thumb turn into the locked position. So much for me waltzing out the back door.

"Think about it, Roger. What are the odds that the one night I decide to try to get a look at that file turns out to be the night someone forgot to lock that door? And then you show up in time for me to explain the situation. Now you get to tell the police about the check, and I can turn my attention to the remaining suspects. All in the name of finding justice for Brittany."

"You talk a good game. I'll give you that." He chuckled as he brushed some dirt from his boot. "Care to tell me who these remaining suspects are?"

"I'd rather not."

"I see." He shrugged. "Maybe you'd be willing to tell the police." He took out his cell. "The choice is yours, of course."

Touché. He'd lost every advantage he had on me, and I sensed he wasn't interested in losing this latest one. There were times when discretion was the better part of valor. This was one of those times.

"You might want to sit down for this." I headed for his office and tried to ignore the image in my mind of an angry and dangerous Roger looming over me as he followed, mere steps behind.

Once we were seated, I told him about my list of suspects—Tommy, Lori, Willie, and the gamblers. I put most of my emphasis on the gamblers. While I had no evidence that Georgie's gambling problem had led to his death, it was easier to accuse nameless criminals of murder than a local business owner, a police officer, and the mayor's daughter.

Plus, the missing check fit into a narrative involving gambling debts as easily as Roger slid his key into the lock I'd picked.

When I was finished, he let out a low whistle. "And you figured all this stuff out by yourself?"

"Being accused of murder is a powerful motivation tool."

"Can't argue with that. I think I need a drink." He opened a desk drawer and pulled out a half-full bottle of brown liquor and two shot glasses. "Care to join me?"

"Thank you." I was a wine girl who occasionally didn't mind a beer. Given my tiny size, hard liquor scared me. Then again, something told me turning down the offer would be a perilous move. Besides, after breaking and entering, how frightening could one drink be?

He filled both glasses to the rim and handed me one. The alcohol had a potent smell that made me wrinkle my nose. I raised my glass to him and sook a sip.

And almost choked on the bitter liquid.

Meanwhile, Roger knocked his back in one swallow and refilled his glass. He kept his gaze on me as I blinked away the burning sensation in my throat. The way he was looking at me had to be some kind of test, so I straightened my spine and downed the rest of the liquor in one eye-watering, breath-robbing swallow.

"You've got guts, Cobb." Roger slapped the desktop with his palm and threw back his second drink. "I admire that. Too many people around here are sheep, content to stay inside the fence because they're afraid of standing out from the crowd."

"My parents taught me that if I believed in something, I needed to give a hundred and ten percent to it. Even if it meant ruffling a few feathers here and there."

He was quiet for a moment, staring at his empty shot glass as he ran his index finger around the rim. At last he let out a long breath. "Do you really think Lori killed him?"

If I was in the middle of a minefield before, now I'd been blindfolded. Well, simple answers and the truth, or at least something coming close to it, had gotten me this far unscathed. "Do I think she did it? I don't know. Do I think she could have done it? It's possible. What I do know is the police haven't interviewed her yet. It's understandable, given the circumstances. Still…"

Roger poured himself another drink. "Beating up on the mayor's daughter wouldn't look good. I see what you mean." In a practiced, single move, he emptied the glass. "What do you want to do now?"

A new theory was forming in my head, but I didn't want to share it, so I kept to the path of being mostly truthful. "I'm going to keep my eyes and ears open for the fallout from your report to the police. While I wait for that, I'm going to keep working on the gambling angle. It's possible—"

"No. I mean now." He tapped the desktop. "Do you want to have another drink, or do you want to leave?"

"Oh." My cheeks started burning, and it wasn't from the alcohol. "I better pass on another drink. The first one's already going to my head. Do you mind if I get going?"

"Nah." He waved toward the door. "Get out of here. Use the front door. I don't want to have to lock the back door again."

I didn't have to be told twice. When I was at the door, I paused. "Do you mind keeping this between you and me?"

"Do you really think you can catch the killer?"

"No doubt about it." It was true. I wouldn't rest until the murderer had been brought to justice.

"Then this never happened. I'll tell my wife the door didn't shut all the way and the wind must have blown it open. Since I was here, I decided to do a little paperwork. Now, if you'll excuse me, I have work do to."

He grabbed a stack of papers from his inbox with one hand and a yellow highlighter with another.

I pulled the door until a click confirmed it was closed. Then I got out of there as fast as my legs would carry me.

When I reached my bike, I jumped on it and pedaled like I was in a final sprint at the Tour de France. At one point, I glanced at my bike computer mounted on the handlebar. The readout said I was going thirty-four miles per hour. Other than going down one of the ultra-steep hills in the state park, I'd never come close to that speed.

My furious pedaling didn't stop until I was within a half mile of my apartment. My lungs were screaming for air. My neck was protesting from my constant looking back to see if Roger had changed his mind and was chasing me. My thighs burned with the heat of a blast furnace from the insane pedaling effort.

It wasn't until I coasted to a stop by the courtyard gate that I realized I wasn't wearing my helmet. Riding helmetless was a mortal sin in my book. I'd gotten lucky when I was hit by a car riding my bike during my college days. It was a glancing blow that sent me to the pavement but left me uninjured. Thinking no harm, no foul, I gave the driver a thumbs-up and went about my business.

When I got home, I removed my helmet. A quarter-sized indentation in the crown, right where my head had impacted the curb, took my breath away. The implication was as clear as fine crystal.

Ever since that fateful day, I'd been a vocal advocate of bike helmets. I bought the twins new helmets every year. I admonished cyclists without helmets about the danger to which they were subjecting themselves.

And I never, ever turned a pedal crank on my bike without having my head protected.

My heart was still thump, thump, thumping away as I checked my saddlebag. The helmet was right where I'd left it. Relief flooded through me. It hadn't fallen off or been left behind for someone to find. My secret was safe with Roger.

As I climbed the steps after putting my bike away, utter exhaustion, both physical and emotional, came over me. My mission was accomplished, but at what cost? I'd thought myself so virtuous for unearthing the secrets of others, while having nothing to hide.

Not anymore.

I could try to justify my actions by telling myself the end justified the means. But it didn't change a key fact.

Now I had my own secrets to hide.

Chapter Twenty

After a night filled with dreams of being chased through the forest by a ten-foot-high lock pick riding a motorcycle covered in skulls and shooting mulch at me, I finally dragged myself out of bed when the snooze alarm went off for the fourth time. The sheets were sweat-soaked, and my muscles ached as though I'd pedaled my bike the entire one hundred sixty miles it took to get from the western border of Indiana to the eastern border.

I rarely deviated from my routine of feeding Ursi, making coffee, and eating breakfast. Over the years, I'd learned a dependable routine in the morning set the stage for a productive day.

This day, I was so gross I headed straight for the shower. After feeding Ursi, of course. She was my number-one priority all day, every day. While she'd never said as much to me, my orange-and-black companion had employed other methods to convey the message in no uncertain terms.

The cool water cascading from the showerhead joined forces with my eucalyptus-infused bath products to elevate me to a zen state for some much-needed meditation. I focused on creating a quiet inner self. In doing so, I set aside, for a while, the questions, doubt, and second-guessing swirling around in my head like a tornado.

When I shut off the water, I was renewed in spirit and reinvigorated in purpose. What was done, was done. I'd made a choice to break into the Parke Landscaping building. Even though my intentions were good, what I'd done was wrong. I'd accept any consequences from my late-night adventure like an adult.

I perused social media while I ate a breakfast of sliced fruit sprinkled with chia seeds. According to Sloane, the tiny seeds were nutritional powerhouses, aiding in everything from heart health to weight management.

Given her outstanding race results over the last six months, it couldn't hurt to give them a try.

It was probably silly to get my hopes up that news of Roger's tip would have made it online already. It was only a little after ten in the morning, after all. Still, when it came to Rushing Creek, the only thing that traveled faster than a juicy rumor was light, and it was a neck and neck race between the two.

Ursi had just jumped from my lap, having had her spine sufficiently scratched, when a notification popped up in my time line that made me smile. After reading it a second time to make sure I wasn't imagining things, I pumped my fist in victory.

Roger had come through.

According to the post, an unnamed tipster had contacted Rushing Creek police suggesting they investigate a twenty-five-thousand-dollar payment to Georgie that might be missing. It claimed a subpoena was in the works so the police could get access to Georgie's bank records.

Now, it was up to me.

I poured another cup of coffee and got comfortable on the couch. First, I updated the notebook with a summary of last night's escapades, edited to avoid incriminating myself. Next, I went to my suspect list and removed Roger. Lastly, I went to the beginning and read through to the end.

My hope was that by reviewing everything in one sitting, something would jump out at me. A piece of information I'd overlooked. A question I'd forgotten to ask. A suspect I hadn't yet identified.

I was bummed, but not surprised, that the key piece of evidence didn't jump off one of the pages and give me a hug. With one suspect eliminated, I was making progress. As it stood, until Al came up with the names of Willie's gambling buddies, I was down to three suspects I could pursue.

Willie seemed like the least likely of the trio. The man made my skin crawl, but if gambling debts truly led to Georgie's demise, the guilty party was probably one of Willie's associates, not the man himself.

Lori checked all the motive, means, and opportunity boxes, but one question lingered. If she wanted to do away with Georgie, why do it in such a convoluted way? She lived with the man, for crying out loud. She could have poisoned him or smothered him with a pillow.

That left me with Tommy.

He checked the boxes better than Lori, but if I was going to enter the minefield of investigating a police officer, I needed to tread with the care of someone walking on thin, cracked ice. On top of that, I needed to figure out how, or if, the million-dollar insurance policy fit with Tommy's status as a suspect.

As I was working on a plan of action, I received a text from Mom. She was going to the 9/11 memorial service. It was being held at noon on the county courthouse lawn. She wanted to know if I was free to join her.

I responded with a thumbs-up, followed with three exclamation points. During my years in New York, I'd met a few family members of those unfortunate souls who didn't survive the attack on the Twin Towers. Those experiences had humbled me and served as reminders of the importance of living a life trying to help others.

A little while later, as I headed down the stairs, the front ones this time, questions formed in my head.

Was I serving anyone by investigating Georgie's murder? Was I being motivated by anything beyond self-preservation and the desire to make sure I didn't go to jail?

As I stepped onto the sidewalk, I gave an emphatic nod. Yes, my efforts to catch the killer were in the service of others. Chief among them were Lori and Brittany. And, of course, Georgie himself.

Georgie might have been a loser, but that didn't mean he lacked the capacity to get his act together and become a good spouse and a good father. The parallels between Georgie and Thornwell were striking. Both were men with serious problems. At least Thornwell had changed, had been given the time to change.

Georgie would never have that chance.

I couldn't let the killer get away with robbing him of that chance.

* * * *

Two dozen rows of white folding chairs had been set out on the courthouse lawn facing the building's main entrance. Every one of them was occupied. The citizens of Rushing Creek weren't lacking in their patriotism.

I found Mom enjoying the shade of a red oak tree in a back corner of the lawn and chatting with people from her office. We hugged as the Rushing Creek High School Choir gathered in front of the crowd to perform "The Star-Spangled Banner."

After that, a couple of local officials gave patriotic, if uninspiring, speeches. The service concluded with a twenty-one-gun salute and the playing of "Taps." The choir's stirring a cappella performance was the highlight of the service. At half past twelve, we were finished.

"Well? What did you think?" Mom's eyebrows were raised, and her head was cocked to the side, indicating that she wanted my honest opinion.

"It was nice. Do they do this every year?"

"Yes." Mom brushed dust from her sleeve. "The exact same thing. Every year. It's gotten stale. You need to get involved with the planning committee for this. Your experience living in New York would add an important perspective."

"Come on, Mom." While she'd let me know how happy she was I'd gotten involved with the park and Angela's election bid, she'd also been after me to join a group that had a long-term function. "It's not like I was living there when the towers came down."

"But you were there when the new One World Trade Center building opened. I remember how excited you were. Nobody here has the kind of experiences you bring to this town. Don't forget that."

Experiences. Yeah, both good and bad. "I'll think about it. Fair enough?"

"Too late." Mom smiled. "I already gave your name to the committee chair. Think of it as penance for keeping your meetings with Luke and Rachel from me."

She had me. We both knew it. There was no point in trying to argue about it.

"I'll let you know when I hear from the committee."

"I'll look forward to it." She hugged me. "I need to get back to work. Luke and Sloane invited me over Friday after work so I can see the fruits of their remodeling. Come with me. I'll pick you up at six."

Aha, now I had the advantage. With Mom's long-standing opposition to her children cohabitating before marriage, she was no doubt having trouble visiting them on her own. She needed a wingman. I could totally do wingman.

"Sure. Should I bring anything?"

"Chips and your homemade guacamole?" When I agreed, she gave me another hug and told me she loved me.

As she walked away, I chuckled. Mom might be having her struggles, but she was still smarter than her three kids combined. She was also going to be okay. That made me happy.

With the service over, I headed for Creekside Chocolates. It had been too long since I'd devoured one of Diane's amazing hot chocolates. I needed to rectify that lapse immediately.

Diane was cleaning her glass counters when I entered the shop. "What's up, girlfriend? Give me a minute to finish my post-lunch-rush tidying up. The usual for you?"

"Yep. I'm in desperate need of your finest."

I went to the tables by the shop's front picture window and threw away cups and napkins that had been left there. Diane was a great friend, so I never passed up a chance to give her a hand around the store. At the moment, I was the only customer, so when I finished cleaning the tables, I straightened the products on the shelves containing the boxes of chocolate samplers.

"One hot chocolate with whipped cream and peppermint sprinkles, also known as the Cobb Special, for your sipping pleasure." Diane handed me the drink, then settled into one of the chairs I'd just wiped off. We spent a few minutes catching up.

"When school lets out for the day, the rack fills up fast." While it had only been in place a short time, the bike rack was paying dividends.

"Any idea who owns the bike out there now? It makes a statement." The bike in question was a cruiser-style machine with a wide seat and chrome handlebars. What made it look like it belonged on a California beach's boardwalk instead of an Indiana town's main street was the shocking-pink paint job and the white tires.

"It ought to. That's why I bought it."

Her response was so unexpected I almost spit out my mouthful of hot chocolate.

She laughed and handed me a napkin. "My doctor told me I have arthritic knees, so if I'm going to exercise, a low-impact approach like cycling is the way to go. I special-ordered that beauty and picked it up Sunday. Now we can go on rides together."

"Only if you remind me to bring sunglasses. That thing's bright enough to blind someone."

"Deal." Her smile lingered for a moment before morphing into a frown. "Have you heard about the rash of vandalism in my neighborhood?"

"No." In my defense, I'd been dealing with other issues, like murder, but mentioning that wasn't going to be helpful. Something else might, though. "Do you want me to talk to Chief Roberson about it? See what I can find out?"

"Don't bother." She shook her head. "The police are looking into it. The reason I brought it up is that, in the past month, five homes have had their storage sheds broken into."

"That's awful. What was taken?"

"Nada. Nothing's missing, so it wasn't burglary. Nothing was tagged with graffiti, so it doesn't seem to be gang activity. Here's the thing." She leaned toward me. "All the sheds had padlocks that were cut off."

It took me a minute, but when I put the puzzle pieces together, I leaned back, bringing the front chair legs off the floor. "Holy samolie. You mean, cut off like by a bolt cutter?"

"Bingo. It gets more interesting, though. The last incident was reported the day before Georgie Alonso was killed."

I returned the chair to a normal position and stared out the window while I processed the information. The Boulevard was quiet. A truck heading south honked its horn, and the driver waved. A couple of seconds later, the mayor rode into my field of vision, headed north on his bike, and returned the motorist's wave. Once again, the combination of a bike helmet to go with his suit and tie made me smile. Then the scene returned to a tranquil state.

Inside, it was a different matter. Over the years, I'd edited enough thriller and mystery novels that I no longer believed in coincidences, especially when criminal activity was involved. To be sure, I asked Diane if she thought the timing was a coincidence.

"Not a chance." She shook her head.

"Agreed. Which means Georgie's killer cut the locks either as practice or to create a distraction." I drummed my fingers on the table as I studied this new piece to the puzzle. It was an intriguing piece that indicated the lengths the murderer went to in planning the crime.

"I'll need the dates the locks were cut. If I could get time estimates of when they were cut, even better."

"Got you covered." She took a piece of paper from under the cash register and handed it to me. "I know a lot of the time frames are pretty wide, but they all happened at night, when people were sleeping."

"This is beyond amazingly helpful. Nice work, Watson."

Diana scrunched up her nose. "Watson? No way. I am so not interested in being a sidekick. Think of me more as a confidential informant, someone wise and mysterious whom the detective visits in times of need."

"You keep coming up with info like this, I'll call you whatever you want." The wheels were already turning inside my head. It would be simple enough to cross-reference the times of the vandalism with the work shifts of my newly designated prime suspect, Tommy Abbott.

One question kept nipping at my heels, though. "This is front-page news for the *Beacon*. Why haven't I heard about this before today?"

"And you say you don't believe in conspiracy theories." Diane scratched her elbow. "Since my house wasn't hit, the police won't tell me anything. They told my neighbor they want to keep it out of the press so whoever did it will try to strike again. A patrol car cruises the neighborhood every night."

"No security video, I assume?"

"Come on, girl. This isn't New York City or Chicago. You know as well as I do. Probably half the people in this town still don't lock their doors at night."

"Just making sure. Awfully convenient for the perp." A cop would likely know if a house had a security camera. I jotted some notes on the piece of paper. My hunch was growing stronger, but something told me to hold off on putting this puzzle piece into place.

Diane gave me a long, probing look, not unlike the look Dad gave me back in school when he asked about my grades. I tried not to squirm while I waited for her question.

"You know who killed Georgie, don't you?"

I let out a long sigh as I leaned back. A car motored past, momentarily blocking Maybelle Schuman from my view. She was pulling an empty wire grocery cart. If I stuck around long enough, I'd see her coming the other way with the cart filled to the brim.

Maybelle was a lesson about maintaining discretion. She'd shot off her mouth about my alleged affair with Georgie without knowing any facts and embarrassed herself. That wasn't going to happen to me.

"Not quite yet." I slipped the paper into a pocket. "But I'm close."

How close depended on the results of a phone call I needed to make.

Chapter Twenty-One

"Come on, come on. Pick up." I tapped my index finger on the bike rack as I waited for Jeanette to answer. Given the request I was about to make, I'd moved outside so Diane couldn't hear me. I didn't want to drag her into this mess any further.

When the voice mail greeting ended, I left a message with the dates and approximate times of the vandalisms. I asked Jeanette to cross-check those dates and times with Tommy's work shifts. I also asked her who'd been assigned to patrol the neighborhood.

As I ended the call, I imagined Tommy in a box. All six sides of the box were closing in on him, inch by inch. There was no escape.

With my mind so laser-focused on the case, I couldn't sit idly by and wait for Jeanette's call. I had to do something, so I took a walk to Winchester-Cobb Memorial Park. I could check on construction and get another look at the crime scene.

After a swing by the apartment to get my construction project file and my case notebook, I arrived to find the park bustling with activity. The playground equipment was installed. One set of workers was leveling the mulch that would give kids a soft and safe landing area as they jumped from slides, crawled through tunnels, and swung from climbing bars.

A different group of workers was finishing the excavation of a walking path from the parking lot to the playground. I checked my time line and did a fist pump. The playground was on schedule. Next week, a swing set would be installed adjacent to the playground, and asphalt would be laid for the path.

I made a note to confirm the date of the swing set delivery. After that, I made my way toward the fitness path that would run along the inside edge of the park. The advantage of having a wealthy benefactor donate the land and the funds to build the park meant we could go first-class all the way. That allowed us to build an asphalt path that was six feet wide, enough to accommodate two lanes of traffic.

The crew was using a backhoe to remove the dirt that would be replaced by the asphalt. I didn't want to bother them by getting too close, but by my estimate, they had only excavated a quarter of the path. I checked my time line again. The asphalt wasn't due for another week. No need to panic.

The final stop on the tour was the gazebo or, to be accurate, the new location where the gazebo was to be installed. The discovery of Georgie's body and the subsequent crime scene investigation had delayed construction of it by a week. During that time, the committee decided that erecting the gazebo at a murder site would be inappropriate. After a flurry of e-mails and phone calls, an area fifty yards away was selected as the new location.

According to the construction schedule, I should have been looking at a leveled piece of ground into which footers had been placed and the framing of the gazebo floor had been built. Obviously, the construction schedule hadn't accounted for a horrific murder, so instead, all I had was the leveled spot of ground. No footers. No framing. Not even stacks of lumber.

I closed my eyes and counted to ten. It wasn't the end of the world. The park's grand opening was a month away. Still, a lot of work, like electrical service and landscaping, couldn't begin until the gazebo was built.

I had a steering committee meeting on Friday. As the chair, I was responsible for an agenda, so I picked out a soft spot of grass nearby and put one together. The status of the gazebo was going to be the first topic of discussion.

A little while later, I had the project's Gantt chart displayed on the grass to my left, the budget on the grass to my right, and a rough draft of the agenda in front of me. I was debating about whether to include a request for signage reminding dog walkers to pick up their pets' droppings when someone blocked the sun.

"Excuse me, Ms. Cobb?"

I had to squint to make out my visitor's features. It was Kim from the *Beacon*. I scrambled to my feet, and we shook hands. I had immense respect for journalists. They had a tough job to do in the best of times.

It didn't matter that Kim was a reporter for a local, weekly paper with a subscription rate in the neighborhood of ten thousand. Her job was to investigate and report on issues of local importance.

It was a job she took seriously. She never missed city council and school board meetings. Though she was only twenty-six, she didn't let people intimidate her, not even those twice her age. She was thorough, fair, and accurate. I liked her, even if I envied her shoulder-length silky, auburn hair.

More importantly, I respected her.

"Good to see you again. We've talked about this before. Call me Allie."

She was sporting a new pair of horn-rimmed glasses that made her look smarter than she already was, which was saying something, since she'd gotten her journalism degree magna cum laude.

"I know." She chuckled. "Trying to maintain that professional distance. And you are the Kickboxing Crusader, after all."

I rolled my eyes. "Thanks to you and Sloane, I'll never live that nickname down." I gestured to my papers. "Looking for a scoop on the park's progress?"

"I was going to take a few pictures and write something up, but since you're here, care to answer a few questions?"

Any chance to talk about the park was free publicity, so I invited Kim to join me as I returned to my spot on the grass.

We spent a half hour talking about construction progress, grand opening plans, and Sloane's vision for its future. Kim's interview technique was impressive. She started with a few softball questions I was happy to answer. Then she moved to more challenging topics, like long-term funding for maintenance and the addition of more amenities.

"The park has a lot of space. There are rumors Ms. Winchester plans to sell the rest of her father's property to a developer who wants to build a hundred or so homes on the site. If that happens, are you prepared to add features like basketball courts or soccer fields to the park?"

I suppressed a frustrated sigh. For one who wasn't much of a fan of traditional stick and ball sports, I appreciated athletic facilities, but not at the expense of open spaces. I'd fought hard against the facilities Kim mentioned.

This was a needle I needed to thread with care. When dealing with public funds and publicly owned facilities, I believed in transparency. Here, the issue was that private dollars, my best friend's dollars, were being used to build and sustain the park. While that distinction mattered to me, it probably didn't matter to the public.

"Sloane and I may be very close, but she doesn't tell me everything about what's going on in her life. I know she doesn't want to keep her father's land long-term. Anything beyond that, you'd have to ask her."

"Hypothetically, then, if the public identified a need for recreational athletic facilities here, would you support that?"

"I prefer to stick to hypotheticals in the stories my clients are working on."

Kim flashed a half-smile. "Indulge me."

"Okay." I scratched an ear. "To be honest, I don't know. When Sloane donated the land, she wanted a place for people who weren't involved with mainstream team sports. That's why the park has a multi-purpose trail, for walkers, runners, cyclists. Groups like that."

"What about the open space? That's a lot of grass to cut."

Aha, here was a chance to talk about the benefits of unstructured play and open spaces. It was a topic close to my heart. After a decade living in the concrete jungle of New York City, I considered open green space to be as precious as gold or platinum.

"Some parts of the park aren't paved or bordered with white lines, but that doesn't mean they won't be used. The trail, the playground, and the gazebo will bring people here, and then they'll use the open spaces to picnic, throw a Frisbee, have fun.

"I believe there's a part of the community that will be grateful to have a place where they can go fly a kite or have a family picnic. I worry those folks may lack the voice the ones involved with organized athletics have. Besides, nothing says people can't come here for informal games of soccer or flag football."

"The Kickboxing Crusader, continuing the fight for those who can't fight for themselves." She ran her fingers through her hair. "Sorry. I shouldn't editorialize like that."

"I get where you're coming from. My sister was a cheerleader. My brother played sports. My niece and nephew are in the youth soccer league. I see the value organized athletics provide. I just want to make sure there's a place in Rushing Creek for those looking for something different, like musical performances at the gazebo."

Kim nodded as she wrote. She'd expressed her skepticism about my argument before, but I trusted her to report my comments fairly.

"On a different topic, since you mentioned the gazebo, do you have any new information on the Alonso matter?"

Oops. For a second, annoyance bloomed in my gut at giving Kim an opening to a subject I didn't want to discuss. I organized my papers as I debated how to respond. Could I afford to give her my full thoughts while asking her to keep it off the record? That seemed problematic at best and unethical at worst.

On the other hand, after being so open about the park, how would it look if I suddenly clammed up? It would look like I was hiding something. Which I was, a few things actually, but Kim didn't need to know that. I'd play it safe and see how things went.

"I heard someone contacted the police suggesting they look into Georgie's bank records. Something about money being unaccounted for."

Kim held a downward gaze as she tapped her pen on her notebook for a few seconds. She took a deep breath and lifted her head until we made eye contact. "Come on, Allie. Don't stonewall me. I know you're looking into this. People deserve to know the truth."

"The truth?" I organized my response while I ran my hand down my sleeve. "I want to find Georgie Alonso's killer as much as anyone. I have this recurring nightmare where Georgie's corpse digs himself out from under a mulch pile and follows me around, moaning, while I turn over rock after rock after rock."

Her eyes went wide. "I'm sorry. I didn't mean—"

"What didn't you mean? You basically accused me of withholding information related to a murder investigation." I wiped away a tear from my cheek with the back of my hand. "I don't know who killed him, but if it's the last thing I do, I'm going to catch whoever did it."

"It wasn't my intent to accuse you of anything. You're a true hero in this town, and deservedly so, after all you did to catch Mr. Winchester's killer. Let me try again. Is there anything you can share about your efforts to find Georgie Alonso's murderer?"

Kim was persistent. I had to give her that. It was a trait I admired, and one I was proud to possess.

"I believe the murder was premeditated. I also think money was the killer's motive. I think Roger Parke deserves a lot of credit for giving the police the tip about the missing money. I can count the number of credible suspects on one hand."

"How do you know Roger was the tipster?"

I had to give Kim credit. She'd noticed my slip-up and seized on it. I hadn't meant to use Roger's name. Now was the time for quick thinking, not lamenting poor word choice.

"Looking for a potential motive, I checked federal and state court records to see if Georgie had sued anybody. The only lawsuit I could find was one he filed against Roger in federal court. It's plausible that if anybody was going to be paying Georgie a large sum of money, it would stem from that."

"Good point. I checked state court records but didn't think about federal court. Lesson learned." She wrote something in her notebook then leaned toward me. "You have a list of suspects, though, right? Can you give me their names?"

The odds were better that I'd beat Serena Williams in a tennis match than that I'd give up the names of my suspects, but I had a brain blast that might help my cause. I hadn't heard from Al yet. Maybe he was still trying to pump Willie for information. Regardless, this was a chance for me to rattle a few cages.

"I can give you one name." I paused for dramatic effect. "Only if you leave me out of your report."

"I can refer to you as an anonymous source."

"Deal." I took a deep breath. "It's no secret Georgie had a gambling problem. I think he may have gotten caught up with some big-time gamblers and gotten in over his head. Gamblers he met through Willie Hammond."

"As in the guy who owns Hoosiers?"

"The one and only."

Kim let out a low whistle. "The owner of the place where Alonso was drinking the night he was killed. Interesting."

"Especially in light of Roger's tip."

My decision to suggest the unnamed gamblers potentially amounted to sending Kim on a wild goose chase. While I couldn't rule out Willie's associates, after receiving Diane's information, I thought them unlikely to be Georgie's murderers. I wasn't proud of my misdirection tactic, but I was close, and I didn't want Kim getting in my way.

"This is helpful. Thanks." She got to her feet. "It shines a whole new light on the situation. I've got work to do."

Once Kim was gone, I put my materials away and made my way to the crime scene. Maybe taking another look at the spot where this crazy thing began would provide some inspiration.

A makeshift memorial consisting of a cross, a teddy bear, and some flowers had been placed where I'd found Georgie's body. I got down on one knee and stared into the shiny, black eyes of the bear. "Who killed you, Georgie?"

My musings were interrupted when I received a text message. It was from Jeanette and contained a single word.

Yes.

Adrenaline surged through me. Another puzzle piece was in place. I took a photo of the memorial and dialed another number. There wasn't time for small talk. I went straight to the point.

"Matt, I know who killed Georgie."

Chapter Twenty-Two

Five minutes later, Matt was marching toward me at a pace just short of a run. Sunglasses shielded his eyes, and a baseball cap shaded much of his face, but his long stride told me all I needed to know.

I had his undivided attention.

He came to a stop a few feet from me and popped a square piece of gum into his mouth. "The nicotine gum's supposed to help. Not sure it's working."

"When the kids get older, they'll appreciate the effort." Unsure of his mood, I figured flattery couldn't hurt.

He opened his mouth, then closed it and shook his head. "Thanks. I hope so." Then he pointed his finger at me. "I told you to stay out of this."

"A man was murdered, Matt." My blood pressure went into the warning zone as I pointed at the memorial. "Right there. It's been ten days, and you haven't made a collar. I'm trying to help."

"I know, and I appreciate it." He shoved his hands into his pants pockets. "The problem is, some people in town believe Maybelle's story."

At the mention of the town's rumormonger, my blood pressure blasted into the red zone. I'd always thought the woman was bored and that spreading rumors gave her something to do and made her feel important. Now I was thinking boredom wasn't behind her gossip, spite was.

"You know that's absurd. It's beyond absurd. It's idiotic, infantile, reckless—"

"I agree, Ms. Thesaurus." Matt smiled then chuckled, which got me laughing, too. He hadn't called me by that nickname in years. Years ago, it had been his way of complimenting me on my smarts without making it sound like he was giving me props.

"I really think I've got something." I led him in a slow circle around the memorial. "You can tell people you wanted to review my statement with me at the scene of the crime."

When we completed the circle, he picked up the teddy bear and rubbed a spot of dirt from one of its paws.

"Tristan had a bear like this when he was little. He played with it every day and slept with it every night until the stuffing started coming out. The last time I saw it, it was in his closet in your sister's house."

After a moment, he took a hard chomp down on his gum and got out his notebook. "What do you have?"

I gave him my Tommy Abbott theory. I included everything I knew, beginning with the time Georgie harassed Tommy's wife. I finished with the information Jeanette had given me.

"Don't you see? Tommy must have planned this for weeks, if not longer. He used the fact he was on duty as cover to practice cutting the locks. When he got the call to follow Georgie home instead of arresting him, he saw his chance and put his plan in motion. He followed Georgie home from Hoosiers and then talked him into breaking into Parke Landscaping."

"Why would they do that?" Matt's tone indicated he wasn't challenging me. He wanted details.

"To mess with Roger for firing him. He probably framed it as a prank. As drunk as Georgie was, it wouldn't have been hard to talk him into it. Then, giving him even more liquor?" I snapped my fingers. "It would have been a walk in the park."

Matt rolled his eyes. "No pun intended, I presume."

My cheeks got hot. I'd pled my case and hadn't convinced him.

After some more note taking, Matt looked at me. "What about Tommy's cruiser?"

"What about it?"

"Georgie's car is missing. We have to assume it was used in some of the crimes committed that night. If they used Georgie's car, they'd have had to leave Tommy's cruiser for a period of time. Why didn't anybody notice it? We canvassed the neighborhood, and nobody reported seeing anything out of the ordinary. Including a police car."

"That doesn't prove anything." Accusing a police officer of murder, and making the accusation to said officer's boss, was tantamount to Pi Patel trying to survive on a lifeboat with a hungry, fully grown tiger for company, but I wasn't going to be deterred.

"All of this went down at night, when the neighbors were asleep. Tommy probably parked a few blocks away. As a police officer, he's also smart enough to make sure he didn't leave any prints." I took a step back and put my hands on my hips, confident my logic was unassailable.

"I don't know." Matt shook his head.

"And another thing. How many times did Tommy have to follow Georgie home instead of putting him in jail? There has to be a report you could run. Imagine being told time after time that you have to ignore the law so the man who cost you a promotion can stay out of trouble, all because that man's living with the mayor's daughter."

"Watch it, Allie. That's a serious accusation you're making."

"Yeah, and a true one, too" Now I was angry. Orwell's *Animal Farm* had made a great impression on me. To this day, the idea of everyone being equal, but some being more equal than others, made me want to puke. "Don't insult me by trying to deny it. You can't."

Matt walked away but returned after taking a few steps. A bead of sweat was trickling down his temple, one I was sure wasn't due to hot weather conditions. "Sorry, Allie. Tommy told me he followed Georgie home. Once Georgie's car came to a stop, Tommy returned to patrol duty. I believe him."

"Did he see Georgie get out of the car or go inside the house?"

"No." Matt scratched his chin. The breeze whistled through a nearby grove of trees, breaking the silence that had developed between us. "Okay, for the sake of discussion, let's say Tommy is the perp. I need hard evidence to tie him to the crime. I can't, I won't, move on him based solely on circumstantial evidence."

"You don't believe me." I laced my fingers together behind my head as I turned away from him. If I maintained eye contact, I'd have said something I'd regret.

He touched me on the shoulder. "It's not that I don't believe you. I have to get this right the first time. I can't take the risk of bringing in one of my own if there's a chance he's not our guy. It could destroy his career."

Matt was one of the good guys. His heart was in the right place.

I had trusted him while I was hunting Thornwell's killer. I needed to trust him now. He'd earned it, after all. "Are you guys looking into Georgie and Lori's banking records?"

"You can be scarier than a hungry junkyard dog." He laughed. "We've requested a subpoena. Do I want to know why you're asking?"

"No, you don't."

"If I ask you to leave this to me and my team, you'll say no, won't you?"

"Yep." In fact, I was already planning my next move.

"Then I won't get in your way if you promise not to get in mine. Deal?"

We shook hands.

After a tip of his hat, he turned to go. He was twenty feet away when he turned back to me. "Be careful, Allie. This town needs you."

I gave him a wave. "Right back atcha, Chief."

Once Matt's cruiser was out of sight, I checked the time. It was a little before four. Plenty of time to swing by the apartment to get Ursi and make it to my next destination, Lori's house, before she got home from work.

While taking Ursi for a walk was always good for her, in this instance, it was also a way to throw Matt or one of his officers off the trail in case they were tailing me. It was unlikely, but after Matt's admonishment to be careful, my level of paranoia had risen to high alert.

Since the weather was sunny and dry, my kitty was thrilled to be outside. During our trek to Lori's house, Ursi dashed as far as her leash would let her after an early-falling leaf or froze and crouched low to the ground when she saw a bird or squirrel.

The only time her tail puffed out in alarm was when a beagle barked at us while its owner stopped to look at his phone. The dog, which was on a leash, and its owner were on the other side of the street, so I was pretty sure we weren't in mortal danger.

I burst out laughing when my fierce feline responded to the barks with a loud hiss. The beagle literally took a step back in response.

"Don't mess with Ursula Cobb, feline huntress." I gave her a kitty treat and scratched her along her spine for a couple of minutes until she calmed down.

Once we got moving again, I started a one-sided conversation with her about the case. Fortunately, nobody was close enough to overhear us. While Ursi was kind enough to respond to a couple of my questions with a half-hearted *meow*, I was sure my crazy cat lady vibe was turned all the way up to eleven.

I didn't care. It was a sunny day with a few clouds to make me appreciative of how intensely blue the sky was. Ursi was enjoying herself being explorer kitty, and I was enjoying stopping from time to time to take pictures of her with my phone.

The exercise was also helping me work off the stress from the day while also letting me talk through the case out loud. While the dialogue didn't provide any *a-ha* insights, it did help me make sense of what I'd learned.

It also forced me to think hard about my conviction that Tommy was the murderer. Yes, my hypothesis had holes in it, including my inability to figure out how the life insurance policy fit, but Matt's rebuttals did, too. That was why I decided to model Kim Frye's approach and go back to the beginning.

To Georgie and Lori's house. The place where he was last seen alive.

Ursi and I came to a stop when we rounded a corner and the house came into view. The neighborhood was populated with modest, bungalow-style homes on small lots. Every now and then, a two-story home rose above the others, like a mother keeping watch on her children.

The homes were well-maintained, with welcoming front porches, tidy lawns, and enough mature oak and maple trees to make me happy I didn't have to rake the millions of leaves that would fall in the next month or so.

My walking shoes were silent on the concrete sidewalk as we approached our target. Situated on a corner lot, the house was a typical southern Indiana starter home. The light blue vinyl siding and white window frames made me think of a warm, sunny day. A four-foot-high chain-link fence enclosed a backyard of lush, green grass that was a little on the tall side. Inside the fence, there was a play set featuring a slide and a two-level fort. A short gravel drive led to a one-car, cinder-block garage at the back of the lot.

The flowers in pots on the front porch and the mums lining the walkway from the street were bursting with yellow, orange, and red. They added a festive touch to the scene and were, no doubt, the result of a lot of hard work. A tulip poplar in the part of the yard between the street and the side of the house towered over the lot. A tire swing hung on a rope from one of the tree's lower branches. Overall, the home emanated a warm, welcoming vibe.

I loved it.

It was the kind of house I would want if I ever built up the courage to become a homeowner.

The mere thought of buying a house sent a shudder through me. Nope, I wasn't ready for that canyon-like leap into full-fledged adulthood. I set the intimidating thought aside as we came to a stop across the street from my destination.

"What do you think, girl? You know as much about this case as I do. Anything jumping out at you?"

Ursi responded by plopping down on the sidewalk and licking her front legs. Okay, maybe she was limited in the amount of help she was capable of providing.

Since Ursi was preoccupied with grooming herself, I tied her leash to a stop-sign post and took a few pictures.

Two things had caught my attention, the garage and the tree. A scan of the neighboring homes indicated one-car garages were the norm around here. So, who parked in the garage, Lori or Georgie? If Lori did, then where did Georgie normally park his car? Was it alongside the house, perhaps taking advantage of the tulip poplar's overhanging branches for cover? Or did he park in front, where he had a straight shot to the front door?

With Ursi still busy with her grooming, I dashed across the street to get a closer look at the area around the tree. Assuming for the moment that Matt was right, could Georgie's killer have used the tree for cover and made his move after Tommy took off? There were no telltale signs like cigarette butts or shoe scuff marks. If someone had hidden in the shadows, he or she left no signs behind.

The hair on the back of my neck standing at attention told me I was on the right track, so I went to the garage. A peek inside through a window in the garage door didn't reveal anything interesting. The middle, where I chose to assume Lori parked her car, was empty. A push mower was in a corner. Above it, a spin trimmer hung from a nail. Paint cans and lawn-care chemicals took up space on wooden shelves.

I was debating the wisdom of getting a closer look at the house when a truck rumbled down the road. Taking that as a sign God didn't want me snooping any further, I snapped a couple more pictures of the house and returned to Ursi, who had stretched out on the sidewalk and was sunning herself.

"Nothing else to see here, girl. Let's head home." As I unwound the leash from the sign post, Ursi batted at my leg. Evidently, just because I was finished with my business didn't mean she was finished with her sunbathing.

I kept my thoughts to myself on the walk home. Ursi was making sure I knew she was unhappy with me by refusing to even look at me. It was fine. I was too busy processing what I'd seen to chat.

By the time we reached the apartment, I'd changed my thought process. I was convinced the answer to the question of who killed Georgie wasn't in what I had seen at Lori's house.

The answer was in what I hadn't seen.

A piece to the puzzle was missing. As I fed Ursi her dinner, along with a few extra kitty treats to get back in her good graces, I made notes to find out where Georgie normally parked his car and to find out where, specifically, Tommy had been when he parted ways with Georgie.

If he actually did part ways. Pending the answers to my two new questions, Tommy was still my top suspect. After all, if he didn't do it, whoever did must have had intimate knowledge of Georgie's whereabouts that night.

That left me with two options. The first was Lori. The second was someone connected to Hoosiers, whether Willie himself or his gambling associates.

The key seemed to be time or, more precisely, timing. I needed to figure out who knew where Georgie was and when they knew it.

Timing.

That was the missing piece I needed to find.

Chapter Twenty-Three

The next morning, I was on the phone with one of my authors discussing a publication offer we'd received when there was a knock on the door. I ignored it. Celebratory times like this were too important to interrupt. If it was that important, the visitor could knock again or slip a note under the door.

"That's right." I glanced at the notes I'd made when the editor called with the offer. "It's a three-book deal, in both e-book and print-on-demand paperback formats."

The knocking came again, more insistent this time, followed by a male voice calling out my name. It was Matt. I opened the door and waved him in while my client asked a question about royalties.

"Yes, the royalty rates are pretty standard. One thing you may like about this publisher is they disburse royalties quarterly instead of semi-annually, like some do." When she asked about an advance, I looked at Matt and pointed toward the coffee maker. "Advances on an offer like this are rare. The important thing to keep in mind is that this offer is from an established publisher with a sterling reputation. For a debut author like you, it's a great opportunity."

While we discussed a few more key points of the offer, Matt poured himself a cup of coffee. I handed my empty mug to him and signaled for him to fill it up.

"Let's do this. Your manuscript is still being considered by three other editors. I'll contact them. I'll tell them you've received an offer and want to know if they want to make an offer as well. Since it's Wednesday, I'll tell them they can have until Monday morning to get back with me. That'll give you time to think about the offer."

My client was amenable to my proposal, so I ended the call by telling her congratulations and promising I'd be in touch. Then I did a little celebratory happy dance.

Matt was staring at me like I'd turned purple and had corn growing out of my ears. "Do you always act that way when you get off the phone?"

"I do when I get to let one of my clients know someone wants to publish their book." I took a seat in front of my computer. The sooner I contacted the other editors with news of the offer, the better. "What brings you by? Ready to admit I was right yesterday?"

"Not exactly." Matt sat in the chair across from me. He took a drink of his coffee and scratched his chin. "There's been a development in the case. This morning, we located Georgie's car."

"Excellent. Where'd you find it?" We exchanged a high five. An examination of the car should help me find the missing puzzle piece.

"A wooded area on Mr. Winchester's property, not far from the new park." He flipped to a page in his notebook. "The car was unlocked. The keys were in the ignition."

"That's great." I pulled up my e-mail and typed a message to the first of the three editors. I came to a complete stop when I couldn't bear Matt staring at me.

"I appreciate you coming by. I wish I could return the favor, but I don't have anything new to share. If you can give me a few minutes, I need to take care of some e-mails, and then we can brainstorm."

"I didn't come to brainstorm. Your fleece that went missing Labor Day was found in the car. I need you to identify it."

The unexpected news took my breath away. When the fleece didn't turn up after a few days, I'd resigned myself to the fact someone had stolen it. I should have been happy to have it located.

Instead, I was horrified that it was found in a murder victim's car.

I tried to take a drink of my coffee, but my trembling fingers made it hard to hold onto the cup.

Matt took it from me before I dropped it. "I'm not accusing you of anything, but I do need you to come with me. Now, please."

"Five minutes." I sent the e-mails as if I was on automatic pilot, then grabbed my purse and followed Matt out the door. I double-checked to make sure the door was locked. It seemed like I shouldn't take anything for granted these days, even something as routine as locking my front door.

By the time we reached his car, I was regaining my grip on the situation. It was Georgie's work ID all over again. It sure looked like someone was working overtime to tie me to the murder.

"Who found the car?" Asking the question gave me a sense of control over circumstances that seemed to have a life of their own.

"Vicky Napier was on the new walking path when she thought she saw something in the woods reflecting the sunlight. It seemed suspicious to her, so she called it in. God love her, she even apologized during the call for using something that hadn't been opened to the public yet. Jeanette responded and found the car."

Vicky Napier was one of my heroes. I had no reason to doubt her intentions. In fact, despite the circumstances, I smiled at the thought of seeing my beloved Mrs. Napier using the walking path at Winchester-Cobb Memorial Park, even though it wasn't finished yet.

We left Matt's cruiser in the park's gravel parking lot. It was on the construction schedule to be paved when the walking path was finished. I followed him across the park around a grove of trees and through a couple of wooden survey sticks to indicate we were crossing from park land onto the Winchester property.

"Any idea how the car got there?"

"I have a theory, but I'll let you take a look first." He gestured me forward.

The now-all-too-familiar yellow police tape had been strung across a twenty-foot span at the edge of the woods and then headed into the greenery until it was lost from sight. There was a gap in the trees in the center of the span that formed the head of a trail that wandered through a wooded area that still belonged to Sloane. A corresponding gap in the police tape provided an entrance to the trail.

At the edge of the trees, I stopped and turned around. We were in a clearing of sorts. Trees on both sides extended outward, shielding the trailhead from view from every angle except straight ahead. Thornwell Winchester's house was a quarter of a mile away in that direction.

"Sloane and I used to hike this trail when we were kids." I wrapped my arms around myself as I broke out in goose bumps, despite the fact that it was sunny and warm. "To protect his privacy, Thornwell wanted to be able to see from his house who was using the trail. He had a pair of binoculars he used when he thought he saw someone."

"My thoughts, exactly. Which means the murderer not only knew Georgie, he or she knew the lay of the land around here. Any ideas about who might fall into that category?"

"Besides Sloane and me?" I rattled off the names of people I thought knew the property well enough to find the trailhead. "Not a lot of people knew about it, but it's not like it was the secret entrance to the Batcave."

Matt popped a piece of his nicotine gum into his mouth when he finished writing down the names. "We've contacted Sloane since the car's on her property. Do you know if any security cameras were installed on the house after Thornwell died?"

"Yes. One by the front door, another by the side door, and one by the back door. I doubt you'd catch anything this far away, though. Sloane's more concerned with making sure the house doesn't get broken into while the property's unoccupied."

"Still can't hurt to check." He slipped on a pair of disposable shoe covers and handed another pair to me. "Let's do it."

When I stared at the covers, he let out a little huff as his shoulders sagged. "They're so our shoes don't contaminate the crime scene."

"Right." I put them on. There was a lot I still needed to learn about investigating crime.

Trepidation filled me as we passed through the opening in the tape. I had no idea what I would find when we reached Georgie's car, and that uncertainty made my anxiety even worse.

The trail surface was hard-packed dirt sprinkled with dead leaves that crunched underfoot with each step. There were no visible tire tracks. Some of the limbs on either side of us were broken, but many more were merely bent or had returned to their normal position. Whoever had driven Georgie's car back here had apparently taken things slow to minimize damage to the plant life. Either that or the murderer knew there was no need to be in a rush.

After twenty feet, the trail bent to the right and the car came into view. Or, at least, the parts of the car I could see came into view. Most of it was covered by leaves and branches that had been cut from nearby trees.

Jeanette was taking pictures of the scene. So much for her being off the case, evidently. She stopped just long enough for us to exchange a quick greeting and shake hands. In evidence-collection mode, my friend was too busy to chat. She was the department's best evidence tech, and I had no doubt that, if there was something incriminating here, Jeanette would find it.

Another officer arrived carrying an evidence-collection kit as Jeanette finished taking photographs. He had gray hair and a belly that would give Santa Claus a run for his money. After a few seconds, his name came to me—Oliver Watson. For as long as I could remember, he'd attended every one of my dad's book-release celebrations.

I smiled at Officer Watson. He tipped his cap in return.

The two officers conferred with Matt for a moment, then put on gloves and spread a tarp on the ground.

"I need your help with two things." Matt took me by the elbow and guided me to the car. He pointed toward the back seat. "First, is that your fleece?"

My beloved Cobb Literary Agency fleece lay across the back seat. The logo was plain to see, as if someone had planted it there on purpose

"That's it. I only had the one made. Any idea how it got here?"

"Not yet. The more relevant question is why is it here? First things first, though." He handed me a pair of exam gloves. "See all the branches leaning against the car? I want you to move them onto the tarp."

I stared at the limbs. They were all sizes, but many were easily three inches thick at the base and ten feet long. Not easy for someone my size to deal with.

At a nod from Matt, I grabbed the first one with two hands and lifted it straight up. It wasn't like it weighted a thousand pounds, but as big as is was, with dozens of smaller limbs shooting off from it in all directions, it was unwieldy. Thanks to the tight quarters in which I was working, it took me the better part of five minutes to maneuver the first one onto the tarp.

Matt told me to stop when I dropped the fifteenth one onto the pile and put a six-inch-long scrape in my arm while doing it.

"Want to tell me what that was all about?" I brushed bark from my shirt while I spit out bits of leaves that had made their way into my mouth.

"Another little test to help prove you're not the murderer. Our perp knew what he was doing. He was methodical." He cracked a half smile. "No offense, but the way you struggled with those branches, there's no way you could have driven the car back here, cut down all these branches, covered the car, and then got out of here without being noticed. Let Jeanette take a few pictures of your arms."

I extended my arms straight out in front of me for better inspection. They were red and scratched. My hands were bleeding from several tiny cuts. My friend grimaced as she photographed my irritated limbs.

"Do you recall her arms and hands looking anything like this the day she discovered Mr. Alonso," Matt asked Jeanette.

"No, sir. She was in short sleeves. I would have noticed." She ran her finger across one of my wrists. "See the beginnings of a contusion there? That's big enough that, even if she had been wearing long sleeves and gloves the night of the crime, some kind of bruising would have been visible the following morning."

"Agreed." Matt jotted down a few things in his ever-present notebook. "When you're finished moving the branches, I want a bumper-to-bumper search of the car. I don't want it moved until you've gone through it with a fine-tooth comb."

At Jeanette's nod, Matt guided me away so his team could resume their work.

"Sorry for putting you through that little exercise—"

"Little?" I held out my bruised, scraped, and aching arms. "Look at me. You call that the result of a little exercise?"

He held up his hands in surrender. "Point taken, but you'll survive. The key thing here is that your demo leaves you one hundred percent in the clear. No more lingering doubts."

"Oh. Well, then." I lowered my arms as the anger that had been building drained away. "That's a relief. Where's that leave you?"

"You said you lost the fleece on Labor Day. Is there any way it could have been earlier?"

"No. Brent can verify I had it that morning. Why?" The empty spot inside me where the venom had been residing was filling up with excitement. Matt seemed to be onto something. The puzzle piece was almost within my grasp.

"This is different than the situation with Georgie's ID. In that scenario, I could see the perp holding onto it and trying to incriminate the first person to find the body. Making a quick trip up the stairs to your apartment and slipping something under the door wouldn't take much in terms of time or guts."

I picked up the thread. "But by the time the killer snagged my fleece, he knew I was the one who found Georgie."

"Exactly. He takes the fleece, then slips out here where the car's been hidden, drops it in the back seat, and waits for them to be found. Then once they're found…"

I swallowed. In the flash of an eye, my throat had gone desert dry. "The killer waits for you to arrest me."

Chapter Twenty-Four

Matt ground a dead leaf into the dirt with the heel of his boot. When he was finished, he raised his head until our gazes met. After a few moments, he sighed and looked away. "Yep, but it's not going to happen. There's no doubt in my mind you didn't do it alone, and I don't see even the tiniest shred of credible evidence you worked in tandem with someone."

"Where's that leave us?" I held off bringing up Tommy. At this point, none of this new evidence pointed conclusively toward him, so there was no point in causing a dustup when we needed to be on the same page.

"Well, one thing's for sure." He rubbed his chin. "Since you didn't kill Georgie, whoever did went to a lot of trouble to pin it on you."

I let out an involuntary laugh. At the moment, it was way better to go with gallows humor than allow myself to drown in self-pity.

That was when I had a brain blast. It started out as a tiny flicker, but as I cupped imaginary hands around it and fed it with tiny breaths of air, it grew until it became a fully grown flame and rocketed around the inside of my skull.

A lot of trouble to pin it on me. I grabbed Matt by the arm and practically dragged him down the trail until we could talk without being overheard.

"What about this? What if the perp killed Georgie as a way to strike out at me?"

Matt raised an eyebrow. "Really? I know you've been under a lot of stress, but that's a stretch, don't you think?"

"Okay, no. I mean…" I closed my eyes and took deep breaths as I silently counted to ten.

The puzzle piece was there, mere centimeters from my outstretched hand. If I grabbed wildly at it, I'd miss, and the piece would spin off into eternal darkness, never to be found. I had to take my time and grasp for the piece with a steady hand.

"We've been working under the assumption the perp killed Georgie and is trying to frame me so he gets away with it, right? After all, what happened after I found the body? My fleece went missing. A few days later, Georgie's ID turned up in my apartment. Now, my fleece turns up in Georgie's car."

Matt nodded. "I'm with you."

"And we're further assuming I'm the one being framed because I'm the one who found Georgie. It could have been anybody, but it just happened to be me."

"Sure, but your point is?"

"What if, instead of killing Georgie and framing me so the murderer gets away, the whole plot was to murder Georgie and silence me, specifically, in one single ploy?"

"That sounds awfully complicated. Why would someone want to do that?"

My mind was racing so fast it was hard to verbalize exactly what I was thinking. I needed to get this right before Matt started thinking I'd cracked under the pressure.

"You can't deny I've rattled a few cages since I came back to town." I shrugged. "And I know more than my fair share of secrets about people around here. What if the murderer hated Georgie enough to kill him and hated me enough to make me look like a criminal"—I snapped my fingers—"to discredit me before those secrets got out?"

"Let's assume for the moment you're right. I can imagine plenty of people who'd had enough of Georgie. Who would want to take you down that hard, though?"

"Jax Michaels, for one. He's never forgiven me for going after him last October. Then there's Charissa Mody—"

"Ah, yes. I'll never forget the video of you going over the bar to get to her at Rushing Creek Winery. I can see how she might hold a grudge."

"Hell hath no fury like a woman scorned. I have plenty of scorn for that woman, and some dirt on her, too. She was working at Hoosiers the night Georgie was killed, wasn't she?"

"Yeah, but she's got an alibi. Witnesses placed her at the bar until eleven, when it closed. She clocked out at midnight and made an ATM deposit fifteen minutes later. Then she went home. Georgie left the bar around ten. There's no way she could have intercepted him."

"But an accomplice could have. What say we go talk to her? Right now."

"Come on, Allie. I really don't think—"

"—Tommy Abbott had anything to do with it. I know. So, humor me. Let's go talk to her. Maybe we'll pick up on something new." I looked over my shoulder toward Georgie's car. "Your team's got this. Come on."

* * * *

Thirty minutes later, I walked into Hoosiers, despite my prior vow to never return. I was wearing a long-sleeved T-shirt to cover my cuts and scrapes, had my case notebook under my arm, and had Matt a step behind me. We'd come up with a strategy during the drive from the park. Matt would do the talking. I would take notes and keep my mouth shut. Given my previous run-in with Charissa Mody, we hoped my silence would unnerve her.

We figured Matt wearing a badge and carrying a gun wouldn't hurt, either.

Since it was a little after eleven, the bar was quiet. An elderly gentleman wearing jeans, a flannel shirt, and a green trucker's cap nursed a beer at the end of the bar. Charissa was taking glasses from a dishwasher, drying them, and hanging them from a rack above her head.

"Morning, Chief Roberson." Charissa shot me a quick glance before returning her attention to Matt. "What can I get you this fine day?"

"I'll have a cup of coffee, and Ms. Cobb will have…" He made a point of turning his whole body in my direction. Message sent.

"Water with lemon, please." *Well done, and thank you, Matt.*

"Of course." With a smile, she nodded at Matt. "Coming right up."

While we waited, I made a production of opening my notebook and going through the pages. If Charissa wanted to play games, I'd play along with her. The only thing that mattered was getting information from the woman.

She placed our drinks and menus in front of us. "Can I get you anything else?"

Matt dumped two packets of sweetener into his coffee and stirred it before answering. "Nothing from the menu, thanks. I'd appreciate it if you'd answer a few more questions about the Alonso matter, though."

"I already told Officer Wilkerson everything I could remember, and the lunch rush will be here soon."

I looked around. The place was as empty as the Boulevard at midnight on a Tuesday.

"We'll be brief." He took a drink. "We understand you made a phone call to someone regarding Mr. Alonso's state of intoxication shortly before he left here the night he died. Who did you call?"

Between the flared nostrils, narrowed eyes, and scrunched-up nose, the way Charissa looked from Matt to me, one would have thought she'd just bit into a fresh lemon. I wasn't proud of schadenfreude-like thoughts directed at her, but I wasn't going to lose any sleep over the issue, either.

"Mayor Cannon."

"Why?" My question was out the instant I realized I'd asked it. Oh, well. Despite Matt's comment to the contrary, I was willing to spend all day asking this woman questions.

"This is insane, Chief. Do I—"

Matt took a long drink of his coffee. "Please answer the question."

"Fine. I called the mayor as a favor to Georgie. I didn't want him to get in trouble."

"Why did you call the mayor instead of the police?" Since Matt had let me ask one question, I was going to keep the questions going until he told me to stop. "Drunk driving's a serious crime. Georgie could have hit and killed someone." The last bit was an attempt to goad Charissa. If I made her mad, she might lose her focus and let something slip.

"Don't lecture me on the dangers of drunk driving. I work in a bar, for God's sake. I called the mayor because he was practically Georgie's father-in-law."

"Had Mayor Cannon asked you in the past to call him when Georgie was too drunk to drive, or did you call him unprompted?"

"He and I were talking a little while after I started here. In case you don't remember, I needed a new job after you got me fired at the winery. Anyway, he warned me about Georgie's drinking problem. He said it would help Lori and Brittany if I'd let him know if Georgie ever needed help getting home. Is that so wrong?"

Before I could respond with a venom-laced yes, Matt cleared his throat. I swallowed the retort and forced a smile.

"We're merely trying to make sure we have our time line and facts straight. I'm sure you can appreciate that. Now, you called Mayor Cannon. What did he tell you?"

Charissa filled Matt's coffee mug. "He told me to call the police station's non-emergency number and request that someone pick Georgie up. I got Officer Abbott. He said he'd take care of it."

I also wanted to ask her in front of Matt how she got the mayor's number. Thanks to my previous sleuthing efforts, I already knew the answer and wanted to make her squirm. Discretion won out, though. I was too close to an answer to get sidetracked.

Two men dressed in similar golf attire, bright Dri-Fit shirts, black polyester pants, and white baseball caps eased onto barstools a few feet away. Charissa left us to take their orders.

I leaned close to Matt to keep my voice low. "What do you think? Anything helpful?"

"Depends on what you consider helpful. Everything she told us lines up with the statement she gave Jeanette. To me, that's helpful."

Keeping my frustration in check, I closed my notebook. When Charissa returned, we thanked her for her time. Matt gave her his business card and asked her to call him if anything else came to mind.

When we were back in the patrol car, he started the engine. "Sorry, Allie. It all fits."

"Sure, it fits. That doesn't mean she isn't hiding something." An idea was niggling me at the base of my skull, like a mosquito bite in need of scratching that was just out of reach. "She may be hiding something and doesn't even know it. Let me go through the conversation out loud. Maybe something will rise to the surface."

After a moment's hesitation, he popped a regular piece of gum into his mouth. "Have at it."

I took Matt's gum choice as a positive sign, so I checked my notes and began my monologue as he drove us out of the parking lot. To his credit, he kept quiet, commenting only when I asked him a question. I was so focused on the task at hand, I didn't realize we'd returned to the park until Matt put the cruiser in PARK.

"I need to check in with Jeanette and see if Sloane's responded. Is there anything else?"

A lump formed in my throat. Sure, Matt wanted to catch Georgie's killer, but I got the sense of something more from our trip to Hoosiers. He knew I was doing all I could to help him, and he wanted to reciprocate.

Thanks to the bad blood that had developed due to his divorce from Rachel, as recently as twelve months ago I wouldn't have been caught dead in the same room with the man. Now look at us. We were working together to solve another murder. I didn't know if I would ever be able to call Matt a friend, but I considered him a trusted ally.

"Don't think so." I stared at my notes and let out a long, cleansing breath. I was still exhaling when my brain zeroed in on a single word. A dose of adrenaline sprinted through me as I considered the word. *Could it really be that simple?*

Matt was halfway out of the car when I grabbed his arm. "Wait. Has anyone talked to the mayor?"

"No. Why?"
I pulled him back into the car.
"He's the missing piece to the puzzle."

Chapter Twenty-Five

"What do you mean he's the missing piece to the puzzle?" Matt pulled his arm out of my grip. His eyes were narrowed, and his hands were balled into fists, reminders he was on duty and on edge. Even someone in my situation, working with a cop, should refrain from touching him or her while they're on duty.

"Hear me out." I put my hands up to lower the emotional temperature. Matt needed to listen to my words and act on what I was about to tell him.

"This case is all about timing. Who knew what and when they knew it. Let's start with the easy stuff. Charissa just told us she called Larry, so he knew where Georgie was and when Georgie would be home."

"But he didn't say he'd take care of it himself. He told Charissa to let the officer on duty handle it."

"Yes. I'll get to that, but let's go back to the morning I discovered Georgie's body. Larry's been working closely with the park planning committee. Because of that, he's had access to the construction schedule." I pounded my fist into my open palm. "He knew the mulch was scheduled to be delivered that morning, so he knew he could use it as a murder weapon."

Matt chewed on his lip. "A lot of people have access to the construction information." He was playing devil's advocate. Since I was accusing his boss of murder, I couldn't blame him.

I ticked off other points to support my new theory, ending with motive. "With Georgie gone, Lori gets the proceeds from the mystery life insurance policy. That's a lot of cash to help your daughter and granddaughter start a new life."

"If you're right, you're asking me to drop the mother of all bombshells on this town. Besides, only yesterday, you wanted me to arrest Tommy." He closed his eyes as he drummed his fingers on the dashboard.

"I was wrong about Tommy. I was trying to force pieces into a puzzle that didn't fit. It's different this time. I know it. We need to go after Larry before he finds out we're looking at him."

"It might explain why he's been leaning on me so hard to make a collar." He started the engine. "Without solid evidence, this stays under wraps. Where to?"

"We can cover more ground if we split up. How about you go to the municipal building? If he's not there, check with his secretary. Drop me off at my place. I want to get a few things, then I'll go to Larry's house."

"Fine, but if you see him, do not engage. Contact me and I'll take it from there. No unnecessary risk-taking. Got it?"

"Acknowledged." He didn't want me to repeat my foolish actions the last time I'd spotted a killer. I couldn't blame him for the safety first reminder.

Matt called Jeanette to tell her he was returning to the office and would touch base with her later. He shook his head as we left the parking lot, as if to say he couldn't believe the killer was the mayor.

I was beside myself, as well. On one hand, I was angry with myself for being so wrong about Tommy. On the other hand, I was disappointed in myself for having missed the signs of Larry's involvement.

As I dashed up the stairs to my apartment, one question kept bothering me. How did Larry get from his house to Georgie's house without being detected?

The answer came to me as I unlocked my front door and glanced at my two-wheeler.

His bike!

First things first, though. I had a bad guy to catch.

Twenty minutes later, I kissed Ursi, gave her some kitty treats, and asked her to wish me luck as I hoisted a backpack full of stakeout supplies over my shoulder. She responded by giving me a *meow* and rubbing her cheek against my shoe. It seemed to be her way of wishing me luck.

Descending the stairs, I hoped I didn't need it.

I hopped on my bike, made sure my helmet was securely strapped in place, and pedaled to Larry's house. I'd received no word from Matt since we parted ways, so evidently our suspect was still at large.

On the ride, I reviewed my new theory that Larry was the killer and wanted to take me down while taking Georgie out. I had to give the man begrudging credit. It was a gambit born of meticulous planning.

Especially since there was no evidence of his involvement.

And therein was the beauty of it. Sick? Yes. Despicable? Absolutely. Horrific? Beyond doubt. It was also elegant in design and nearly flawless in execution. The nearly part was what I was banking on as I rolled to a stop in front of Larry's house.

The lights in the house were off. No surprise, given it was late afternoon and Larry and his wife were still at work. While I'd gotten to know the man, or thought I had, over the past few months, I didn't know much about his wife, Anita, other than that she worked as a nurse at a hospital a half hour away in Columbus, Indiana.

It didn't seem prudent to hang out in the open where Larry could see me when he got home, so I parked my bike behind a neighbor's hedgerow and got comfortable at the base of a nearby beech tree.

Despite Matt's instructions, I was prepared to confront the man if the situation warranted it. My goal was to approach him as soon as he arrived so he'd have no time to prepare for my accusation. By engaging him outside, I'd avoid the hazards that came with going up against a killer in a confined space. If things went south, I could run away.

As the minutes ticked by, I went over and over what I was going to say. I had to convince him it was in his best interest to give himself up without a lot of fuss. To that end, I pulled up Matt's number on my phone. That way I could show it to Larry to let him know I was serious.

Would it work? I had no idea. That was why I took some zip strips out of my backpack and stuffed them into my pocket. If worse came to worst, I'd drop him with a kickboxing move and bind him with the zip strips.

The question of whether I'd bind him too tight remained to be answered.

I was reading a text from Matt saying the mayor hadn't been located when a dented and rusty blue pickup pulled into Larry's driveway. I responded that I had him in sight, then got to my feet and double-timed it up the driveway.

He did a double take as he got out of his truck. "Allie. This is a surprise. What brings you by?"

"Stopped by to chat. What have you been up to?" Between the orange cap and camo clothing, I knew exactly what he'd been doing. While I wasn't among them, lots of folks in southern Indiana hunted. Deer, wild turkey, and small furbearers were plentiful and among the most common game animals found in the Hoosier State.

"Been out in the field." He reached into his truck and pulled out a rifle. "Squirrel hunting with my buddy Jax Michaels."

Jax Michaels. If I was right that Larry had been playing me for months, the fact that he'd spent the day with someone who despised me probably wasn't helpful.

He held the rifle in one hand and waved it in my general direction before pointing it straight at my chest. The message was clear, but I held my ground. The intimidation tactic was, for all intents and purposes, an admission of guilt.

"Squirrels are so small, you can't hunt them with a more powerful rifle like a shotgun or a thirty-aught-six." He laughed. "It's still plenty dangerous, though. If you're not careful around it, you could get hurt. A bullet placed in the proper location can be lethal."

"Oh, I know. Luke has a rifle like that. He took me to the firing range a couple times when I was younger." I leaned against the truck. To further the illusion of confidence, I yawned and peeked in the truck's bed. A gray canvas tarp covered most of it, but something metallic caught my attention. Without giving Larry another look, I pulled back the tarp.

"Well, lookie here. What's this?" A shiny bolt cutter lay among a few other tools.

"I have a lot of tools in there. I was raised to work with my hands."

"Maybe I'm just a little city girl, but what could you possibly use a set of bolt cutters for when you're out squirrel hunting?" I took a half-step toward him, ready to spring into action, the zip strips safely stashed in my pocket.

"You think you're so smart. You don't know anything." He bit his lip as his eyes darted back and forth.

The odor of cheap alcohol was on his breath. If he was drunk, things could get out of hand in the blink of an eye. Or in the squeeze of a trigger. I'd have to be more careful than I'd ever been in my life, while still goading him into making a mistake.

"Oh, I don't know. I know bolt cutters have a lot of uses. I'll admit I don't know why you'd need bolt cutters for squirrel hunting. But I know it's the perfect tool to cut locks off the doors of a bunch of storage barns around town and to cut the lock off the gate at Parke Landscaping."

"I've had enough of your meddling. You're worse than those annoying kids from *Scooby-Doo*."

The world slowed as Larry pulled the trigger. A puff of smoke rose from the rifle as the bullet rocketed toward me. My kickboxing instincts took control, and I leaned to my right.

Searing pain knifed through a spot just below my left shoulder blade as the bullet made contact. The force knocked my breath from me, and I stumbled backward until I hit the corner of the house. Another shock of pain charged up and down my spine as I crumpled to the ground.

While I blinked back tears and fought for breath, the truck door slammed shut. My vision cleared as the engine rumbled to life and peeled back down the driveway. I struggled to my feet as the squeal of tires was followed by the crunch of metal against metal. Despite the pain in my chest, I smiled as Larry struggled to separate his truck from a neighbor's SUV he'd plowed into.

My hand went to the bullet wound. There was blood and some intense pain, but I'd live. I made it to my bike, grabbing the handle bars as Larry's truck finally broke free from the other vehicle and headed down the street.

I'd watched a few broadcasts of the Tour de France over the years. Those athletes were tough. I mounted the bike and began the chase. I was every bit as tough those pro bike racers and was going to prove it by catching Larry.

And bringing him to justice.

The bullet wound burned like a blast furnace, but I gritted my teeth and took up the chase. A check of my bike computer showed I was riding at more than twenty miles per hour. That was a good speed for a car in downtown Rushing Creek. My efforts at channeling the pain into pedal power were working. For now, at least.

Lacking the ability to call Matt, I focused on the blue tailgate ahead of me. Larry was the matador. I was the bull. This time the bull was going to be victorious.

As we neared the Boulevard, the truck's red brake lights flared to life. I kept pedaling, closing the distance to within ten feet before Larry hit the gas. His tires spit pebbles at me as he leapt into the intersection and turned left.

A left turn meant he was heading south, for the state highway that ran through the southern portion of Rushing Creek. Somehow, I had to stop him before he reached the highway. Once there, his getaway would be easy, and more importantly, he'd have time to manufacture a story about why I was chasing him. And why he had to flee my pursuit.

I barreled through the intersection without giving a second thought to tapping my brakes. Midway through my turn, a car's horn blasted as if it was inches from my right ear. Long-dormant bike-handling skills from my daredevil college days returned in the nick of time, and I kept the rubber on the road and the pedals cranking.

A combination of motorized traffic and pedestrians crossing the Boulevard helped me stay close. Larry couldn't weave through the obstacles, but I could. The all-out effort was causing my thighs to burn, though. Before long, my lungs would join the protest.

I was running out of time.

What I needed was enough of a distraction to cause him to lose control and spin out. I almost had my chance as we motored past the Rushing Creek Inn. Larry was forced to slow enough that I pulled even with him and managed to pound on the driver's side door.

My maneuver got his attention, and the truck veered away from me and sped ahead. The gap between us grew, but Larry overcorrected, and the truck veered sharply to the left, like a pinball bouncing off a bumper.

The Rushing Creek Bridge came into view. As Larry fought to regain control of the truck, I ignored the agonized protests from my body and stayed with him. If he crossed the bridge, he was out of options. The span led directly to the entrance of Green Hills State Park. He'd have no choice then and would have to stop at the park gate.

If I could hold on that long.

As we closed in on the bridge, the truck drifted to the right, back to the left, and then back to the right. Too far to the right. The passenger side of the truck hit the guardrail, producing a shower of sparks and an earsplitting screech as metal rubbed against metal until it ground to a stop.

I slammed on my brakes and dismounted, sucking in lungfuls of air as I crept toward the truck.

"Larry? It's over. Don't make this worse than it already is." I reached for my cell when there was no response. Between the physical exertion and the bullet wound, my fingers were trembling so hard I struggled to key in the code to unlock the phone.

During my third attempt, the truck's driver door swung open. Larry hobbled out. He had a gash across his forehead that was bleeding like something out of a horror movie. That was less of a problem than the rifle he had in his hands, though. It was pointing right at me.

"You're wrong. It's not over. Not by a long shot."

Chapter Twenty-Six

"Long shot." He jabbed the rifle at me and laughed. "Get it?"

I kept my distance as a wave of nausea coursed through me. A quick glance at my shirt showed a red splotch that was expanding with each breath I took. The physical exertion needed for my insane race hadn't done the wound any favors. My scraped-up forearms were throbbing, too.

I gritted my teeth and focused on the rifle barrel. "Very funny, Larry. What I *get* is that you're a murderer. You killed Georgie and tried to make me take the fall."

"Of course I did." He leaned against the truck's open door and used his sleeve to wipe away blood that was trickling into his eye. "Been planning it for months. Years, actually. I hated that worthless bum since the day I met him. And then he had the audacity to ruin my Lorelei's life by getting her pregnant. When she wouldn't get rid of him, I had to."

"You took out the insurance policy." I figured if I could keep him talking, help would arrive. Our dash down the Boulevard couldn't have gone unnoticed.

"Who else? One of the advantages of being mayor is having access to the files of every city employee. When Roger fired Georgie, it gave me the perfect opportunity to swoop in and look like a kindhearted father-in-law by giving him a job working for your brother."

"Wow. You're more devious than I thought. I figured you were just a womanizer when I learned about your affair with Charissa. That's still going on, I take it?" I was trying again to unlock my cell when the gun went off. I screamed and dropped it.

"Don't even try reaching for it."

"Okay." I stepped away from the phone. Where was the cavalry when you needed it? "But I'm done keeping your and Charissa's secret. I kept it under my hat because I thought it was a private matter. Not anymore. Was she simply another pawn on your chessboard? Did you manipulate her just like you've manipulated everyone else in this town?"

"Not really, but when she started working at Hoosiers—at my suggestion, I might add—I saw an opportunity I couldn't pass up. She was the perfect person to keep me up to speed on Georgie's comings and goings."

And then the final puzzle pieces dropped into place. The realization would have taken my breath away if I wasn't already struggling to breathe.

"You told Charissa to call the police to buy you time to get from your house to Lori's house. You couldn't take your SUV or this thing." I waved at the truck. "Those were too noticeable. You rode your bike and hid in the shadows of the big tree in the yard."

He made a half bow. "I knew Abbott wouldn't tail Georgie any longer than he had to. I cut Georgie off before he'd gotten five feet from his car. Told him I had an idea to prank Roger Parke. He loved it, especially when I showed him a backpack that had the bolt cutter and booze."

"Then it was you who stole my fleece and slipped Georgie's ID under my door." A faint siren's wail caught my attention. While it was a relief to have help on the way, I couldn't let him get back in his truck. I stepped toward him.

"Don't come any closer. I'm taking these shots in self-defense, you understand. I won't let you use your dangerous kicking skills on me." He lowered the rifle barrel and pulled the trigger. The shot hit the pavement mere inches from my left foot.

"And, yes, I did those things. Bringing you down was going to be the icing on the cake." He fired again, this time barely missing my right foot.

The siren's undulating call grew louder. Larry looked past me.

Now was my chance.

"Don't worry. I won't kick you." I lunged at him, bringing my right arm back to deliver a roundhouse punch. Once I was close enough, I let out a roar and brought my fist forward. It connected with his jaw and sent him spiraling, first into the truck's door, then to the ground.

The gun clattered to the pavement between us. I scooped it up before he could make a move for it.

"Don't you dare move an inch." I kept the rifle pointed at him while I grabbed my phone and dialed Matt. I told him where we were. He said he was already en route.

A police cruiser skidded to a halt beside me seconds later. My knuckles were throbbing like a bass drum keeping time with a clock. A few of them were probably broken, but I kept the firearm pointed at Larry until the officer was out of the car.

It was Jeanette.

"Stay down. Put your hands behind your head." Her shouts carried so much authority, Larry followed them without a hint of argument. In what seemed like the blink of an eye, she was on one knee and putting Larry in handcuffs.

"You okay, Allie?" She responded to my nod with a frown and used her microphone to request an ambulance.

Matt arrived, bringing his cruiser to a stop in front of the truck. With his gun drawn, he sprinted to my side. "My God. You've been shot."

"That's the rumor." A chuckle was cut off by a lightning bolt of pain from the bullet hole. I handed the rifle to Matt and crumpled to the ground, using Jeanette's car as a backrest.

While Jeanette dealt with Larry, Matt ran to his car. He returned with a thick pad of gauze, which he placed over my wound. Then he put my injured right hand, which was still balled into a fist, on top of the gauze.

"Keep that covered until the paramedics get here." He gave me a long look, then shook his head. "You actually chased down a killer on your bike."

"With my arms scraped like with a cheese grater and a bullet in my chest." I winced at the discomfort the pressure on the wound was causing to both my chest and my hand. "Getting shot made me mad. Don't make me mad."

Matt laughed. "You ought to put that on a shirt. You'd make a fortune."

Evidently convinced I wasn't going to die anytime soon, he gave my uninjured shoulder a squeeze and went to help Jeanette as she dealt with Larry.

A few minutes later, the paramedics arrived. I wanted to walk to the ambulance, but they insisted on using a stretcher, overruling my protests that lying down on the job would damage my Kickboxing Crusader cred.

* * * *

Mom met me at the emergency room. She wasn't happy.

"Last year you got strangled. Now you get shot. What am I going to do with you?" Her watery eyes belied her harsh words.

"All in a day's work." The pain medication I'd been given in the ambulance was doing an A-plus job, so I was in a jovial mood. "Guess you're going to have to visit Luke and Sloane on Friday by yourself, huh?" I tried to wink but ended up closing both eyes at the same time. At least my clumsy attempt at winking made Mom laugh.

* * * *

I woke up in a hospital bed. My right hand was wrapped in a thick bandage. My left upper chest was covered in gauze, and an IV was stuck in my arm. Bandages covered the most serious cuts and scrapes on my arms.

My best friend was in a chair in the corner of the room, working on her laptop.

"Can I get a drink?" My throat was parched, so my request was akin to a frog's croak.

"Omigod, Allie. One sec." Sloane practically dropped her computer on the floor in her rush to my bedside. A plastic cup with a straw sticking out of it was on a stand next to my bed. She guided the straw into my mouth and held the cup while I sucked the frigid water down my throat. When the cup was empty, she refilled it.

"The Kickboxing Crusader strikes again." Sloan was smiling from ear to ear. "I can't believe you caught the murderer, again. I mean, I *can* totally believe it, but still." She tapped me on my good shoulder. "You're amazing, girlfriend."

"It was either find the killer or go to jail. And you know orange isn't my color." I sucked down another cup of water as she laughed.

A nurse came in to check my vital signs and dressings. The woman's eyes were wide open, and she barely said a word before promising the doctor would be in shortly and then hurrying out the door.

"That was weird."

"I think taking care of the woman who busted the mayor has her freaked out. Plus, your mom can be a little intimidating. She's taking a break in the café." Sloane ticked out a message on her phone. "I just let her know you're awake."

"How long have I been out?" While the water had revived me, I was still a little groggy and had absolutely no sense of time.

"They took you into surgery around five and you've been out ever since. It's almost nine in the morning. You had a good night's sleep. And don't worry. I checked in on Ursi last night. She's fine. She told me to tell you *meow*."

I glanced at the ceiling. *I was out all night?* Sloane must have read my mind because she patted my foot as she sat on the corner of the bed.

"Thanks to your superhero crime fighting efforts, removing the bullet was more complicated than normal. Cleaning the wound to prevent infection was a challenge. Then they needed to fix your hand."

I was about to ask after Larry when Mom came in with a bouquet of flowers in one hand and a balloon in the other. Once we made eye contact, she handed the decorations to Sloane and rushed to give me a hug.

"How do you feel? Any dizziness? Does the area around the gunshot wound feel hot? Can you move the fingers on your broken hand?"

"Mom." I waited until she stopped fussing over me. "I'm fine. No dizziness. No infection-related discomfort." I lifted my right hand and wiggled my fingers, ignoring the throbbing caused by the demonstration. "You can relax, okay?"

"How am I supposed to relax with news crews from Indianapolis crawling all over town asking about you?" Despite her cross tone, Mom couldn't hide a smile and burst out laughing when Sloane said it was business as usual for the Kickboxing Crusader.

A little while later, I talked to Brent, who only stopped freaking out about my injuries when Mom assured him I would be fine. Then it was breakfast time, which was good because I was famished. I was plowing through a bowl of oatmeal and some sliced fruit when there was a knock at the door.

Sloane stepped aside to let Matt in. After exchanging hugs with the others, he asked me how I was doing.

"Getting better by the minute. My surgeon was here earlier. He said if I'm feeling okay, I can go home this afternoon."

"That's great. I don't want to keep you from your breakfast, but I've got good news. Last night, Larry made a full confession to Georgie's murder."

"No way." It was better than good news. It was the best news I could imagine. "How'd you manage that?"

"You're not going to believe this, but when word got out he was in custody, Charissa came to see him. About ten minutes later, Anita showed up." Matt paused as he covered his mouth, evidently trying to maintain a sense of decorum. "And Charissa was still there. A lot of harsh words were exchanged. After I managed to get both women out of the station, he confessed. He said something about it being safer inside behind bars than outside at the mercy of two angry women."

"You should have let him out and made him fend for himself," Sloane said. "He killed Georgie and tried to screw over Allie. Whatever happened to him, he had it coming."

"Don't think that option didn't cross my mind. Especially after it became obvious neither woman had any involvement in his scheme." Matt straightened the collar of his shirt. "Let's just say neither will be testifying on his behalf as a character witness."

I let out a contented sigh as I looked from Mom to Sloane to Matt. I had a bullet hole in me and three broken knuckles, but I'd caught the bad guy. That felt good.

"What's next?" I popped a grape in my mouth and savored the soft texture. It was easy to chew, despite the pain in other parts of my body. I was ready for easy things for a while.

Matt looked from Sloane to Mom, as if he wanted their approval before saying anything more. They both nodded.

"The press would like to talk to you. Do you think you're up to it?"

"Come on. Do I have to?"

"No, but fair warning, if you don't talk to them, I'm sure Maybelle will be happy to tell them everything. And you know she won't let the truth get in the way of a good story." He winked.

That settled it. If anyone was going to tell my story, it was going to be me.

"Then let's do it. All part of the drill for the Kickboxing Crusader, right?"

Chapter Twenty-Seven

"Ready for your big speech?" Brent helped me into my suit jacket.

I thanked him with a kiss. The ceremonial ribbon cutting to officially open Winchester-Cobb Memorial Park was set to begin in an hour. It was almost showtime.

"A small speech, yes. A big speech, no."

"Regardless of length, you'll be amazing." He straightened his bow tie and flicked some pet hair from the lapel of his tweed suit jacket. When he was dressed up, he really looked like a stereotypical librarian, which made him the sexiest man around.

"I hope so. Public speaking's not my strong suit."

"Catching criminals wasn't either, and look at you now. You're a legend in this town."

I rolled my eyes. "A legend who would be perfectly happy going back to being a literary agent and nothing else."

Things had been returning to normal in the month since I'd solved Georgie Alonso's murder. At least as normal as things could be for a town whose mayor was a confessed murderer. The clerk-treasurer had been sworn in as mayor until a new one was elected. Angela was now running unopposed, so she was a shoo-in to be Rushing Creek's next chief executive.

I was happy with that development, if not the way it came about. I hadn't thought Angela would lose to Larry, but I hadn't thought Larry was a murderer, either, so there you go.

Construction of the park finished on budget and only three days late. The community really stepped up the last week to make sure all the final details, like signage and landscaping around the gazebo, were completed to Sloane's satisfaction. The park wouldn't have existed if not for her incredible generosity, so the community owed it to her to unveil a park she could be proud of. They did that. And then some.

In short, the park was stunning.

Now, all I had to do was say a few words about my father and Thornwell, thank Sloane for her gift, and cut an oversized red ribbon with a pair of scissors almost as big as me. Physical therapy had helped restore much of the range of motion to my left shoulder, but there were still some things I couldn't do, like put on a suit jacket by myself and lift heavy weights. It remained to be seen if operating a pair of oversized scissors would have to be added to the list.

I coaxed Ursi off her perch by the front window and into her harness while Brent roused Sammy, who'd been napping in her doggy bed in a corner of the living room. The grand opening was being billed as a family affair. To me, that meant four-legged family members were welcome, too.

After a few drizzly, gray days, the clouds had departed, and the sun was out in all her celestial glory. With a spring to our steps, we left my building, ready to enjoy the Chamber of Commerce weather. The skies were blue as far as the eye could see, and the temperature had risen to the mid-sixties. The air was still, which made for excellent viewing of the vibrant green, red, and orange fall leaves.

Perfect conditions for a stroll to the park.

We stopped and said hi to dozens of folks on our walk. A lot of people asked how I was feeling. I was happy to show off my right hand, which had been out of a hard cast for a couple of days and would be in a soft cast for another two to three weeks. The knuckles had healed well, the cuts and scrapes on my arms were gone, and the bullet was going to leave a tiny scar, at most. It didn't look like I was going to have any long-term issues with any of my injuries. Thank goodness.

When the park came into view, Brent stopped. "I've been thinking about how you figured out Mayor Cannon was the killer. It was brilliant. I wanted to tell you how lucky I am to have such a brilliant, persistent, caring woman in my life."

My cheeks got warm. The man had a knack for saying the perfect thing at the perfect time.

"Thank you. I'm glad you have me in your life, too." As we laughed at my little joke, I took his hand in mine. "Seriously, though, I feel like I got lucky. If I hadn't had been at the chocolate shop when they were taking pictures of the new bike racks with Larry, I wouldn't have seen him wearing the jacket and dress shirt. If not for that, I wouldn't have realized Larry was keeping his arms covered to hide scratch marks from the limbs he used to cover Georgie's car."

"But you did realize it. That's what matters. No detail ever gets past you, Allie. That's why you're so amazing in everything you do. Just promise me one thing."

"Maybe. Depends on what you want me to promise." After a compliment like that, it was hard to imagine me ever turning Brent down, but one could never be too sure.

"Will you promise to make crime fighting a thing of the past? I mean, the Kickboxing Crusader moniker is cool, and you're two for two when it comes to cases you've solved. Why not retire while you're on top?"

The request warmed my heart. Brent cared about me and wanted me to be safe. I wanted that, too. I also wanted my town to be safe. I didn't have any interest in prowling the streets of Rushing Creek, Indiana, at night searching for miscreants and scoundrels, but if my town needed me, I'd be there.

No doubt about it

"I'll promise you this. As long as no more murders are committed in Rushing Creek, I will stick to my life as mild-mannered Allie Cobb, literary agent."

"Fair enough" He looked toward the park.

A crowd the size of half the town was gathering. It was going to be the perfect kickoff to the annual Rushing Creek Fall Festival.

"Ready to cut that ribbon?"

"You bet."

As we wound our way through the crowd and joined my family, Sloane, and the planning committee members at the park's main entrance, it was like my father was residing on my left shoulder and Thornwell was on my right shoulder. Their presence gave me confidence to address the crowd and reminded me that, no matter what, I had friends and family by my side.

The acting mayor opened the ceremony by saying a few words and presenting Sloane a key to the city as a token of gratitude for her generous donation. With tears in her eyes, but a smile on her face, she thanked the mayor and said she hoped the park would provide generations of Rushing Creek residents hours and hours of enjoyment.

When it came time for me to speak, I ignored the statement I'd prepared. This was a moment to speak from the heart. So, I did.

"My father, Walter Cobb, and his best friend and client, Thornwell Winchester, were lovers of words. They also loved the community of Rushing Creek, Indiana. I think, as we stand here today, under this cloudless sky, they'd agree words aren't adequate to describe the beauty of this park. That the best thing would be to experience it, so it is my honor and pleasure to declare Winchester-Cobb Memorial Park open for your enjoyment."

I took the scissors and sliced through a red ribbon being held at one end by my nephew, Tristan, and the other by my niece, Theresa. A raucous round of applause erupted. A tear trickled down my cheek as I exchanged hugs with my family while the crowd streamed through the entrance and toward the gazebo, where refreshments were being served.

As I stood between Sloane and Brent, cuddling Ursi in my arms and welcoming old friends and new to the park, I was complete. The last year had been full of change and challenges, but I'd survived.

Not only had I survived, I'd thrived. I had everything I'd ever wanted and couldn't wait to see what new adventures were in store for me. There was no doubt in my mind that they'd be moments to remember.

Printed in the United States
by Baker & Taylor Publisher Services